ESCAPE ON VENUS

ESCAPE ON VENUS

EDGAR RICE BURROUGHS

NEW ENGLISH LIBRARY
TIMES MIRROR

To
Brigadier General Kendall J. Fielder

Originally published as four novelettes in *Fantastic Adventures Magazine*
under the titles "Slave of the Fishermen", "The Goddess of Fire",
"The Living Dead" and "War on Venus", copyright © 1941, 1942 by
Edgar Rice Burroughs Inc. Published in book form under the title
"Escape on Venus", copyright © 1946 by Edgar Rice Burroughs.

*

First Four Square Edition November 1966, copyright © Edgar Rice Burroughs Inc.
FIRST NEL PAPERBACK EDITION AUGUST 1972
Reprinted March 1973

*

NEL Books are published by
New English Library Limited, from Barnard's Inn, Holborn, London E.C.1.
Made and printed in Great Britain by Hunt Barnard Printing Ltd., Aylesbury, Bucks.

45001168 2

FOREWORD

Any patriotic citizen can give you the name of the astronaut commonly believed to be the first American in space, and inform you of the exact time and date of liftoff from the pad at Cape Kennedy; but any student of Burroughs knows that the first American in space was a tow-headed, blue-eyed, young man named Carson Napier.

Napier, a former British subject, was an American by choice. He did not lift off from a Cape Kennedy rocket pad, but was blasted into the heavens in a rocket torpedo of his own design —more than thirty years ago!

This "Wrong-way" Corrigan of space was attempting to reach Mars but landed on Venus instead. There he encountered races primitively bestial and super-scientifically advanced. There he battled with strange beasts and giant insects. There he lost his heart to Duare, daughter of a Vepajan *jong*, whose beauty could mean death to the beholder.

Carson Napier's amazing adventures on *Amtor* are recorded in four volumes, of which this is the fourth, as communicated directly from him to Edgar Rice Burroughs, through the marvelous medium of telepathy.

Impossible? Science-fiction fantasy? You don't believe it? Well, if you cannot believe in the reality of the worlds of Edgar Rice Burroughs after reading the first few pages of this book, then there is no Tarzan of the Apes! For it is the unique style of making the impossible plausible that made Edgar Rice Burroughs the most popular and best selling author in the world.

VERNELL CORIELL
Founder, The Burroughs Bibliophiles

EDITOR'S FOREWORD

Venus, at its nearest approach to Earth, is still a little matter of twenty-six million miles away—barely a sleeper jump in the vast reaches of infinite space. Hidden from our sight by its cloak of enveloping clouds, during all time its surface has been seen by but a single Earth man—Carson of Venus.

This is the fourth story of the adventures of Carson of Venus on the Shepherd's Star, as narrated by him telepathically to Edgar Rice Burroughs at Lanikai on the Island of Oahu. It is a story complete in itself. It is not necessary even to read this foreword, unless you happen to be curious to learn how Carson navigated interplanetary space and something of the strange lands he has visited, the vast, deserted oceans he has navigated, the savage beasts he has encountered, the friends and enemies he has made, and the girl whom he won over apparently insuperable obstacles.

When Carson of Venus took off from Guadalupe Island off the west coast of Mexico in his giant rocket ship his intended destination was Mars. For more than a year his calculations had been checked and rechecked by some of the ablest scientists and astronomers in America, and the exact moment of his departure had been determined, together with the position and inclination of the mile long track along which the rocket ship would make its take-off. The resistance of the Earth's atmosphere had been nicely calculated, as well as the earth's pull and that of the other planets and the Sun. The speed of the rocket ship in our atmosphere and beyond had been as accurately determined as was scientifically possible; but one factor had been overlooked. Incomprehensible as it may appear, no one had taken into consideration the pull of the Moon!

Shortly after the take-off, Carson realized that he was already off his course; and for some time it appeared likely that he would score a direct hit upon our satellite. Only the terrific velocity of the rocket ship and the pull of a great star saved him from this; and he passed over the Moon by the narrowest of margins, scarcely five thousand feet above her loftiest mountains.

After that, for a long month, he realized that he was in the grip of the Sun's attraction and that he was doomed. He had long since given up hope, when Venus loomed far ahead and to his right. He realized that he was going to cross her orbit and that there was a chance that she might claim him rather than the Sun. Yet he was still doomed, for had not Science definitely proved that Venus was without oxygen and incapable of supporting such forms of life as exist upon Earth?

Soon Venus seized him, and the rocket ship dove at terrific speed toward the billowing clouds of her envelope. Following the same procedure that he had purposed using in making a landing on Mars, he loosed batteries of parachutes which partially checked the speed of the ship; then, adjusting his oxygen tank and mask, he bailed out.

Landing among the branches of giant trees that raised their heads five thousand feet above the surface of the planet, he encountered almost immediately the first of a long series of adventures which have filled his life almost continuously since his advent upon Amtor, as Venus is known to its inhabitants; for he was pursued and attacked by hideous arboreal carnivores before he reached the tree city of Kooaad and became the guest-prisoner of Mintep, the king.

It was here that he saw and loved Duare, the king's daughter, whose person was sacred and upon whose face no man other than royalty might look and live.

He was captured by enemies of Mintep and put upon a ship that was to carry him into slavery in a far country. He headed a mutiny and became a pirate. He rescued Duare from abductors, but she still spurned his love. Again and again he befriended, protected her, and saved her life; but always she remained the sacrosanct daughter of a king.

He was captured by the Thorists, but he escaped the Room of the Seven Doors in the seaport of Kapdor. He fought with tharbans and hairy savages. He sought Duare in Kormor, the city of the dead, where reanimated corpses lived their sad, gruesome lives.

He won renown in Havatoo, the perfect city; and here he built the first aeroplane that had ever sailed the Amtorian skies. In it he escaped with Duare after a miscarriage of justice had doomed her to death.

They came then to the country called Korvan, where Mephis,

the mad dictator, ruled. Here Duare's father was a prisoner condemned to death. After the overthrow of Mephis, Duare, believing Carson dead, flew back to her own country, taking her father with her. There she was condemned to death because she had mated with a lesser mortal.

Carson of Venus followed in a small sailing boat, was captured by pirates, but finally reached Kooaad, the tree city which is the capital of Mintep's kingdom. By a ruse, he succeeded in rescuing Duare; and flew away with her in the only airship on Venus.

What further adventures befell them, Carson of Venus will tell in his own words through Edgar Rice Burroughs who is at Lanikai on the Island of Oahu.

THE EDITOR

ONE

If you will look at any good map of Venus you will see that the land mass called Anlap lies northwest of the island of Vepaja, from which Duare and I had just escaped. On Anlap lies Korva, the friendly country toward which I pointed the nose of our plane.

Of course there is no good map of Venus, at least none that I ever have seen; because the scientists of the southern hemisphere of the planet, the hemisphere to which Chance carried my rocket ship, have an erroneous conception of the shape of their world. They believe that Amtor, as they call it, is shaped like a saucer and floats upon a sea of molten rock. This seems quite evident to them, for how else might the spewing of lava from the craters of volcanoes be explained?

They also believe that Karbol (Cold Country) lies at the periphery of their saucer; whereas it is, as a matter of fact, the Antarctic region surrounding the south pole of Venus. You may readily perceive how this distorts their conception of actual conditions and is reflected in maps, which are, to say the least, weird. Where actually the parallels of longitude converge toward the pole, their conception would be that they converged toward the Equator, or the center of their saucer, and that they were farthest apart at the periphery of the saucer.

It is all very confusing to one who wishes to go places on the surface of Amtor and must depend upon an Amtorian map, and it seems quite silly; but then one must bear in mind the fact that these people have never seen the heavens; because of the cloud envelopes which enshroud the planet. They have never seen the Sun, nor the Planets, nor all the other countless suns which star the skies by night. How then might they know anything of astronomy or even guess that they lived upon a globe rather than in a saucer? If you think that they are stupid, just bear in mind that man inhabited the Earth for countless ages before it occurred to anyone that the Earth was a globe; and that within recent historic times men were subjected to the Inquisition, broken on the rack, drawn and quartered, burned at the stake for holding to any such iniqui-

11

tous theory. Even today there is a religious sect in Illinois which maintains that the Earth is flat. And all this in the face of the fact that we have been able to see and study the Heavens every clear night since our earliest ancestor hung by his tail in some primordial forest. What sort of astronomical theories do you suppose we would hold if we had never seen the Moon, the Sun, nor any of the Planets and myriad stars and could not know that they existed?

However erroneous the theory upon which the cartographers evolved their maps, mine were not entirely useless; though they required considerable mental mathematical gymnastics to translate them into usable information, even without the aid of the theory of the relativity of distance, expounded by the great Amtorian scientist, Klufar, some three thousand years ago, which demonstrates that the actual and the apparent measurements of distance can be reconciled by multiplying each by the square root of minus one!

So, having a compass, I flew a little north of west with reasonable assurance that I should eventually raise Anlap and Korva. But how could I foresee that a catastrophic meterological phenomenon was soon to threaten us with immediate extinction and literally hurl us into a series of situations as potentially lethal as that from which we had fled on Vepaja?

Duare had been very quiet since we had taken off. I could understand why, and I could sympathize with her. Her own people, whom she loved, and her father, whom she worshipped not only as her father but as her jong, had condemned her to death because she had mated with the man she loved. They all deplored the stern law of the dynasty as much as she, but it was an inexorable commandment that not even the jong himself might evade.

I knew what she was thinking; and I laid my hand on hers, comfortingly. "They will be relieved when morning comes and they discover that you have escaped—they will be relieved and happy."

"I know it," she said.

"Then do not be sad, dear."

"I love my people; I love my country; but I may never return to them. That is why I am sad, but I cannot be sad for long; because I have you, and I love you more than I love my people or my country—may my ancestors forgive me it."

I pressed her hand. We were silent again for a long time.

The Eastern horizon was lighting faintly. A new day was breaking on Venus. I thought of my friends on Earth, and wondered what they were doing and if they ever thought of me. Thirty million miles is a great distance, but thought travels it instantaneously. I like to think that in the next life vision and thought will travel hand in hand.

"What are you thinking?" asked Duare.

I told her.

"You must be very lonely sometimes, so far from your own world and your friends," she said.

"Quite the contrary," I assured her. "I have you; and I have many good friends in Korva, and an assured position there."

"You will have an assured position in that Heaven of yours of which you have told me, if Mephis ever gets hold of you," she said.

"I forgot. You do not know all that transpired in Korva," I said.

"You have told me nothing. After all, we haven't been to-gether for very long—"

"And just being together seemed enough, didn't it?" I inter-rupted.

"Yes, but tell me now."

"Well, Mephis is dead; and Taman is now jong of Korva." I told her the whole story in detail and of how Taman, having no son, adopted me in gratitude for my having saved the life of his only daughter, the Princess Nna.

"So now you are Tanjong of Korva," she said, "and if Taman dies you will be jong. You have done well, Earthman."

"I am going to do even better," I said.

"Yes! What?"

I drew her to me and kissed her. "That," I said. "I have kissed the sacrosanct daughter of an Amtorian jong."

"But you have done that a thousand times. Are all Earthmen as silly?"

"They all would be if they could."

Duare had put her melancholy from her; and we joked and laughed, as we flew on over the vast Amtorian sea toward Korva. Sometimes Duare was at the controls, for by now she was an excellent pilot, and sometimes I. We often flew low to observe the strange and savage marine life which occasionally broke the surface of the sea—huge monsters of the deep, some

13

of which attained the dimensions of an ocean liner. We saw millions of lesser creatures fleeing before fearsome carnivorous enemies. We saw titanic battles between monstrous leviathans —the age-old struggle for survival which must exist upon every planet of the Universe upon which life exists; the reason, perhaps, why there must always be wars among nations—a cosmic *sine qua non* of life.

It was mid-afternoon. The thing that was to change our lives was about to happen. The first intimation of it was a sudden lightening of the sky far ahead. We noticed it simultaneously.

"What is that?" asked Duare.

"It looks as though the Sun were trying to break through the cloud envelopes of Amtor," I said. "I pray Heaven that he doesn't succeed."

"It has happened in the past," said Duare. "Of course our people knew nothing of the Sun of which you tell me. They thought it the all-enveloping fire which rose from the molten mass upon which Amtor is supposed to float. When a break came in our protective cloud envelopes, the flames struck through, destroying all life beneath the cloud rift."

I was at the controls. I banked sharply and headed north. "I am going away from there," I said. "The Sun has broken through one of the cloud envelopes; he may break through the other."

TWO

We watched the increasing light upon our left. It illumined the whole sky and the ocean, but it was intensest at one spot. As yet it resembled only bright sunlight such as we are accustomed to on Earth; then, suddenly, it burst through like blinding flame. There had been coincidental rifts in both cloud envelopes!

Almost instantly the ocean commenced to boil. We could see it even at a distance. Vast clouds of steam arose. The heat increased. It was fast becoming unendurable.

"The end," said Duare, simply.

"Not yet," I replied, as, with throttle wide, we raced toward the north. I had chosen flight to the north because the rift was a little southwest of us and the wind was from the west. Had I turned back toward the east, the wind borne heat would have followed us. In the north lay what hope we had.

"We have lived," said Duare. "Life can hold nothing better for us than that which we have enjoyed. I am not afraid to die. Are you, Carson?"

"That is something that I shall never know until it is too late," I said, smiling down at her, "for while I live I shall never admit the possibility of death. Somehow, it doesn't seem to be for me—at least not since Danus injected the longevity serum into my veins and told me that I might live a thousand years. You see, I am curious to know if he were right."

"You are very silly," she said, "but you are also reassuring."

Enormous clouds of steam blotted out everything in the southwest. They rose to the clouds, dimming the sunlight. I could imagine the devastation in the sea, the myriad of living things destroyed. Already the effects of the catastrophe were becoming plainly discernible below us. The fleeter reptiles and fishes were fleeing the holocaust—and they were fleeing north! Instinct or intelligence, or whatever it was, it filled me with renewed hope.

The surface of the ocean was alive with them. Mortal enemies raced side by side. The stronger creatures pushed the weaker aside, the fleeter slithered over the tops of the slower. How they had been warned, I cannot guess; but the flight was on far ahead of us, though our speed was greater than the swiftest of the creatures racing with us from death.

The air was becoming no hotter; and I had hopes that we should escape unless the cloud rift enlarged and the Sun took in a larger area of Amtor's surface; and then the wind changed! It blew in a sudden furious gust from the south, bringing with it stifling heat that was almost suffocating. Clouds of condensing vapor whirled and swirled about us, drenching us with moisture and reducing visibility almost to zero.

I rose in an attempt to get above it; but it was seemingly everywhere, and the wind had become a gale. But it was driving us north. It was driving us away from the boiling sea and the consuming heat of the Sun. If only the cloud rift did not widen we might hope for life.

I glanced down at Duare. Her little jaw was set; and she was staring grimly ahead, though there was nothing to see but billowing clouds of vapor. There hadn't been a whimper out of her. I guess blood will tell all right, and she was the daughter of a thousand jongs. She must have sensed my eyes upon her, for she looked up and smiled.

"More things happen to us!" she said.

"If you wished to lead a quiet life, Duare, you picked the wrong man. I am always having adventures. That's not much to brag about, though. One of the great anthropologists of my world, who leads expeditions to remote corners of the Earth and never has any adventures, says that having them is an indication of inefficiency and stupidity."

"I don't believe him," said Duare. "All the intelligence and efficiency in the world could have neither foreseen nor averted a rift in the clouds."

"A little more intelligence would probably have kept me from attempting to fly to Mars, but then I should never have known you. No; on the whole, I'm rather glad that I am no more intelligent than I am."

"So am I."

The heat was not increasing, but the wind was. It was blowing with hurricane force, tossing our sturdy anotar about as though it were a feather. I couldn't do much about it. In such a storm the controls were almost useless. I could only hope that I had altitude enough to keep from being dashed on some mountain, and there was always the danger from the giant Amtorian forests which lift their heads thousands of feet into the air to draw moisture from the inner cloud envelope. I could see nothing beyond the nose of the anotar, and I knew that we must have covered a great distance with the terrific tail-wind that was driving us furiously toward the north. We might have passed the sea and be over land. Mountains might loom dead ahead, or the mighty boles of a giant forest. I was not very happy. I like to be able to see. If I can see, I can face almost anything.

"What did you say?" asked Duare.

"I didn't know that I said anything. I must have been thinking aloud—that I would give almost anything to be able to see."

And then, as though in answer to my wish, a rift opened in the swirling vapor ahead; and I saw. I almost leaped at the controls because of what I saw—a rocky escarpment looming high above us and dead ahead.

I fought to bank and turn aside, but the inexorable wind

16

carried us toward our doom. No scream broke from Duare's lips, no faintest echo of the fear that she must have felt—must have, because she is human and young.

The thing that appalled me most in the split second that I had to think, was the thought of that beautiful creature being broken and crushed against that insensate cliff. I thanked God that I would not live to see it. At the foot of the escarpment we should lie together through all eternity, and no one in all the Universe would know our resting place.

We were about to crash when the ship rose vertically scarcely a dozen yards from the cliff. As the hurricane had toyed with us before, it did again.

Of course there must have been a terrific up-draft where the roaring wind struck the face of the escarpment. It was this that saved us, combined with the fact that when I had discovered that I could not maneuver away from the cliff, I had cut my engine.

Now we rose high above a vast tableland. The vapor, torn to shreds, floated off in little cloud-like wisps; and once more we could see the world below us. Once more we breathed.

But we were still far from safe. The tornado had not abated. I glanced back in the direction of the cloud rift, but now there was no brightness there. It had closed, and the danger of incineration had passed.

I opened the throttle a little in a rather futile effort to battle the elements and keep the anotar on an even keel; but we were dependent more upon our safety belts than upon our engine for salvation, for we were so tossed about that often our landing gear was above us, and we dangled helplessly in our belts.

It was a harrowing experience. A down draft would plummet us toward the ground with the velocity of a power dive; and when it seemed that we must surely crash, the giant hand of the storm would toss us high aloft.

How long we were the plaything of the Storm God, I may only guess; but it was not until almost dawn that the wind abated a little, and once more we were permitted to have some voice in the direction of our destiny; and even then we must still go where the wind willed, for we could not fly against it.

For hours we had not spoken. We had made an occasional

attempt, but the howling of the wind had drowned our voices. I could see that Duare was almost spent from the buffeting and the nervous strain, but there was nothing that I could do about it. Only rest could revive her, and there could be no rest until we could land.

A new world lay below us with the coming of the new day. We were skirting a great ocean, and I could see vast plains, and there were forests and rivers and, far away, snow-capped mountains. I believed that we must have been driven thousands of miles toward the north, for much of the time the throttle had been wide open, and all the time that terrific wind had been at our tail.

Where could we be? I felt confident that we had crossed the Equator and must be in the north temperate zone; but where Korva lay I could not even guess, and might never know.

THREE

The tornado died out in a last few fitful gusts. The air was suddenly calm. It was like the peace of Heaven.

"You must be very tired," said Duare. "Let me take the controls. You have been fighting that storm for sixteen or seventeen hours, and you have had no sleep for two days."

"Well, neither have you; and do you realize that we've had neither food nor water since before we left Vepaja?"

"There's a river down there, and game," said Duare. "I hadn't realized before how thirsty I was—and hungry, too. And so sleepy! I don't know which I am the most."

"We'll drink and eat, and then we'll sleep," I told her.

I circled around, looking for some sign of human habitation; for it is always men that must be feared most. Where there are no men, one is comparatively safe, even in a world of savage beasts.

In the distance I saw what appeared to be a large inland lake, or an arm of the sea. There were little patches of forest, and the plain was tree dotted beneath us. I saw herds grazing. I dropped down to select my quarry, run it down, and shoot it from the ship. Not very sporting; but I was out for food, not sport.

My plan was excellent, but it did not work. The animals

discovered us long before we were within range, and they took off like bats out of Hell.

"There goes breakfast," I said.

"And lunch and dinner," added Duare, with a rueful smile.

"The water remains. We can at least drink." So I circled to a landing near a little stream.

The greensward, close cropped by grazing herds, ran to the water's edge; and after we had drunk, Duare stretched out upon it for a moment's relaxation and rest. I stood looking around in search of game, hoping that something would come out of the near-by forest into which it had fled, effectively terminating my pursuit of it in the anotar.

It couldn't have been more than a minute or two that I stood there in futile search for food on the hoof, but when I looked down at Duare she was fast asleep. I didn't have the heart to awaken her, for I realized that she needed sleep even more than she did food; so I sat down beside her to keep watch while she slept.

It was a lovely spot, quiet and peaceful. Only the purling murmur of the brook broke the silence. It seemed very safe, for I could see to a considerable distance in all directions. The sound of the water soothed my tired nerves. I half reclined, supporting myself on one elbow so that I could keep better watch.

I lay there for about five minutes when a most amazing thing happened. A large fish came out of the stream and sat down beside me. He regarded me intently for a moment. I could not guess what was passing in his mind, as a fish has but one expression. He reminded me of some of the cinema stars I had seen, and I could not repress a laugh.

"What are you laughing at?" demanded the fish. "At me?"

"Certainly not," I assured him. I was not at all surprised that the fish spoke. It seemed quite natural.

"You are Carson of Venus," he said. It was a statement, not a question.

"How did you know?" I asked.

"Taman told me. He sent me to bring you to Korva. There will be a great procession as you and your princess ride on a mighty gantor along the boulevards of Sanara to the palace of the jong."

"That will be very nice," I said; "but in the meantime will you please tell me who is poking me in the back, and why?"

19

At that the fish suddenly disappeared. I looked around, and saw a dozen armed men standing over us. One of them had been prodding me in the back with a three pronged spear. Duare was sitting up, an expression of consternation on her face. I sprang to my feet. A dozen spears menaced me. Two warriors were standing over Duare, their tridents poised above her heart. I could have drawn my pistol, but I did not dare use it. Before I could have killed them all, one of us would have been killed. I could not take the chance, with Duare's life at stake.

As I looked at the warriors, I suddenly realized that there was something very peculiar and inhuman about them. They had gills, which their heavy beards did not conceal; and their fingers and toes were webbed. Then I recalled the fish which had come out of the stream and talked to me—I slept, and I was still dreaming! That made me smile.

"What are you smiling about?" demanded one of the warriors, "me?"

"I am laughing at myself," I said. "I am having such an amusing dream."

Duare looked at me wide-eyed. "What is the matter with you, Carson?" she demanded. "What has happened to you?"

"Nothing, except that it was very stupid of me to fall asleep. I wish that I could wake up."

"You *are* awake, Carson. Look at me! Tell me that you are all right."

"Do you mean to tell me that you see what I see?" I demanded, nodding toward the warriors.

"We both slept, Carson; but now we are awake—and we are prisoners."

"Yes, you are prisoners," said the warrior who had spoken before. "Come along with us, now."

Duare arose and came and stood close to me. They did not try to prevent her. "Why do you want to make us prisoners?" she asked the warrior. "We have done nothing. We were lost in a great storm, and we landed here for food and water. Let us go our way. You have nothing to fear from us."

"We must take you to Mypos," replied the warrior. "Tyros will decide what is to be done with you. I am only a warrior. It is not for me to decide."

"Who are Mypos and Tyros?" asked Duare.

20

"Mypos is the king's city, and Tyros is the king," He said *jong*.

"Do you think he will let us go then?"

"No," said the warrior. "Tyros the Bloody releases no captives. You will be slaves. The man may be killed at once, or later, but Tyros will not kill you."

The men were armed with tridents, swords, and daggers; they had no firearms. I thought I saw a possibility for Duare's escape. "I can hold them off with my pistol," I whispered, "while you make a run for the anotar.'

"And then what?" she demanded.

"Perhaps you can find Korva. Fly south for twenty-four hours. You should be over a great ocean by that time; then fly west."

"And leave you here?"

"I can probably kill them all; then you can land and pick me up."

Duare shook her head. "I shall remain with you."

"What are you whispering about?" demanded the warrior.

"We were wondering if you might let us take our anotar with us," said Duare.

"What would we do with that thing in Mypos?"

"Maybe Tyros would like to see it, Ulirus," suggested another warrior.

Ulirus shook his head. "We could never get it through the forest," he said; then he turned suddenly on me. "How did you get it here?" he demanded.

"Come and get in it and I'll show you," I told him. If I could only get him into the anotar, along with Duare, it would be a long time before Ulirus would see Mypos again; and we would never see it. But Ulirus was suspicious.

"You can tell me how you did it," he countered.

"We flew it here from a country thousands of miles away," I told him.

"Flew it?" he demanded. "What do you mean?"

"Just what I said. We get in it, and it flies up into the air and takes us wherever we wish to go."

"Now you are lying to me."

"Let me show you. My mate and I will take it up into the air, and you can see it with your own eyes."

"No. If you are telling me the truth about the thing, you would never come back."

21

Well, finally they did help me shove the anotar among a clump of trees and fasten it down. I told them their jong would want to see it, and if they let anything happen to it he'd be very angry. That got them, for they were evidently terribly afraid of this Tyros the Bloody.

We started off through the forest with warriors in front and behind us. Ulirus walked beside me. He wasn't a bad sort. He told me, in a whisper, that he'd like to let us go; but that he was afraid to, as Tyros would be sure to learn of it; and that would be the end of Ulirus. He was much interested in my blond hair and gray eyes, and asked me many questions about the country from which I came.

I was equally interested in him and his fellows. They all had beautiful physiques—smooth-flowing muscles and not an ounce of unnecessary fat; but their faces were most peculiar. Their full black beards and their gills I have already mentioned; these, with their protruding lips and pop eyes, resulted in a facial pulchritude of something less than zero.

"They look like fish," Duare whispered to me.

Just how piscine these Myposans were we were to learn later.

FOUR

We followed a well marked trail through the forest, a typical Amtorian forest, a forest of exquisite loveliness. The lacquer-like bark of the trees was of many colors, and the foliage of soft pastel shades—heliotrope, mauve, violet. Flowering parasitic plants added to the riot of color, flaunting blooms beside which our most gorgeous Earthly orchids would have appeared as drab as a church mouse at a Mardi gras.

There are many types of forests on Venus, as there are on Earth; but this through which we were passing is the most common, while the most awe inspiring and amazing are those such as cover Vepaja, the tops of which rise fully five thousand feet above the ground, and whose trees are of such enormous girth that, as at Kooaad, the palace of a king is carved within one a thousand feet from its base.

I am an inveterate worshipper of beauty; so that even though Duare and I were marching to an unknown fate, I could still be thrilled by that which met my eyes on every side.

22

I could still wonder at and admire the gaily plumaged birds and insects and the tiny flying lizards which flitted from flower to flower in the eternal routine of pollination, but I could also wonder why Ulirus had not taken my pistol from me.

Perhaps there are few people more gifted with telepathic powers than I, yet I do not always profit by my knowledge. Had I, I should not then have thought about my pistol, for while I was wondering why Ulirus had not taken it from me, he pointed to it and asked me what it was. Of course it might have been only coincidence.

"It is a charm," I told him, "which protects me from evil."

"Let me have it," he said, holding out a hand.

I shook my head. "I wouldn't do anything like that to you, Ulirus," I said, "for you have been very decent to my mate and me."

"What do you mean?" he demanded. Several of the other warriors were looking on interestedly.

"This is my personal charm," I explained; "anyone else touching it might die." After all it was not exactly a lie. "However, if you would like to take the chance, you may." I took the weapon from its holster and proffered it to him.

He hesitated a moment. The other warriors were watching him. "Some other time," he said; "we must be getting on to Mypos now."

I glanced at Duare. She was keeping a very straight face; though she was smiling inwardly, I guessed. Thus I retained my weapon for the time being at least; and though the warriors showed no further desire to handle it, they did not lose interest in it. They kept eyeing it, but I noticed that they were very careful not to brush against it when they were close to me.

We had marched through the forest for about a mile when we came into the open again, and ahead I saw the body of water that I had seen from the anotar before I made my fateful landing. On its shore, and perhaps a mile away, was a city, a walled city.

"That is Mypos," said Ulirus. "It is the largest city in the world."

From where we stood, on slightly higher ground, I had a good view of Mypos; and should say that it covered perhaps a hundred acres. However, I didn't dispute Ulirus's claim. If he wished to believe that it was the largest city in the world, that was all right with me.

We approached a large gate which was well guarded. It was swung open when Ulirus was recognized. The officer and members of the guard gathered around us, asking many questions of our captors; and I was delighted that among the first things that they were told was of the magical charm that I carried, which dealt death to whomever else touched it.

"They curl up like worms and die in horrible convulsions," explained Ulirus. Ulirus was quite a propagandist, however unintentionally.

Nobody, it seemed, wished to touch it.

"Now," I said, "I wish that you would take us at once to Tyros."

Ulirus and the officer appeared astounded. "Is the man mad?" demanded the latter.

"He is a stranger," said Ulirus. "He does not know Tyros."

"My mate and I," I explained, "are of the royal family of Korva. When the jong dies, I shall be jong. The jong of any other country should receive us as befits our rank."

"Not Tyros," said the officer. "Perhaps you do not know it, but Tyros is the only real jong in the world. All the others are impostors. You had better not let Tyros know that you claim to be related to a jong. He would have you killed immediately."

"What are you going to do with us, then?" I asked.

Ulirus looked at the officer as though for instructions.

"Take them to the slaves' compound at the palace," he directed; "they look fit to serve the jong."

So Ulirus marched us off again. We passed along narrow, crooked streets flanked by one storied houses built of frame or limestone. The former were of roughly split planks fastened to upright framework, the latter of carelessly hewn blocks of limestone. The houses were as crooked as the streets. Evidently they had been built by eye without benefit of plumb-line. The windows and doors were of all sizes and shapes and all manner of crookedness. They might have been designed by a modernist of my world, or by a child of five.

The city lay, as I later learned, on the shore of a great freshwater lake; and as we approached the lake front we saw buildings of two stories, some with towers. The largest of these is the palace of Tyros.

The compound to which we were taken adjoined the palace grounds. Several hundred tiny cells bounded an open court, in the center of which was a pool. Just before we were admitted, Ulirus leaned close to me.

"Do not tell anyone that you are the son of a jong," he whispered.

"But I have already told you and the officer at the gate," I reminded him.

"We will not tell," he said, "but the slaves might in order to win favor."

I was puzzled. "And why won't you tell?" I asked.

"For one reason, I like you; for another, I hate Tyros. Everyone hates Tyros."

"Well, I thank you for the warning, Ulirus; but I don't suppose I can ever do anything to repay you;" then the guard opened the gate and we were ushered into our prison.

There must have been fully three hundred slaves in the compound, mostly creatures like ourselves; but there were also a few Myposans. The latter were common criminals, or people who had aroused the ire of Tyros the Bloody. The men and women were not segregated from one another; so Duare and I were not separated.

Some of the other slaves gathered around us, animated by curiosity, a part of which was aroused by Duare's great beauty and a part by my blond hair and gray eyes. They had started to question us when the officer who had admitted us strode into the compound.

"Look out!" whispered one of the slaves. "Here comes Vomer;" then they drifted away from us.

Vomer walked up to me and eyed first me and then Duare from head to feet. His bearing was obviously intentionally insulting.

"What's this I hear," he demanded, "about something that you ride in that flies through the air like a bird?"

"How should I know what you heard?" I retorted.

One couldn't tell, from their facial expressions, the mental reactions of these Myposans; because, like true fish, they didn't have any. Vomer's gills opened and closed rapidly. Perhaps that was a sign of rage or excitement. I didn't know, and I didn't care. He annoyed and disgusted me. He looked surprisingly like a moon fish, numbers of which I had seen seined off the Florida Keys.

"Don't speak to me in that tone of voice, slave," shouted Vomer; "don't you know who I am?"

25

"No, nor what,"

Duare stood close to me. "Don't antagonize him," she whispered; "it will only go the harder with us."

I realized that she was right. For myself, I did not care; but I must not jeopardize her safety. "Just what do you wish to know?" I asked in a more conciliatory tone, though it griped me to do it.

"I want to know if Ulirus spoke the truth," he said. "He told me that you rode in a great thing that flew through the air like a bird, and the other warriors with him said the same thing."

"It is true."

"It can't be true," objected Vomer.

I shrugged. "If you know it can't be true, why ask me?"

Vomer looked at me steadily with his fishy eyes for a moment; then he turned and strode away.

"You have made an enemy," said Duare.

"They are all our enemies," I said. "I should like to punch his face."

A slave standing near smiled. "So should we all," he said, He was a nice looking chap, well put up; a human being and not a freak of nature like the Myposans. I had noticed him before. He had been surreptitiously eying me. It was evident that my appearance had aroused his curiosity. "My name is Kandar," he said, by way of opening up a conversation with me. "I am from Japal."

"I am Carson of Venus," I told him. "I am a citizen of Korva."

"I have never heard of such a country, and I have never before seen a man with hair and eyes the color of yours. Are all the men of Korva like you?"

I tried to explain the matter to him; but of course he couldn't grasp the fact that there was another world far from Amtor, nor could he readily accept my statement that Korva lay thousands of miles to the south.

"In that direction lies the edge of Amtor," he objected, "not more than four or five hundred kob; and no country could exist beyond that, where all is fire and molten rock."

So he, too, thought that his world was flat; but at that his was a more tenable theory than that of the inhabitants of the southern hemisphere.

I questioned him about our captors and the treatment that we might expect from them.

"Our work ashore is not heavy," he explained, "and we are not treated so very badly; but at sea—that is different. Pray that you are not sent to sea."

FIVE

The slaves, other than the Myposans, were from various countries—mysterious lands with strange names; lands which lay east and west and north, but none that lay south. That was the *terra incognita,* the land of terror into which no one ever ventured.

Nearly all of the slaves had been captured after being shipwrecked on the shores of the great lake on which the city of Mypos lay, or on the coast of an ocean which they said lay about ten miles from the city.

Kandor told me that the lake was about five hundred miles long and that Mypos lay close to the lower end of it and Japal at the upper end.

"We of Japal," he said, "trade with several friendly countries which lie along the coast of the great sea, and we have to pass Mypos on our voyages. Sometimes we are wrecked and sometimes a ship of Japal is attacked by the Myposans and captured. Most of the wrecks occur where the lake empties into the ocean through a narrow channel. Only at high tide can a ship pass through the channel, for at low tide the waters of the lake rush madly into the ocean; and no ship can make headway against the current. When the tide is high the waters of the ocean flow into the lake, and then a passage can be made."

Duare and I had a little cubicle to ourselves, and we only hoped that they would leave us together until I could perfect some plan of escape. We slaves were fed twice a day—a stew of something that looked a little like shrimp and which also contained chopped tubers and flour made from the ground seeds of a plant which grows in profusion with little or no cultivation.

Kandar said it might not be very palatable, but that it was nutritious and strength giving. Occasionally meat was added

27

to the stew. "They want us to be strong," Kandar explained, "so that we can do more work. We build their ships and their houses and row their galleys; till their fields, carry their burdens. No Myposan does any work if he has sufficient slaves."

The day following our capture Vomer came into the compound with some warriors and selected a number of male slaves, whom he ordered to accompany him, Kandar and I were among them. We were marched down to the water front, where I had my first glimpse of Myposan ships. Some of them were quite large, being over a hundred feet in length. They were equipped with sails as well as oars. The largest, which lay at anchor, sheltered by a rude breakwater, I took to be warships. These were biremes, with large, flat overhanging decks above the upper bank of oars, capable of accommodating hundreds of warriors. There was a small deck house both fore and aft, upon the tops of which were mounted some sort of engine, the purpose of which I could not determine but which I was to learn later greatly to my discomfiture and sorrow.

I asked Kandar if the Myposans had any motor driven ships, but he did not know what I meant. This aroused my curiosity, and further questioning confirmed my suspicion that we had been carried far north of the Equator into what was, to the inhabitants of the southern hemisphere, the terra incognita of Venus, where an entirely different culture prevailed. Everything here was quite different, there being nothing to compare with the advanced civilization of Vepaja, Korva, or Havatoo, the countries with which I was most familiar.

There were signs of old age and disease here among both the Myposans and their prisoners, indicating that they knew nothing of the longevity serum of the south. Their weapons and customs differed widely. Their language, however, was similar, though not identical with that of the southern peoples.

Vomer put us to work loading a barge with rock that was to be used to strengthen the breakwater. He walked among us with a sort of bull whip, flicking first one and then another on bare legs and bodies. The act was purely sadistic, as the best workers received as many lashes as the shirkers. I saw that he had his eyes on me, and that he was slowly working his way toward me. I wondered if he would dare.

At last he came within striking distance of me. "Get to

work, slave!" he growled, and swung his whip hand back for a terrific blow.

I dropped the rock I had lifted; and faced him, my hand upon the butt of my pistol. Vomer hesitated, his gills fluttering rapidly—a sign of rage or excitement in these strange creatures, who have no facial muscles with which to register emotion.

The warriors with us, and the other slaves, were watching. Vomer was on a spot, and I wondered what he would do. His reaction was quite typical of the petty tyrant and bully. "Get to work!" he blustered, and turned and struck another slave.

The warriors were staring at him with fishy eyes. One couldn't tell what they were thinking, but the second-in-command didn't leave me in doubt long.

"Give me your whip," he said to Vomer. "If you are afraid to punish the slave, I am not." The fellow had a most repulsive countenance, looking not at all unlike a sculpin with whiskers. His gills were palpitating, and I could see that he meant business.

"Who said I was afraid?" demanded Vomer.

"I do," said the warrior.

"I am in command here," blustered Vomer. "I can punish a slave, or not, as I please. If you are so anxious to punish him, take my whip."

The fellow seized it, and came toward me.

"Hadn't you better tell him about this?" I said to Vomer, tapping my pistol.

"What about it?" demanded the warrior.

"It kills," I said. "It can kill you before you can strike me."

The fellow's protruding lips formed an O, and he sucked air in noisily through his teeth. It was a Myposan laugh. When angry, they often reverse the operation and blow the air out with a whistling sound. He continued to advance upon me.

"I don't want to kill you," I said; "but if you attempt to strike me with that whip, I will."

My only reason for not wishing to kill him was based upon the certainty of reprisal that might jeopardize Duare's safety. Otherwise, I should have been glad to kill him and all his kind.

"You'd better use your trident on him," cautioned another warrior.

"I've whipped slaves to death before," boasted the fellow, "and I can whip this one to death," then he rushed at me with upraised whip.

I whipped out my pistol, the r-ray pistol that destroys flesh and bone; and let him have it. There was no smoke, nothing visible; just a sharp, staccato buzz; then there was a great hole in the center of the fellow's face; and he sprawled forward, dead.

All about me the slaves stood, wide eyed and terrified; and the gills of the fish-men opened and closed rapidly. The warrior who had advised the dead man to use his trident, raised his weapon to hurl it at me; and he went down too, with a hole in his heart.

I swung around then, so that I was facing them all. They looked at Vomer, as though awaiting orders. He hesitated. I let the muzzle of my pistol swing in his direction.

"Get to work, slaves," he said, "we have wasted enough time." Both his voice and his knees shook.

Kandar was working beside me. "One of us must always keep an eye on him," he said; "otherwise he'll get you when your back is turned. I'll help you watch."

I thanked him. I felt that I had a friend.

SIX

When we got back to the slaves' compound Kandar told Duare what had happened. I would have stopped him could I have done so, for the poor girl had enough to worry about as it was.

"I knew that you had made an enemy of Vomer," she said, "the very first time he came out to speak to you. This thing had to come. It is just as well that it is over, so that we may know where we stand."

"If I could get an audience with Tyros," I said, "it is possible that we might receive better treatment—even our release."

"What makes you think so?" inquired Kandar.

"He is a jong, and it seems reasonable to believe that he would accord to people of our station in life the ordinary amenities of decent and civilized society. My mate is the daughter of a jong, and I am the son of one." I referred to my adoption by Taman, Jong of Korva.

Kandar smiled and shook his head. "You do not know Tyros," he said, "nor the psychology of the Myposans. They consider themselves a superior race and the rest of us on a par with the beasts. I have even heard them voice their wonder that we are endowed with speech. It is Tyros' ambition to conquer the world, carrying the Myposan culture to all benighted races and at the same time enslaving or destroying them. He is well aware of the fact that I am the eldest son of the Jong of Japal, yet I receive no better treatment than the meanest slave. No, my friend, it would do you no good to have an audience with Tyros, even if you could obtain one, which, of course, you cannot. The best that you can do is hope for the impossible."

"And what is that?" asked Duare.

"Escape."

"You think that that is impossible?" I asked.

"Well, let us say improbable," Kandar replied; "for after all nothing is impossible to the man of imagination and initiative, such as I assume you to be."

"And may we count on your co-operation?" I asked.

"Absolutely. I do not intend remaining a slave here indefinitely. Death would be far preferable."

"You have been here longer than we," I said. "You must have given much thought to escape. Perhaps you already have a plan."

"I wish I had," he replied, "but you will find it difficult to plan, where one is not the master of one's simplest acts and where one is constantly under the watchful eyes of armed warriors and traitorous spies."

"Spies?" asked Duare. "What do you mean?"

"I mean that among the slaves there are always those who will inform against their fellows in the hope of currying favor with their masters. You cannot be too careful with whom you discuss even your hopes. You do not even know that *I* am not a spy," he added with a smile.

"I'll take a chance on that," I told him. "I think I am a sufficiently good judge of human nature to know a man of honor even upon only short acquaintance."

"Thank you, but don't be too sure," he laughed; which made me all the surer of him.

31

I liked Kandar, and so did Duare. He was quite genuine—the sort of fellow you might meet in the officers' club at Schofield or San Diego. Had he not been captured by the Myposans he would one day have been jong of Japal; and he probably had a family tree the roots of which reached way back into antiquity, as did those of most of the royal families of Amtor with which I was acquainted.

Unlike the Polynesians, whose genealogies were handed down by word of mouth for hundreds of years and are all mixed up with myth and legend, these people had a written language; and the records were true and exact for ages. On my mother's side, I can trace my ancestry back to Deacon Edmund Rice, who came to Sudbury, Massachusetts about 1639; and from him to Cole Codoveg, who was King of Britain in the third century; yet, by comparison with Duare or Kandar or Taman, I am a parvenu.

These people are extremely proud of their ancestry, yet they can still accept others at their face value, regardless of their background.

About mid-forenoon of the day following my encounter with Volmer, he came swaggering into the compound with a number of warriors—his bodyguard, I called them; for I was quite sure that, hated as he was, he dared not come alone among the slaves.

In a loud voice he summoned Duare to step forward. Instantly I was alert and antagonistic. I didn't know what he wanted of Duare; but whatever it was, I was against it; so I stepped up beside her.

"I didn't call *your* name, slave," growled Vomer in the most insulting tone of voice he could conjure. I said nothing. "Back to your kennel, slave!" he shouted.

"Not until I know what you want of my mate," I told him.

His gills flapped, and he pursed his hideous lips and blew out air like a spouting whale. The flapping of the gills by these Myposans has an almost obscene sound, and the blowing of air when they are angry is equally disgusting. But, disgusting or not, it was quite evident that Vomer was angry; and I could endure his obnoxious manifestation of anger for the pleasure that it gave me to have made him angry. As you may have gathered, I did not like Vomer.

He took a step toward me, and then hesitated; then he looked at his warriors; but they were looking the other way. Evidently they had heard of or seen the lethal possibilities of the r-ray.

Between his flapping gills and his blowing, he had difficulty in controlling his voice; but he managed to scream, "Carson of Venus, step forward!"

"I am already here," I said. This he ignored.

"Kandar of Japal, step forward!" he wheezed. He would probably have liked to bellow; but his gills were still flapping, and he was still blowing spasmodically, which would, naturally, interfere with bellowing. I had to laugh.

"What are you laughing at, slave?" It was only a gurgle.

Duare laid a hand upon my arm before I could reply. She has far more sense than I. I wanted very much to say that I had seen moon fish seined off the Florida Keys; but that I had never before seen moon fish with whiskers; and that I thought them very amusing.

Vomer called a couple of more names, and the slaves stepped forward and took their places beside us; then he told us to fall in and follow him. The warriors formed before and behind us, and we left the slaves' compound and marched out into the streets of the city. Where were we going? To what new scenes, what new adventures, what new dangers were we being conducted?

SEVEN

The streets of Mypos are narrow and winding. As the Myposans have neither wheeled vehicles nor beasts of burden, their streets need not be wide; and the fact that they are narrow and winding would make the city easier to defend in the event of invasion. A single stalwart Horatius might hold any one of them against a greatly superior force.

In many places our little party of slaves and warriors were compelled to move in single file, the pedestrians we met flattening themselves against the walls of the buildings as we squeezed past. And so we progressed to an open plaza near the water front. Here there were a number of Myposans surrounding a small platform, near which we were halted. Immediately a number of the Myposans congregated there came among us and commenced to examine us, and one with a huge beard mounted the platform. One of those who moved among us attracted his attention and touched Duare on the shoulder.

The bearded one caught Vomer's eye. "Bring the woman to the platform," he directed.

I waited as Vomer led Duare up the three or four steps to where the other man stood. What was going to happen? I did not know, but I had my suspicions.

"What do you know of this woman?' asked the man of Vomer.

The fellow who had touched Duare's shoulder moved forward to the platform, and the others crowded about him.

"She was captured beyond the forest with a man who says that she is a janjong in some country of which no one ever heard," replied Vomer. "Beyond that I know nothing of her. She has behaved well, but the man is insubordinate and dangerous. He is down there," and he pointed to me. The man with the large beard fixed his fishy eyes upon me, while Vomer whispered to him earnestly. They spoke together thus for a moment, and then Vomer left the platform.

The man standing beside Duare looked down on the little crowd below him. "Who wishes to buy this fine female slave?" he asked.

So that was it! Well, I had guessed correctly; but what was I going to do about it?

"I will buy her," said the man who had touched Duare.

I could kill many of them with my pistol; but eventually they would overpower me; and Duare would be, if anything, worse off.

"What will you pay?" demanded the auctioneer.

"One hunred kloovol," replied the man.

A vol has about the same purchasing power as our fifty-nine cent dollar. Kloo is the prefix forming the plural. So this creature had dared to appraise Duare, daughter of a thousand jongs, at fifty-nine dollars! I fingered the butt of my pistol longingly.

"And who will pay more?" asked the auctioneer.

"Yes, who?" grumbled a Myposan standing near me. "Who would dare bid against Kod, who buys for Tyros?" He spoke in a very low voice to one who stood near him.

There were no other bids, and Duare was knocked down to Kod. I was furious. Duare was to be taken away from me; and, worse still, she was to became the chattel of a heartless

34

tyrant. All my moderate intentions went by the board. I determined to fight it out, killing as many as I could, seize Duare and blast my way to the city gates. With any luck at all I might make it, for the element of surprise in my action would give me a great advantage.

Vomer and the warriors were pressed pretty closely around me. I had not noticed it before; but they had been closing in on me; and now, before I could put my plan into action, they leaped upon me and by weight of numbers bore me to the ground. It was evidently the fruit of Vomer's whispered conversation with the auctioneer.

Before I could whip out my pistol they bound my hands behind my back, and I was helpless. They did not take my weapon from me, and I knew why. I had said that whoever touched it would die, and they believed me.

While I was down Vomer kicked me in the ribs, and after they had jerked me to my feet he struck me in the face. I don't know how much further he would have gone had not the auctioneer commanded him to desist.

"Do you want to ruin a valuable piece of property?" he cried.

"I wouldn't give one vol for him," snapped Vomer.

I was smarting under the indignities that Vomer had heaped upon me, but I was more concerned about Duare's future. The man, Kod, was leading her away; and she was looking back at me with a brave little smile.

"I shall come for you, Duare!" I cried after her. "Somehow, some way I shall come."

"Silence, slave!" snapped Vomer.

Kandar was standing near me. "Duare is fortunate," he said.

"Why?" I asked.

"She was bought for Tyros," he replied.

"And what is fortunate about that?" I demanded. "It seems to me to augur a future worse than death for a woman such as Duare."

"You are mistaken. She will serve one of the women of the royal family."

"Not after Tyros has seen her," I argued.

"Skabra will see her, and Skabra will see that Tyros does not get her."

"Who is Skabra?" I asked.

"Tyros' mate, the Vadjong of Mypos—a she-tharban and a

35

jealous one. You need have no fear that Duare will fall into the hands of Tyros while Skabra lives; she is too beautiful. Were she ill-favored, Skabra might let Tyros have her."

Well, that offered a ray of hope; and I was thankful for even the slightest glimmer.

Just then a man came and touched Kandar on the shoulder, and he went to the slave block. A number of Myposans swarmed around him, feeling of his muscles, examining his teeth.

The bidding for Kandar was spirited. He brought three hundred fifty kloovol—three and one half times as much as Duare; but then he was a strong, husky man; and as he was not being bid in by an agent of Tyros, the bidding was open to all.

After Kandar had been purchased, the man who had bought him touched me on the shoulder; and it was my turn to go to the block. I went with my hands bound tightly behind my back.

"Who wishes to buy this fine male slave?" he droned.

No one spoke. There was no bid. The auctioneer waited a moment, looking first at one potential bidder and then at another.

"He is very strong," he said. "He has fine teeth. I have examined them myself. He could do a great deal of work for many years. I am sure that he is quite as intelligent as any members of the lower orders. Who wishes to buy him?"

Again there was silence. "It is too bad to destroy such a fine slave," urged the auctioneer. Almost, he had tears in his eyes. And that was understandable, since he received a commission on every slave sold, and every unsold slave was a blot on his escutcheon.

Suddenly he got quite angry. "Why did you touch him?" he almost screamed at the man who had laid a hand on my shoulder.

"I didn't touch him for purchase," snapped the fellow; "I only wanted to see if his flesh was firm—just a matter of curiosity."

"Well, you had no business to do it. Now you will have to bid on him. You know the law of the slave market."

"Oh, all right," said the fellow. "I don't want him, but I'll pay ten kloovol for him."

"Anybody else crave this fine male slave?" inquired the auctioneer.

It seemed that no one did. "Very well," he said, "this fine male slave has been sold to the agent of Yron for ten kloovol. Take him away!"

So I had been sold for five dollars and ninety cents! That was certainly a blow to my ego. It is a good thing that I have a sense of the ridiculous.

EIGHT

Well, at least I would not be separated from Kandar; and that was something, for he had been in Mypos long enough to become more or less familiar with the city and the manners and customs of its inhabitants. If an opportunity for escape arose he would be invaluable as an ally.

Yron's agent motioned us to accompany him; and Kandar started to comply, but I stood still.

"Come, slave!" commanded the agent. "What are you standing there for? Come with me!" He raised a whip he carried, to strike me.

"My wrists are bound," I said.

"What of it?" he demanded. "Come along!"

"Not until you free my hands," I told him.

He struck me then with his whip. "Get going, slave!" he cried.

"Not until my hands are freed," I said, stubbornly; then he struck me again; whereupon I lay down.

The fellow became furious; and struck me again and again, but I would not budge.

"If you want your slave alive," said Kandar, "you will free his hands. He will never come until you do."

I knew that it was a hell of a way for a five dollar and ninety cent slave to act, but I felt that by asserting myself at the beginning I might find the going easier later.

The agent hit me a couple of more blows for good luck; then he stooped and freed my hands.

"Get up!" he ordered, and as I rose to my feet he swelled visibly, exhaling wind through his teeth. "I am a great slave driver," he said; "they always obey me."

I was glad he was satisfied, and winked at Kandar. Kandar grinned. "Be careful," he cautioned. "They make short shrift of slaves who are recalcitrant, and don't forget that you didn't cost Yron very much. He could easily afford to do away with you."

Vomer had been standing around evidently enjoying the whipping I had received. "You shouldn't have freed his hands," he said to Yron's agent.

"Why?" demanded the fellow.

"Because now he can kill you with that thing," he explained, pointing at my pistol.

"Give it to me!" commanded the agent.

I slipped it from its holster and proffered it to him, muzzle first.

"Don't touch it!" cried Vomer. "It will kill you if you touch it."

The man drew back. He was in a quandary.

"You needn't be afraid," I told him, "you would never have touched it, and as long as you treat Kandar and me well I'll not kill you." I slipped the weapon back into its holster.

"You've bought something for Yron," said Vomer, venomously. "When he finds out what, he'll lop off your head."

I suppose the fellow was unhappy, for his gills fluttered. I couldn't tell, of course, by the expression on his face; as that never changed. Like all the rest of his kind, he had no facial muscles to reflect his moods.

"Come along, slaves!" he ordered, and led Kandar and me away.

It was not far from the slave market to Yron's house, and we presently found ourselves in a large patio in the center of which was a pool about fifty feet wide and a hundred long. There were trees and shrubs and flowers and an expanse of lawn, all in the soft pastel shades of Amtorian verdure. Several slaves were pruning and trimming and cultivating, and there were three armed with wooden tridents standing like sentries about the pool. I noticed that these often glanced up at the sky. Naturally, I looked up also; but I saw nothing. Glancing into the pool, I saw a few fishes swimming about; but they did not interest me—then.

Some one had notified Yron that two new slaves had arrived; and presently he came out into the patio to inspect us, much as a gentleman farmer on Earth would inspect a couple of new cows or horses.

There was nothing distinctive about Yron, except that his

trappings and weapons were more ornate than those of common warriors. He looked us over carefully, felt of our muscles, examined our teeth.

"A fine specimen," he said, indicating me. "What did you have to pay for him?"

"Ten kloovol," said the agent.

"They must have paid you to take this one, then," he said, nodding toward Kandar.

I gave Kandar the laugh, then.

I think the agent was not very happy then. Casting about for an out, he said, "I was very fortunate. I got both these fine male slaves for three hundred sixty kloovol."

"You mean to tell me you paid three hundred and fifty for that," he yelled, pointing at Kandar, "when you could buy magnificent specimens like this for only ten?"

"Nobody wanted this one," said the agent. "That is why I got it so cheap. No one else bid."

"Why?" demanded Yron.

"Because he is insubordinate and dangerous. They had to tie his hands behind his back to keep him from killing people."

Yron's gills fluttered and flapped; and he blew, and he blew, and he blew, reminding me of the Big Bad Wolf in the Three Little Pigs. "So!" he fairly screamed. "So! you bought a dangerous slave that no one else would have, and you brought him here!"

"The auctioneer made me buy him," pleaded the agent; "but if you don't want him, I'll kill him and repay you the ten kloovol."

I laid my hand upon the butt of my pistol, and the agent saw the gesture.

"All right," said Yron. "Kill him."

I drew the pistol from its hoster, and the agent changed his mind. "On second thought," he said, "I'll buy him from you and then resell him. Perhaps I can make some profit from him."

"Listen," I said to Yron, "this is all very foolish. If I am well treated and my friend here is well treated, I will kill no one."

"And you will work for me and obey orders?" demanded Yron.

"As long as we are well treated," I said.

"What is your name?"

"Carson."

39

"And yours?"

"Kandar."

Yron called to a funny looking little man whose mouth appeared to be beneath his chin. He looked like a shark. He was a sort of major domo. "Carson and Kandar," said Yron, "will go to the ship the next time we sail; in the meantime keep them around the pool and let them guard the children; and as for you," he shouted at the agent, "if this Carson causes any trouble, you'll go to the ship;" then he came and examined me closely. "Where did you come from?" he demanded. "I never saw any of your kind who looked like you. I never saw anyone with yellow hair and gray eyes before."

As there was no use trying to explain something to him that he couldn't possibly understand, I simply told him that I came from a country far to the south.

"There is no country to the south," he said, "only molten rock and fire;" so that settled that. Yron, the great noble, walked away and re-entered his house.

The major domo approached us. He seemed to undulate toward us. Momentarily I expected to see him roll over on his back and bite somebody, so sharklike was his appearance. He handed us each a wooden trident.

"You will remain close to the pool," he said, "until you are relieved. Let nothing harm the children. Let no one enter the pool other than Yron or one of his women. Be constantly on the lookout for guypals. Never forget that you are very fortunate to be in the service of so great a man as the noble Yron;" then he undulated away.

Kandar and I walked over beside the pool where the other three slaves were patrolling, and one of them instantly recognized Kandar and greeted him most respectfully. "You do not recognize me, of course," he said. "I was a warrior in the bodyguard of Jantor, Jong of Japal, your father. My name is Artol. I am sorry to see a prince of Japal here. As I served your father, I will serve you in whatever way I can."

"We are neither common warrior nor royal prince here," said Kandar. "Let us serve one another."

"Whatever you wish," replied Artol, "but you are still my Prince."

Kandar smiled and shrugged. "How came you here?" he asked.

So Artol told his story.

NINE

"We were twenty," he said, "twenty warriors of the Jong's own bodyguard. A great ship with two banks of oars manned by a hundred slaves and carrying a huge sail for fair winds was fitted out to carry a great cargo of wares to Torlac, which lies five hundred klookob to the west on the shores of the Noellat-gerloo.

'We knew that the cargo was valuable because we twenty were sent along to guard it—twenty warriors of the Jong's own bodyguard, picked men all, from the best warriors of Japal.

"It was to be a long journey—two hundred klookob down the great Lake of Japal, five hundred klookob along the coast of the Noellat-gerloo to Torlac; and then back—fourteen hundred klookob (3500 miles) altogether."

(Note: Noellat-gerloo, the name of the ocean, means mighty water. *Ellat* is might, and the prefix *no* is identical with our suffix y; so *noellat* means mighty. *Gerloo* is water.)

"But it turned out to be a short journey," said Kandar; "you came only as far as Mypos."

"On the contrary, my prince, we completed our journey to Torlac; but not without incident. While we were lying at the lower end of the Lake of Japal, waiting for the tide that would float us through the channel into the Noellat-gerloo, we were attacked by a Myposan ship of war—fifty oars and a hundred warriors.

"They slipped up upon us at night and swarmed our deck. It was a great battle, Prince—twenty against a hundred; for our galley slaves were no good to us, and the sailors of our ship were little better.

"Our officer was killed in the first clash; and I, Artol, took command. The captain of the ship, terrified, was in hiding; so the command of the ship as well devolved upon me. We fought as only the jong's bodyguard knows how to fight, but five to one are heavy odds. And then they armed their galley slaves and turned them upon us, forcing them to fight.

"Still we held our own. The decks were red with blood. As we cut them down, more threw themselves upon us—two for every one we killed; and then I saw that the tide had changed —it was running out of the lake into the ocean.

"So far we had been able to hold the hatch leading from the fighting deck to the deck where the galley slaves sat at their oars, and I sent a good man down there with his orders; then, with my own hands, I slipped the anchor. I shouted the command to row, and leaped to the tiller.

"The ship swung around and headed for the ocean, dragging the enemy ship with it. It was certain that one of the ships would be wrecked, and quite probably both. The Myposans ran for their own ship just as some of their fellows cut her loose from us. We were caught in the swirling rush of the waters racing from the lake into the ocean.

"I could hear the crack of the whips on the slaves' backs as the galley masters urged them to greater effort, for only by tremendous effort could they give the ship steerage way in that racing torrent.

"I am a soldier and no sailor, but I guided the ship through the channel in the darkness of night until it floated at last on the bosom of the ocean; then the captain came out of hiding and took command. Instead of thanking me for saving his ship, he berated me for slipping the anchor.

"We had words, then; and I told him that when we returned to Japal I should report to the jong himself that he had hidden all during the battle when he should have been on deck defending his ship. That is why I am here."

"But I do not understand," said Kandar.

"Wait. I am not through. Presently you shall know. When I checked up after the fight, I found that only ten of us remained; and five of these were wounded. Also, we had eleven Myposan prisoners—eleven who had been unable to reach the deck of their ship after it had been cut loose. These were sent down to the galley masters to help man the oars.

"In due time we reached Torlac, unloaded our cargo and took on another for Japal. The return trip was uneventful until after we entered the Lake of Japal. We lay to at the lower end of the lake so that we should pass Mypos after dark, as is the custom. Then we rowed slowly and silently up the lake, with no lights showing on the ship.

"It was quite dark. One could not recognize faces on deck. There was a great deal of movement there I thought, men passing to and fro constantly. We came opposite Mypos. The lights of the city were plainly discernible.

"Some one said, 'What is that—right there to starboard?' At that, I and my warriors moved to the starboard rail. I had no more than reached it than some one seized me around the waist, leaped to the rail with me, and then into the lake.

"It was a Myposan! You know how these fellows swim, my prince. Half the time he had me under water, half drowned; but at last he dragged me ashore at Mypos, more dead than alive. When I could gather my breath and my wits I found myself in a slave compound with all my men. Later I learned the truth.

"The captain, fearful that we would report him to the jong, had liberated the Myposans with the understanding that they would take us prisoners. As a matter of fact he had stipulated that they were to drown us, but the temptation to take us in as prisoners whom they might sell into slavery was too much for them. It saved our lives.

"So that, my prince, is how I came to be a slave in Mypos; and I live only to return to Japal and have the life of the coward and traitor who sent ten of the jong's bodyguard into slavery."

"Who was this captain?" asked Kandar.

"His name is Gangor."

Kandor nodded. "I know much of him," he said, "but nothing good. It was rumored that he was high in the councils of the party that has long sought to overthrow the jong, my father."

That name meant nothing to me then. It was to mean much, later.

TEN

As we three talked, the major domo came sinuously toward us, more shark-like than ever. "You stand here and talk, slaves," he accused, "when you should be watching for guypals. For this you should be beaten. Separate! Patrol the pool. If a child is harmed you all die—most unpleasantly."

So we fell to walking around the pool with the other two guards, and some of us were always looking up at the sky; though for what, I hadn't the remotest idea.

After the major domo left the patio, I fell in beside Kandar. "What are guypals?" I asked.

"They are large birds of prey," he said—"really very dangerous. If it were not for the guards they would come down and carry off the children. As it is, guards or no guards, you never can tell when they will come. If they do, some of us may be killed. They are terrific fighters and absolutely without fear."

It seemed to me a lot of foolishness, guarding children against birds, when there weren't any children nor any birds. At least I hadn't seen any. It would have been much more sensible, I thought, to let us sit down and rest until the children came out into the patio.

As guypals don't fly at night, we were dismissed as soon as it got dark, and taken to the slaves' compound, where we were fed a nasty mess and herded into a shed to sleep on filthy grass mats. Yron's slaves evidently didn't fare any too well.

I wondered about Duare. Was she being well treated? Was she safe? Would I ever see her again? I fell into a fitful sleep worrying about her.

At dawn the next day, after a vile breakfast, we were taken to the patio again and told to look out for guypals and guard the children. "If the guypals are as dangerous as you say," I remarked to Kandar, "why do they give us wooden tridents? What can we do with a piece of wood against such fierce birds?"

"All we can do is the best we can," he said. "They are afraid to arm us with metal tridents—we might turn on them. You know, these Myposans are at heart arrant cowards."

"Well, I hope I see a guypal today," I said—"anything to break the monotony. I'd even like to see one of their children— it might attract a guypal or two. Where do they keep these children of theirs, anyway?"

Kandar laughed and pointed into the pool. "There," he said. "There are the children."

I looked into the pool, but saw nothing but the few strange looking fishes I had occasionally see the previous day. "I see nothing in there," I said, "but a few weird looking fishes."

"Those are the children," said Kandar.

I looked at him in surprise for a moment, until I got the idea.

"I see," I said. "We have people like that in my own world;

44

being childless, they lavish their affection on dogs and cats. These people have adopted fishes."

Kandar shook his head. "You are quite wrong on both scores," he said. "In the first place these people have no affection to lavish on anything; and, in the second, these *are* their children," and he pointed to the fishes swimming playfully about the pool.

"You are very amusing," I said.

"I didn't intend being. I am really quite serious. You see, these fishlike creatures are really the children of Yron and his mate."

"It is incredible," I said.

"But a fact. Human beings, such as we, bring forth young that somewhat resemble themselves. Many of the beasts do likewise. Some creatures lay eggs in which the embryo develops. The Myposan females bring fish into the world—fish that eventually develop into Myposans.

"If you look closely you will see that the largest of these creatures is already developing hands and feet. Later it will slough its tail; then it will become an amphibian and crawl out on land. Slowly its head and face will change, becoming more human; it will walk erect, and it will become a Myposan; but it will still have gills as well as lungs and be partially amphibious."

I looked closely at one of the darting fishes, and plainly saw rudimentary hands and feet. Somehow it seemed shockingly obscene.

"I owe you an apology," I said to Kandar, "but I really thought that you were joking. So these are the 'children' we are guarding! The little darlings. Papa seems quite solicitous about their safety, but he and Mamma don't pay much attention to them otherwise."

"The Myposans are absolutely devoid of affection. They have no word for love. Their protective instinct is strong, however—a purely biological reaction against racial extinction. They will protect these little monstrosities with their lives."

"These are very young, I suppose," I said.

"They are more than a year old. The females come into their pools to spawn once a year, and give birth to thousands of tiny fishlike creatures—some say as many as a million. These almost immediately find their way out into the lake through the subterranean channels which connect all these pools with the Lake of Japal. Where they go is not definitely known; but probably out into the ocean, where those that survive remain for a year. Of course most of them are devoured by the larger denizens of the sea. In the case of Yron's mate only three survived from last year's spawning."

"These may not even be hers," I suggested.

"Oh, yes they are," Kandar assured me. "Some instinct always guides the little rascals back to the pool in which they were spawned."

"I don't see how anyone can tell," I demurred.

"Instinct again," said Kandar. "These creatures are endowed with a congenital antipathy for similar creatures devoid of identical genes. If one of another spawning should blunder into this pool in search of his own, these creatures would set upon it and either drive it out or kill it.

"The parents, especially the females, have the same instinctive power of recognition of their own. Myposan slaves have told me that it is not uncommon for none of a female's own spawning to return, all having been devoured at sea. If, in such a case, the young of another female blunders into her pool, she immediately recognizes that it is not hers and destroys it."

"I presume that is a provision of Nature to prevent inbreeding," I suggested.

"On the contrary it is a provision of Nature to insure inbreeding," said Kandar. "The Myposans never mate with offspring outside their own families. After you have been here a little longer, you will be struck by the startling family resemblances and characteristics. You will see that Yron and his mate look and act alike; and if you ever witness a gathering of the clan, you will be struck by the remarkable resemblances."

I was about to ask some further question; what, I do not now recall, when I heard a shrill scream from overhead and the whir of wings.

"The guypals!" cried Artol.

ELEVEN

Guypals! They were large birds and ferocious. There must have been a dozen of them. They dove for us and for the pool. We poked and struck at them with our wooden tridents, and they zoomed and dove again.

People came running from the house. Yron and his mate were among them. There was a great deal of noise and a great deal of excitement. The warriors who came had metal tridents, but these the guypals eluded. They seemed to know that the wooden weapons wielded by the slaves could not do much damage.

The Myposans were blowing furiously and flapping their gills. All were screaming orders and advice. It was bedlam. The noise should have frightened off almost anything. We were doing pretty well; and keeping the guypals at a distance, when one of them eluded us and dove straight for the pool. It looked as though one of Mrs. Yron's little darlings was about to get his.

You can't get up much enthusiasm about succoring a fish. At least I can't; but I had a job to do; and it was only natural that, being what I am, I should do the best I could to acquit myself worthily.

I imagine that I just don't think such things out. I act quite mechanically. Had I stopped to think, I should have said to myself, "These may be children to some; but they are just fish to me, and if I save them they will grow up to be three more enemies. I shall let them die;" but I said nothing of the kind to myself. I imagine that what crossed my mind and influenced me was a subconscious reminder that I had been given the job of protecting these creatures and that nothing else counted.

Of course it all happened in the fraction of a second. The guypal dove for the pool, and I drew my r-ray pistol and blew a hole through it. It crumpled and fell into the pool; then I turned the pistol on the others which were circling about awaiting another opportunity to elude us. Three more dropped, and the others flew away.

Yron approached me. I though he was going to express his

indebtedness to me, but he did nothing of the sort. He didn't even thank me for saving his little darlings.

"What is that thing?" he demanded.

"A pistol," I replied.

"What is a pistol?" he asked.

"This," I said.

"And it killed the guypals?" he asked.

"*I* killed the guypals. Without me the pistol could not kill them—unless," I added, "they had touched it."

"Could it kill anything else?" he asked.

"Certainly—anything."

"Me?"

"You and all your people," I assured him.

"Give it to me, slave," he demanded.

"Certainly," I said, holding it out toward him, "but if you touch it it will kill you."

He drew back, and commenced to blow. His gills flapped. "Throw it away!" he commanded.

He might as well have asked me to cut off my right hand and throw it away. I was saving that pistol for some future emergency. You may wonder why I had never used it on these people in a break for freedom. It was because I had never yet found conditions such that I might hope to escape and take Duare with me, and I certainly had no intention of trying to escape without her.

I just grinned at Yron and shook my head. "I may need it," I said, "If the people of Mypos do not treat my mate and me well."

Yron fairly danced up and down. "Throw it away, slave!" he screamed. "I, Yron, a noble of Mypos and your master, command you."

"And I, Carson of Venus, a prince of Korva, refuse."

You could have heard Yron's gills flap a city block away, and he was blowing like a whale—which he didn't at all resemble. I don't know whether or not fish have high blood pressure; but I am sure Yron didn't, as otherwise he would have exploded. I think I have never seen any other creature in the throes of such a terrific rage—the more terrific because of its futility.

"Seize him!" he screamed at several of his warriors who had come to the pool following the alarm. "Seize him and destroy that thing!"

The warriors had been interested listeners to our altercation. They had heard me say that whoever touched my pistol would die; so they came forward warily, each one intent upon permitting some one else to be first. They were very polite in this respect. There was no rude elbowing of others aside in order to be the first to seize me.

"That is close enough," I said, pointing the pistol at them.

They halted in their tracks, looking very uncomfortable.

"Spear him!" commanded Yron.

I pointed the pistol at Yron. "When the first spear is raised, you die," I told him. The warriors looked questioningly at him.

"Hold!" cried Yron. "Do not spear him—yet. Wait until I have gone."

"You are not going until you have countermanded that order," I told him. "I think that perhaps we had better discuss this matter so that there may be no more misunderstandings; they are always annoying and sometimes fatal."

"I do not discuss anything with my slaves," replied Yron, haughtily.

I shrugged. "It is all the same to me," I said, "but remember this: If my mate and my friend Kandar, here, and I are not treated well, you die. I can kill you any time I wish."

"Your mate? You have no mate here."

"Not here, but in the palace of Tyros. She was purchased for him in the slave market. You'd better advise him to treat her well. At the same time arrange to release us and return us to the place where we were captured."

"Such insolence!" he cried. "Wait until Tyros hears of this. He will have you killed."

"Not before I have killed Tyros. Tell him that." I thought I might as well play up my advantage while I could, for it was evident that he was already afraid of me.

"How can you reach Tyros in his palace?" he demanded.

"By killing every one who tries to stop me—commencing with you," I said, twirling my pistol around my index finger.

"I don't believe that you could do it; you are just boasting," said Yron.

"I shall prove it," I said, leveling my pistol at him.

At that, he dove into the pool and disappeared. I found it difficult not to laugh, he cut such an amusing figure in his fright. All the slaves and warriors were standing around watching me—at a respectful distance.

I waited for Yron to come to the surface. I was going to give him another scare, but he didn't come up. Five minutes passed, and nothing happened—except that the warriors slowly dispersed, going back into the building. Finally only we slaves remained in the patio.

"Yron must have drowned," I said to Kandar.

"By no means," replied Kandar. "He may be out in the lake by this time, or in a grotto at the bottom of the pool, or back in his palace."

"But how?" I asked.

"These people are amphibians," explained Kandar. "They can remain under water for considerable periods of time. Also, they have underwater corridors that lead from their pools out into the lake, as well as other corridors that lead to smaller pools within their palaces; and there are usually grottos, which are really parts of the pools, far under water, where they can remain in hiding, breathing through their gills."

Kandar told me a great deal about these Myposans, but nothing that was later to stand me in better stead than the description of these underwater corridors. He did not like the Myposans, upon whom he looked with the utmost contempt. He said that they were neither fish nor human, and their arrogant egotism irked him no end.

"They consider themselves supermen whose destiny it is to rule the world, forcing what they call their culture on all other peoples. Culture!" he snorted, and then words failed him.

"We have had peoples like that in my own world," I said, "led by such men as Genghis Kahn and Attila the Hun who wrecked the culture and civilization of their times and set the world back many centuries; and I suppose we shall have others."

"And what happened after them?" asked Kandar.

"Civilization struggled slowly from the mire into which they had plunged it, as I suppose it always will struggle back after each such catastrophe; but to what glorious heights it might have attained had they never lived!"

TWELVE

The next day dawned like any other day. The intense light of the Sun, filtering through the two cloud envelopes, imparted a brilliance comparable to that of an April day in our own northern hemisphere when the sky is lightly overcast by fleecy clouds; yet, for me, it was to be no ordinary day. It was to mark a definite, a drastic change in my fortunes.

With other slaves, I was still guarding the horrid little creatures in the pool. I day-dreamed of Duare. I lived again the high moments of our lives together. I planned. I schemed fantastic schemes for our escape; but, when all was said, I was still a slave.

The major domo came into the patio with four warriors. They were garbed differently from those I had seen on the grounds of Yron's palace or elsewhere. Their trappings were more ornate.

Kandar was patrolling at my side. "Members of the jong's guard," he said. "I wonder what they are doing here."

We were soon to learn. Led by the major domo, they approached us. The major domo confronted me. His gills flapped idly; and he blew a little, as befits one who addresses a low slave.

"Slave," he said, "You will accompany these warriors."

"Why?" I asked.

Then his gills *did* flap, and he blew angrily. "Because I say so," he bellowed.

"That is not enough," I said. "I don't like it here, but I don't intend going some place that may be worse."

"Enough of this," snapped one of the jong's warriors. "Come, slave! and come alive, or we will take you dead." He came toward me.

I drew my pistol, and the major domo seized the arm of the warrior. "Careful!" he cautioned. "With that thing he can kill you—and he will."

"He threatens one of the jong's guard?" demanded the warrior.

"I do," I said. "I threaten them all and I can kill them all. Ask any of Yron's people if I speak the truth."

"Why hasn't that thing been taken from him?" demanded the warrior.

"Because whoever touches it dies," said the major domo.

"Tell me where I am going and why," I insisted, "and then perhaps there will be no reason for killing."

The major domo and the warriors stepped to one side and whispered together; and the former said to me, "There is no reason why you should not know. The noble Yron, as a mark of his loyalty and high esteem, has presented you to our beloved jong."

So! The noble Yron was getting rid of a dangerous and undesirable alien by passing him on to his ruler. The loyal Yron! I had to smile. Had the German Kaiser presented Trotsky, armed with a bomb, to the Czar of Russia the acts would have been somewhat analogous.

"Why are you smiling?" demanded the warrior spokesman.

"I am happy," I said. "I shall be delighted to go to the palace of Tyros, and I will go willingly on one condition."

"Slaves do not make conditions," growled the warrior.

"I am an exception," I said; "you have never before seen a slave like me." I twirled my pistol about my finger.

"Well, what do you want now?" demanded the major domo.

"I think that Yron should also present Kandar to his jong. Kandar is a much more valuable slave than I, and if Yron really wishes to demonstrate his loyalty and high esteem he should present a really royal gift to his jong—two princes instead of one; the Crown Prince of Japal and the Crown Prince of Korva." Of course I didn't say Crown Prince; I said Tanjong.

I made this condition not only because I had grown very fond of Kandar but because I felt that he could be very helpful to me in effecting the rescue of Duare and the eventual escape of all three of us.

"That," said the warrior, "is an excellent suggestion."

"But Yron only mentioned the slave Carson," objected the major domo.

"Should I return to Tyros with only one slave and have to report that Yron refused to give two, the jong might be very angry with Yron," suggested the warrior.

The major domo was on a spot. So was Yron. "I shall have to consult my master," said the former.

"We will wait," said the warrior, and the major domo disappeared within the palace.

"I hope you don't mind going with me," I said to Kandar. "I felt that we might work together, but I had no opportunity to discuss the matter with you."

"I was delighted when you mentioned it," he replied. "I only wish that Artol might accompany us."

"I wish so, too; but perhaps I have gone as far as is safe. Tyros might become suspicious if he learned that he had acquired three slaves who were bound together by ties of friendship and that one of them had proved highly insubordinate. I have a feeling that Yron has pulled a boner."

The shark-like major domo came weaving back into the patio. His gills were moving gently, and he sucked air in between his teeth as he addressed the warrior. "The noble Yron is delighted by the opportunity to present two slaves to the mighty Tyros. He would be delighted to give three slaves."

"That is noble of him," I said, "and if this warrior of the jong's guard would like to select an unusually fine slave I suggest that he have a look at this one, with whom I have been particularly impressed since I have been in the palace of Yron;" and I indicated Artol.

The major domo glared at me with his fishy eyes, his gills flapped, and he blew noisily. Artol was one of Yron's best and most valuable slaves. The warrior looked him over, felt his muscles, examined his teeth.

"An excellent specimen," he said. "I am sure that our jong will be well pleased with this gift."

Artol was pleased, too, for now he would not have to be separated from his beloved Tanjong. I was pleased; Kandar was pleased; the jong's warriors were pleased. The major domo was not pleased, but I was sure that Yron was glad to get rid of me at any price. Now he could come out into his patio without fearing for his life. Perhaps I could make Tyros so anxious to be rid of me that he would give us all our freedom.

The leader of the warriors stood looking at me. He seemed to hesitate. I guessed that he was wondering what other demands I might make if he again attempted to take me away, and hesitated to subject his authority to any further embarrassing contretemps.

Kandar, Artol, and I were standing together. The other

slaves and warriors and the major domo were watching the ranking warrior. The situation was becoming strained and difficult, and I was on the point of relieving it by suggesting that we leave for the palace of Tyros, when a whir of wings and a shrill whistle attracted our attention upward.

"Guypal!" someone cried; and, sure enough, a huge guypal was diving straight for the pool.

The warriors with their metal tridents and the slaves with theirs of wood rushed about frantically, screaming, and raising such a din as should have frightened away a battalion of guypals; but it never deterred this one. It was diving straight for the center of the pool well out of reach of the tridents. A dozen were cast at it, and all missed.

What has taken so long to tell happened in a few seconds; and in those few seconds I whipped out my pistol; and as the guypal touched the surface of the pool, I sent a stream of r-rays through its body. It cut the water, staining it red with its blood; and then it floated to the surface, dead.

The warriors looked at me in open mouthed astonishment. The major domo nodded his head. "You see, " he said to the warriors, "that what I told you is true. This is a very dangerous man."

"And so Yron is giving him to Tyros!" exclaimed the leader of the warriors.

"You do not understand," hedged the major domo. "This is Yron's most valuable slave. All alone he can guard the children against guypals. Twice now has he proved this. Yron thought that Tyros would be glad to have such a guard for the royal children."

The warrior grunted. "Perhaps," he said.

"And now," I said to the warrior, "why don't you take us to Tyros? Why are we hanging around here listening to this little man?"

The major domo was speechless from blowing.

"Very well," said the warrior. "Come, slaves!" and thus at last we started for the palace of Tyros; Kandar, Artol, and I.

THIRTEEN

I thought that now I should see Duare often, but I was doomed to disappointment. The palace of Tyros sprawls over many acres; and the compound where the common slaves are confined is far from the precincts allotted to royalty, where Duare served, as I learned soon after arriving.

The slaves' quarters were open sheds forming a quadrangle in the center of which was a pool. There was no growing thing within the quadrangle, just bare earth, pounded hard by the passage of bare and sandaled feet. We slept upon mats. The pool was for bathing. Its connection with the lake was by a conduit too small to permit of escape. Fresh water was being constantly supplied it from a stream which ran down from the distant hills; so it was always clean and fresh. The entire compound was kept in immaculate condition, and the food rations of the royal slaves were far better and more generous than those I had before seen. Insofar as these matters were concerned, we had little of which to complain. It was the arrogance and brutality of the guards that made the lives of many of the slaves miserable.

My reputation and I arrived simultaneously. I could tell it by the way the guards eyed me and my pistol; and it soon spread to the slaves, with the result that I was immediately the center of attention. Kandar and Artol had to tell over and over the story of my encounters with Yron and his major domo, and so great became the laughter that the guards came among us with their whips and laid onto many a back. I called Kandar and Artol to my side; and when the guards came slashing in our vicinity I laid my hand upon the butt of my pistol, and the guards passed us by.

Among the slaves was a Myposan named Plin who was very friendly. Now, I do not like Myposans; but a friendly Myposan might some time be a handy thing to have around; so, while I did not particularly cultivate Plin, neither did I discourage his friendly advances.

He was much interested in my pistol, and asked many questions about it. He said that he was surprised that I had not been murdered while I slept; as a slave with such a weapon as mine was a very dangerous person for any master to have around. I told him that Kandar, Artol, and I took turns standing watch every night to prevent just that very thing.

"And it will really kill anybody who touches it?" he asked.

"Certainly," I said.

He shook his head. "Maybe the other things you have told me are true, but I do not believe that anyone would be killed just by touching it. If that were true, you would be killed."

"Would you like to touch it and prove your theory?" I asked.

"Certainly," he said. "I am not afraid of it. Let me have it."

I shook my head. "No," I said. "I would not let a friend kill himself."

He grinned. "You are a very smart man," he said.

Well, I thought he was rather smart, too. He was the only Myposan who had had the brains to pierce my ruse. I was glad that he was my friend, and I hoped that he would keep his suspicions to himself.

In order to change the subject, which was growing distasteful to me, I asked him why he was in slavery.

"I was warrior to a noble," he explained, "and one day this noble caught me making love with one of his concubines; so he sold me into slavery, and I was purchased by Tyros' agent."

"And you will have to remain a slave the rest of your life?" I asked.

"Not if I am fortunate enough to win the favor of Tyros," he said. "Then I should be freed and probably be permitted to enter the service of Tyros as a warrior."

"And you think that this may happen?" I asked.

"Something tells me that it may happen very soon," he replied.

"You have been a slave in the palace of Tyros for some time?" I asked.

"Yes."

"Then perhaps you can give me some information that I should very much like to have."

"I shall be glad to, if I can," he assured me. "What is it?"

"My mate, Duare, was purchased by Tyros' agent. Have you seen her? Do you know where she is and how she fares?"

"I have seen her," said Plin. "She is very beautiful, and she

56

fares quite well. She is serving the Vadjong Skabra, Tyros' queen. That is because she is so beautiful."

"I don't understand," I said.

"Well, you see Tyros has many concubines, some of which have been slaves; but none of them is very beautiful. Skabra sees to that. She is very jealous, and Tyros is much afraid of her. She has let him have a number of ill favored concubines; but when a beautiful woman like your mate comes along, Skabra takes her for herself."

"So my mate is safe?"

"As long as she serves Skabra, she is safe," he said.

Life in the slave compound of the jong of Mypos was monotonous. The guards took us out in shifts for odd jobs around the palace grounds. As a rule they were too bored themselves to even wield their whips on those who were too helpless or too poor to protect themselves. They left Kandar, Artol, and me alone because of my pistol; and Plin, who was able to receive money from outside, won immunity and favors by bribery. He hung around me a great deal, and was always fawning on me and flattering me. I got rather tired of him.

I chafed under the enforced inaction which offered not the slightest suggestion of a hope for escape. I wished that they would give me more work to occupy my time. "Wait until you're sent to the ships," said one of my fellow slaves; "you'll get work enough there."

The days dragged on. I longed for Duare and for freedom. I commenced to concoct fantastic and wholly impractical schemes for escape. It became an obsession with me. I didn't discuss them with Kandar or others; because, fortunately, I realized how silly they were. It was well that I didn't.

Then, one day, Tyros sent for me. Tyros, the great jong, had sent for a slave! The compound buzzed with excitement. I had an idea why I was being thus signally honoured. The gossip of the slave compound and the guardroom had reached the ears of Tyros, and his curiosity had been aroused to see the strange slave with yellow hair who had defied nobles and warriors.

It was curiosity that killed the cat, but I feared it might work with reverse English in this instance. However, the summons offered a break in the monotony of my existence and an opportunity to see Tyros the Bloody. It would also take me into the palace proper for the first time, and I had been anxious to gain some knowledge of it against the day that I might attempt to take Duare away.

So I was escorted by a strong detachment of warriors to the palace of the jong of Mypos.

FOURTEEN

The Myposans have little or no sense of the artistic. They seem to be form and line blind. Their streets are crooked; their houses are crooked. The only harmony that abounds is that of disharmony. The palace of Tyros was no exception. The throne room was a shapeless, polyangular space somewhere near the center of the palace. In some places the ceiling was twenty feet high, in others not much more than four. It was supported by columns of different sizes, irregularly spaced. It might have been designed by a drunken surrealist afflicted with a hebephrenic type of dementia praecox; which of course, is not normal, because surrealists are not always drunk.

The dais upon which Tyros sat on a wooden bench might have been rolled out of a giant dice box and left where it came to rest. Nobody could possibly have placed it where it was, for the major portion of the room was behind it; and Tyros' back was toward the main entrance.

I was led around in front of the dais, where I had my first sight of Tyros. It was not a pleasant sight. Tyros was very fat—the only Myposan I had seen whose physique was not beautiful. He had pop eyes and a huge mouth, and his eyes were so far apart that you could see them bend inward to focus. His great gills were terribly inflamed, appearing diseased. On the whole, he was not a pretty sight.

The room was full of nobles and warriors, and among the first that I saw was Yron. His gills were palpitating and he was blowing softly. I knew by these signs that he was distraught. When his eyes alighted on me, his gills flapped angrily.

"How is the noble Yron this morning?" I inquired.

"Silence, slave!" ordered one of my guard.

"But Yron is an old friend of mine," I objected. "I am sure that he is glad to see me."

Yron just stood there and flapped and blew. I saw some of the nobles near him sucking air through their teeth; and I guessed that they were laughing at his discomfiture, for that is as near as they can come to laughing.

I saw Vomer there, too. I had almost forgotten him. He stared at me with his dull, fishy eyes. He hated me, too. In all the room full of people, I had no friend.

When I was halted below the dais, Tyros focused his eyes upon me. "Yellow hair!" he commented. "A strange looking creature. Yron says that he is a very valuable slave. What makes him so valuable—his yellow hair? I have heard many things about you, slave. I have heard that you are insubordinate and disrespectful and that you carry a weapon that kills people if you merely point it at them. What foolishness is that? They've been lying to me, haven't they?"

"Yron probably has," I said. "Did he tell you that I was a valuable slave?"

"Silence!" cried a noble at my side. "Slaves do not question the great jong."

Tyros waved the man to silence. "Let him speak. I asked him a question. His answer interests me. Yes, slave, Yron said that you were very valuable."

"Did he tell you what he paid for me?" I asked.

"It was some very large amount. I do not recall that he stated it exactly, but I know that he gave me the impression that you had cost him quite a fortune."

"He paid just ten kloovol for me," I said. "I didn't cost him much and he was afraid of me; those are the reasons that he presented me to you."

"Why was he afraid of you?" demanded Tyros.

"Because he knew that I could kill him any time I wished; so he gave me to you. Perhaps Yron wanted you killed."

All gills were flapping by this time, and there was a great blowing. Every eye was upon Yron. "He lies," he screamed. "I gave him to you, Tyros, to guard your children. Twice he saved mine from guypals."

"But he cost you only ten kloovol?" demanded Tyros.

"I got a very good bargain. I—"

"But he cost only ten kloovol and you were afraid of him; so you gave him to me." Tyros was screaming by this time. Suddenly he focused his popeyes on me, as though struck by a new idea. "How do I know that that thing can kill anybody?" he demanded.

"The noble Yron has told you so," I reminded him.

"The noble Yron is a liar and the son of a liar," snapped Tyros. "Fetch a slave!" he shouted at a warrior standing near him.

While he was waiting for the slave to be brought, he returned his attentions to the unhappy Yron. He vilified and insulted him and his ancestors back for some ten generations; then he started in on Yron's wife, her ancestors, and her progeny; nor did he desist until the slave was brought.

"Stand him up with his back to that pillar," ordered Tyros; then he turned to me. "Now kill him with that thing, if you can," he said.

"Why should I kill a fellow slave when there are so many of my enemies about me?" I demanded.

"Do as I tell you, slave!" ordered Tyros.

"I kill only in self-defense," I said. "I will not kill this man."

"You can't kill him; that is the reason," fumed Tyros. "That thing wouldn't kill anybody. You are a great liar; and you have frightened others with your lies, but you can't frighten Tyros."

"But I can easily prove that it will kill," I said, "without killing this defenseless man."

"How?" demanded the jong.

"By killing you," I told him.

Figuratively, Tyros went straight through the ceiling. His gills flapped wildly, and he blew so hard that he couldn't speak for a full minute.

"Seize him!" he cried to the members of his bodyguard. "Seize him and take that thing from him."

"Wait!" I ordered, pointing the pistol at him. "If anyone comes nearer me or threatens me, I'll kill you, Tyros. I can kill every one in this room if I wish. I do not wish to kill any one unless I am forced to. All I ask is that you set free my mate, Duare, myself, and my two friends, Kandar and Artol. If you do that, we will go away; and you will be safe. As long as I am in Mypos no one is safe. What do you say, Tyros?"

His warriors hesitated, turning toward him. Tyros was on a spot. If he showed fear of me, he would lose face. If he insisted on his bodyguard carrying out his orders, he might lose his life. He decided to hedge. He turned on Yron.

"Traitor!" he screamed. "Assassin! You sent this man here to kill me. Because he has refused to do your bidding, I forgive him what he has said to me. After all he is only an ignorant creature of a lower order. He knows no better. But you, knave! You shall die! For high treason I condemn you to death, and this man shall be your executioner.

"Send that other slave back to his quarters and place Yron against the pillar in his place," he ordered; then he turned again to me. "Now let's see what that thing will do. Kill Yron!"

"I told you once that I kill only in self-defense. If you want some one killed, come and attack me yourself, or shut up."

Like most tyrannical despots, Tyros was half mad. He had little or no control of his temper, and now he was frantic. He fumed and bellowed and flapped and blew and tore at his beard; but I saw that he feared me, for he made no move to attack me himself, nor did he order others to do so.

"Listen," I said. I had to shout to be heard above the racket he was making. "Free us, as I suggested, and let us go away in peace. If you don't I may be forced to kill you in order to effect our escape."

"You would be well rid of him at any price," said one of his nobles.

This was all Tyros required to give him a slender out. "If that is the wish of my people," he said, "I will consider it. In the meantime return this slave to the slaves' quarters, and let me see no more of him."

FIFTEEN

When I returned to the compound, I found that the slave whom I had refused to kill had spread the story of my encounter with Tyros; and, as is usually the case with such a story, it had lost nothing in the telling. The other slaves looked at me as they might at one who had returned from the grave; or, what might probably be a better simile, as one on his way to the death chamber. They crowded around me, asking many questions; some of them just content to touch one who had bearded the lion in his den. Plin was loudest in his praise. Kandar seemed worried. He thought that I had finally sealed

61

my doom. Artol was genuinely proud of me. He had the warrior's reaction—that what I had done was worth dying for. Somehow Plin's praise seemed tinged by envy. After all, Plin was a Myposan.

Kandar, Artol, and I finally detached ourselves from the others and sat down on the hard packed ground to talk. They were both very grateful that I had included them in my demand for freedom, but neither of them thought that there was the slightest chance that Tyros would free us.

"He'll find some way to destroy you," said Kandar. "After all, one man can't overcome a city full of enemies."

"But how?" asked Artol. "Have you a plan?"

"S-s-s-t!" cautioned Kandar. "Here comes Plin."

So Kandar mistrusted the Myposan. I was not surprised. The fellow was too oily, and his protestations of friendship were overdone.

Kandar, Artol, and I had maintained something of a night watch, one of us always trying to remain awake; but we must have slipped up that night, for the next morning my pistol was gone. It had been stolen while we slept. I discovered my loss almost immediately I awoke; and when I told the others, Kandar said, "Where is Plin?"

Plin was not in the slaves' compound. We wondered how he had dared touch the weapon. Either the proffered reward or the threat of punishment had been too great for him to resist. You see, we did not doubt that it was Plin.

I expected to be put to death immediately, but a circumstance intervened to save me temporarily. It was a royal celebration. One of Tyros' young had developed arms, and legs, and lungs, and was ready to emerge from the pool—the future jong of Mypos. Many slaves were required in connection with this celebration, and we were all herded into the great royal patio, covering several acres, in the center of which was the jong's pool, where the royal monstrosities developed.

The patio was filled with nobles, warriors, women, and slaves. I saw Plin and approached him, but he went quickly away into that part of the garden reserved for free men. So that had been Plin's reward! Of course I could not follow him there. Warriors saw to that.

A palace slave saw the little drama as Plin eluded me and the warriors roughly turned me back. The fellow smiled at me.

"You must be the slave from whom Plin stole the strange weapon," he hazarded.

"I am," I said. "I wish I knew where it was."

"It is in the pool," he said. "Tyros was so afraid of it that, in his terror, he ordered Plin to throw it into the pool."

Well, at least I knew where my pistol was, but little good it would do me. It might lie there forever, for it would never corrode. The metal of which it was fabricated insured that. And, doubtless, no Myposan would dare retrieve it.

There was a great deal of drinking going on, mostly a potent brew that the Myposans concoct. Tyros was drinking a great deal, and getting rather drunk. I saw Skabra, his vadjong—a most brutal looking female. I did not wonder that Tyros was afraid of her. And I saw Duare, too; but I could not catch her eye. I could not get close enough to her; and there were hundreds of people there, constantly milling.

In the afternoon a great cry arose; and every eye was turned upon the pool, from which a hideous little amphibian emerged. It still had the head of a fish. Nobles ran forward to catch it; but it eluded them, scampering here and there to avoid capture. Finally, however, it was brought to bay; and a net was thrown over it; then it was borne away to the royal nursery, where it would have a private pool and could complete its development.

By this time Tyros was quite drunk. I saw him approach Duare, and I saw Skabra rise from her bench and move toward them. I couldn't hear what Tyros said to Duare, but I saw her little chin go up as she turned her back on him. Skabra's voice was raised in anger—shrill, harsh—and Tyros, ordinarily afraid of her, screamed back at her, brave with liquor. They were calling each other all the unroyal names they could lay their tongues to. Every eye was upon them.

Suddenly Tyros seized Duare and started to drag her away; then it was that I started for him. No one paid any attention to me. All were too interested in the actions of the principals in this royal triangle, for now Skabra had started in pursuit.

Tyros was running toward the pool, carrying Duare with him. He reached the edge; and, to my horror, dove in, dragging Duare beneath the surface with him.

SIXTEEN

A warrior tried to bar my way as I ran toward the pool. I swung a right to his chin, and he went down. A trident whizzed past my head as I dove, and another cut the water beside me after I had submerged. But no one followed me. Perhaps they felt that Tyros was safe in his own element and needed no protection. Perhaps they didn't care what happened to Tyros, for they all feared and hated him.

The pool was deep, very deep. Ahead of me and below I could see the figures of Tyros and Duare going deeper and deeper. Could I reach them before Duare drowned? Could either of us survive a struggle with the amphibian king and reach the surface alive? These questions harassed me, but I swam on.

As I reached the bottom, I saw Tyros slither into a dark hole at the very bottom of the pool's side wall; and as I followed him, my lungs seemingly on the verge of bursting, I saw something lying on the floor of the pool. It was my pistol, lying where Plin had thrown it. I had only to reach out my hand and pick it up; then I was in a dark corridor fighting for my life and Duare's.

I thought that corridor would never end, nor did it add any to my peace of mind to realize that it might end in a watery cavern from which there would be no escape for me or for Duare. My only hope and encouragement lay in what Kandar had told me of these pools and passageways. I prayed that this passageway led to another, near-by pool. It did. Presently I saw light ahead and then above. Almost unconscious from suffocation, I shot to the surface—just in time. Another second, I honestly believe, and I should have been dead.

I saw Tyros dragging Duare from the pool. Her body was limp. It was evident that she was dead. Had I been absolutely certain of that, I could have shot Tyros then; but I hesitated, and in the brief instant of my indecision he bore her through a doorway and was gone.

I was absolutely exhausted. I tried to climb from the pool only to discover that I did not have the strength. What I had gone through had sapped it all. I looked about me as I clung to the edge of the pool. I was in a small apartment or court, which the pool almost entirely filled. It had no roof. Several doors led from it. There was one small window.

My strength came back rapidly, and I dragged myself from the pool and followed through the doorway which had swallowed Tyros and Duare. Here I encountered a veritable labyrinth of corridors. Which way had Tyros gone? There was no clew. Every precious moment counted if, Duare alive, I was to rescue her; or, Duare dead, I was to avenge her. It was maddening.

Presently I heard a voice, and I followed it. Soon I recognized it. It was Tyros' drunken voice exhorting, commanding. At last I found him. He was bending over the lifeless form of Duare demanding that she arise and follow him. He was telling her that he was tired of carrying her. He didn't seem to realize that she was dead.

When he saw me and my levelled pistol, he screamed; then he swept Duare's body up and held it before him as a shield; as he hurled his trident. It was a poor cast, and missed. I advanced slowly toward him, taking my time, gloating over my vengeance.

All the time, Tyros was screaming for help. I didn't care how much help came—I could always kill Tyros before they could kill me. I expected to die in that chamber; and I was content; because I would not live without Duare.

Tyros tried to draw his sword as he saw me coming nearer, but Duare's body interfered. At last he let it slip to the floor; and, still screaming, he came toward me. It was then that a door flew open and a dozen warriors burst into the room.

I let Tyros the Bloody have it first. He collapsed in a heap; then I turned the weapon upon the advancing warriors. They nearly got me as a veritable shower of tridents drove through the air at my almost naked body. It was the very number of them that saved me. They struck one another and their aim was diverted—just enough to permit me to dodge and elude them. After that it was simple. The warriors with their swords were no match for me. I mowed down ten of them before the remaining two turned and fled.

At last I was alone with the body of my mate. I turned toward it. Duare was sitting up, looking at me wonderingly.

"How did you do it, Carson?" she demanded. "However in the world did you do it?"

"I could do much more than this for you," I said, as I took her in my arms.

"What now?" asked Duare presently. "We are trapped. But at least we shall die together."

"We are not dead yet," I said. "Come with me!"

I led the way to the pool from which we had just emerged. Through the one small window I could see the great lake scarcely a hundred yards away. I was certain that a corridor led from this pool to the lake. "Can you swim another hundred yards under water?" I asked her.

"I can try," she said.

"Wait until I make sure that there is a corridor leading to the lake;" then I dove into the pool. I found an opening near the bottom of the end of the pool nearest the lake; so I was reasonable certain that it led into a corridor that would take us out of the city of Mypos. The only drawback to the plan was that we should be swimming in the lake right off the quays of Mypos in broad daylight. It didn't seem possible that we could escape detection.

As I broke the surface of the pool after locating the corridor, Duare whispered to me that she heard someone approaching. I listened. Yes, I could hear them plainly—the sound of sandalled feet and the rattling of accoutrements; then we heard men shouting, and the sounds were very near.

"Come, Duare!" I called and she dove in.

I led her to the mouth of the tunnel and followed her in. I must have been wrong in my estimate of the distance to the lake. It was far more than a hundred yards. I marvelled at Duare's endurance, for I was almost all in and virtually at my last gasp, had I dared to gasp, when I saw light shining from above. As one, we shot up to the surface; and as our heads broke it, almost simultaneously, Duare flashed me a reassuring smile. Ah, what a girl! In two worlds; yes, even in all the Universe I doubt that there is her like.

We found ourselves in a small, circular pool in the bottom of a roofless, windowless tower. A ledge, a few feet wide, encircled the pool. We dragged ourselves on to it to rest and plan. We decided to remain where we were until after dark; then try to reach the lake. If we were followed into this pool, I could account for our pursuers as fast as they stuck their heads above the surface. How I thanked Heaven for that pistol!

Well after dark we swam through the remainder of the passageway to the lake; and followed the shore line to a point beyond the city. What hideous terrors of the deep we were fortunate enough to escape, I can only guess; but we came through all right. More by intuition than anything else, I made our way back to the point at which we had left the anotar. Our hearts were in our mouths as we searched for it. The night was dark. Even the strange Venusian luminance seemed lesser than usual. At last we gave up, disheartened, and lay down on the soft grass to rest.

We both must have fallen asleep almost instantly, for the next I remember it was daylight. I sat up and looked around. Duare lay asleep beside me; and a hundred yards away, just inside the forest, was the anotar!

I shall never forget with what a sense of gratitude to God and with what relief we felt the ship rise above the menaces of this inhospitable land.

The only blemish on our happiness was that Kandar and Artol were still prisoners in Mypos.

SEVENTEEN

There are, fortunately, recorded indelibly upon our minds moments of great happiness that we have enjoyed. Standing out among mine, I am sure, will be the moment that the anotar rose from the ground that day and I realized that Duare and I were reunited and that she was safe.

Safe! That word has its nuances. Safety is relative. In relation to her immediate past, Duare was quite safe; but we were still thousands of miles from Korva, with only a very hazy idea of the direction of our goal.

We had enough concentrated fuel to fly the ship for, probably, some fifty years; but we would have to make occasional landings for food and water, and it seemed as though every time we landed something terrible happened to us. But that is Venus. If you had a forced landing in Kansas or Maine or Oregon, the only thing you'd have to worry about would be the landing; but when you set a ship down in Venus, you

67

never know what you're going to run up against. It might be kloonobargan, the hairy, man-eating savages; or a tharban, that most frightful of lion-like carnivores; or a basto, a huge, omnivorous beast that bears some slight resemblance to the American bison; or, perhaps worst of all, ordinary human beings like yourself, but with a low evaluation of life—that is, your life.

But I was not so much troubled by consideration of these possibilities as I was of the fate of Kandar and Artol. They were splendid fellows, and I hated to think of their having to remain slaves in Mypos.

Duare had evidently been watching my face, for she said, "What is troubling you, Carson? You look worried."

"I was thinking of Kandar and Artol," I replied. "We had hoped to escape together."

"Who is Artol?" she asked. "I do not recall a slave by that name."

"I met him after I was taken to Yron's palace," I explained. "He was a warrior in the bodyguard of Jantor, jong of Japal—Kandar's father, you know."

"We should help them to escape, if we can," said Duare.

"I can't risk your safety again," I said.

"They are our friends," she said. "We cannot abandon them without making an effort to save them." That was like Duare.

"Well," I said, "we might fly over the city and see what can be done about it. I have a plan. Perhaps it will work, and perhaps it won't. That will depend more upon Kandar and Artol than on us. Take the controls a minute."

As she flew the ship, circling back toward Mypos, I found writing materials in one of the storage compartments; and wrote a note to Kandar. I showed it to Duare, and after she had read it, she nodded her approval.

"We can do our part easily enough," she said; "I hope they can do theirs."

I tied the note to a spare bolt, and took the controls. We were now about a thousand feet above Mypos, and I started a wide spiral down toward the city, aiming at Tyros' palace.

As we got closer, I could see people staring up at us from the streets and from the palace grounds; and I could see others scurrying for safety. Of course none of them had ever seen an aeroplane before, for our anotar is the only one in Venus

—as far as I know; at least none of them had seen one except the Mypos warriors who had captured us. Of course they had told every one about it, but nobody believed them.

I headed for the slave compound in the palace grounds, flying very low and looking for Kandar or Artol. At last I recognized them both; they were standing together, looking up at us. Although I had told Kandar all about the anotar, he looked now as though he couldn't even believe his eyes.

As I circled again, some of Tyros' warriors ran into the compound and commenced to hurl spears at us—the three pronged tridents with which they are armed. As far as we were concerned they were quite harmless; but they fell back among themselves; and after one impaled a warrior, they desisted.

I didn't want the warriors in the compound; because I didn't wish them to see me drop the note to Kandar. But how to get rid of them? Finally I hit upon a plan. The only trouble was that it might chase Kandar out of the compound, too; but I could only try it.

I zoomed to a thousand feet, and then banked and dove for the compound. You should have seen slaves and warriors scurry for safety! But Kandar and Artol never moved from their tracks. If the compound had only been a little longer and there had been no pool in it, I could have landed and taken off again with Kandar and Artol before the terrified warriors could have been aware of what I was doing.

Duare gave a little gasp as I flattened out and just missed the cornice of one of the palace buildings by a hair; then I banked again and came back. This time I dropped the note at Kandar's feet; then I rose and circled back low over the compound. I saw Kandar pick up the note and read it. Immediately he raised his left hand above his head. That was the signal I had written him to give if he would make the attempt to escape that I had suggested. Before I flew away, I saw him destroy the note.

I rose high and went inland. I wanted the Myposans to think that we had gone away for good. After we were out of sight of the city. I turned north and gradually circled back toward the lake on which Mypos is situated. Still well out of sight of the city I found a secluded cove, and made a landing a short distance off shore. Here we waited until after dark.

EIGHTEEN

It was very peaceful on the waters of that little cove. We were not even threatened by any of the fearsome creatures which swarm the lakes and seas of Venus. In fact, none came near us. Our only discomfort was hunger. We could see fruits and nuts and berries growing on shore, but we could also see kloonobargan watching us from behind trees and bushes. Fortunately, we were on a fresh-water lake; so we did not suffer from thirst; and we were so happy to be together again and so contented to be temporarily safe that we did not notice the lack of food particularly.

After dark, we took off again, heading for Mypos. The motor of our anotar is noiseless; so I didn't anticipate being discovered. I took to the water about a mile above the city and taxied slowly toward it, avoiding the galleys anchored in the roadstead off the city.

Venus has no moon, and no stars are visible through her solid cloud blankets. Only a mysterious, eerie light relieves the gloom of the nights; so that they are not utterly black. One can see faintly for a short distance.

We came at last to a point about a hundred yards off the palace, and here we waited. The night dragged on. We could see the ghostly shapes of ships out beyond us, with here and there a light on them. We could hear the sounds of men's voices on ship and on shore, and on shore there were many lights.

"I am afraid they have failed," I said.

"I am afraid so," replied Duare, "but we must not leave before daylight, They might come yet."

Presently I heard shouts on shore, and very dimly I saw a boat put off. Then a torch was lighted in it, and I could see that the boat was full of warriors. The boat was not coming directly toward us, but was quartering. I could hear men shouting from the shore: "Not that way! Straight out!"

"They must have escaped," said Duare. "Those men are searching for them."

"And they're coming our way now," I said, for the boat had changed its course, following the directions from shore.

I searched the surface of the water for some sign of Kandar and Artol, but I could not see them. The boat was coming straight for us, but not rapidly. Evidently they were moving cautiously so as not to overlook the fugitives in the darkness.

Presently I heard a low whistle—the prearranged signal. It seemed to come from off our port bow. The ship was lying with its nose toward the shore, and the boat-load of warriors was approaching from slightly to starboard.

I answered the signal and started the motor. We moved slowly in the direction from which that low whistle had come. Still I saw no sign of Kandar or Artol.

Some one in the approaching boat shouted, "There they are!" and at the same time I saw two heads break the water a few yards from us. Now I knew why I had not seen them: they had been swimming beneath the surface to avoid discovery, coming up to signal and then going under again when they heard the answer. Now they were swimming strongly toward us; but the boat was approaching rapidly, twenty paddles sending it skimming across the water. It looked as though it would reach us about the same time that Kandar and Artol did.

I shouted to them: "As I pass you, grab the side of the ship and hang on! I'm going to tow you out until we're away from that boat far enough to stop and get you on board."

"Come on!" cried Kandar; "we're ready."

I opened the throttle a little and bore down on them. The Myposans were very close. They must have been surprised to see the anotar on the water, but they kept on coming. A man in the bow raised his trident and called on us to stop.

"Take the controls, Duare," I said. She knew what to do. Duare always does. For a girl who had led the cloistered life she had in the palace of her father before I came along, she is a marvel of efficiency and initiative.

I turned and faced the boat just as the fellow in the bow cast his trident. It was a close shave for us: the weapon whizzed between Duare's head and mine. Two other warriors had risen and were poising their tridents; then I let them have it. The hum of my r-ray pistol sounded no warning to them, but almost simultaneously three Myposan warriors crumpled and fell—two of them over the side of the boat into the lake.

Kandar and Artol had seized the side of the ship and

71

Duare had given her more throttle. Two more tridents were hurled, but this time they fell short. We were pulling away rapidly, when Duare saw another boatload of warriors ahead of us. The boat had evidently been lowered from one of the ships in the roadstead.

Thinking quickly, Duare throttled down. "Climb aboard!" she cried to the two men, and they lost no time in obeying her; then she opened the throttle wide and bore straight down on the second boat. I heard the frightened cries of its crew and saw the frantic efforts they were making to get out of our way, as Duare pulled up the anotar's nose and we rose gracefully above them.

"Nice work!" I said.

"Beautiful!" said Kandar.

Artol was speechless for a moment. It was his first flight. This was the first plane he had ever see. "Why don't we fall?" he said presently.

Kandar was thrilled. He had heard me talk about the anotar, but I imagine that he had taken all that I said with a grain of salt. Now he could scarcely believe the testimony of his own senses.

I was planning to return Kandar and Artol to Japal, where Kandar's father, Jantor, was jong. It lies at the upper end of the Lake of Japal, about five hundred miles from Mypos; and as we didn't wish to arrive there before dawn, I determined to make a landing and ride the night out on the surface.

There was no wind, and the surface of the lake was like glass; so we made an easy landing and prepared to lie there until morning. We settled ourselves comfortably in the two cockpits, content to wait out the night.

I asked Kandar if they had much difficulty in making their escape.

"It was not easy," he said. "As you know, the outlet from the slaves' pool to the lake is too small to permit the passage of even a small man; so we had to find some way to reach one of the palace pools.

"After you killed Tyros, things were in a chaotic condition. Skabra, his wife, proclaimed herself sole ruler; but she is so generally hated that several factions sprang up, insisting that their particular candidate be made jong. There were so many of them that they have, at least temporarily, defeated their

72

own purpose; and Skabra rules; but the discipline of the palace guards has been undermined. Naturally, they want to favor him who may be next jong; and, as they are hoping that it won't be Skabra, they are not very loyal to her. They spend most of their time holding secret meetings and scheming; so the interior palace guard is extremely lax.

"Artol and I decided to take advantage of this; and we also decided upon a bold move. We knew that the royal pool connected with the lake; that much we were positive of; so we agreed that the royal pool was the one we would use.

"The slaves' compound is usually heavily guarded, but tonight was the exception. Only one warrior stood at the gate that leads into the palace grounds. We had no weapons, not even the wooden trident with which we are furnished when we guard the royal pool. We had nothing but our bare hands."

"And a tremendous desire to escape," added Artol.

"Yes," admitted Kandar, "that was our most powerful weapon—the will to escape. Well, we worked our way around to the guard, a great bearded fellow, who had always been extremely cruel to all of us slaves."

"That made it easier," said Artol.

"Whatever the cause, it was not difficult for Artol," said Kandar, grinning. "When we approached close to him, the guard asked what we were doing in that part of the compound, and ordered us back to our shelters; and he supplemented the order with a poke of his trident. That was what we had expected and hoped for. I seized the trident, and Artol leaped on the fellow and got him by the throat.

"You have no idea how powerful Artol is, or how quick. The guard didn't have time to cry out before his wind was shut off; and then he was down on his back with Artol on top of him, choking the life out of him; and I had the trident. I knew what to do with it, too.

"We took his sword as well as his trident; and, leaving his body where it lay, walked out into the palace grounds. This portion of them is not well lighted, and we came to the wall surrounding the royal pool without being discovered. Here was another guard. He proved a much simpler obstacle to overcome; because now we had a sword and a trident.

"Leaving his corpse resting peacefully on the ground, we entered the enclosure wherein lies the royal pool. This was well lighted, and there were several people loitering on the other side of the garden. As we approached the pool, one of them came toward us. It was Plin."

"The fellow-slave who turned traitor and stole my pistol," I explained to Duare.

"Oh, by the way, how did you get it back?" asked Kandar.

"Plin threw it into the royal pool," I replied; "and when I dove in after Tyros and Duare, I found it lying at the bottom —but go on, what happened then?"

"Well," continued Kandar, "Plin screamed for the guard. We didn't wait any longer then; we both dived into the pool, hoping we could find the corridor leading to the lake and not drown before we could swim through it."

"And we barely made it," said Artol. "I think I did drown a couple of times before my head finally broke the surface. As it was I was practically unconscious, and if Kandar hadn't held me up for a couple of minutes, I'd have been a goner."

"So that's how the search started for you so quickly," I said; "it was Plin."

Kandar nodded. "Yes," he said, "and my only regret at leaving Mypos is that I shall now not be able to kill Plin."

"I can take you back," I said.

Kandar grinned. "No thanks," he said; "I am not that mad at anybody. Then, too, having such a friend as you outweighs Plin and all my other enemies. I shall not try to thank you for what you and Duare have done for us—not in words. There are none adequate to express my gratitude."

"I am only a common warrior," said Artol, "and know but few words; but, after my jong, you have all my loyalty."

NINETEEN

As dawn approached, we took off and headed up the lake toward Japal. Kandar thought that we had better set the ship down outside the city, when he and Artol could go to one of the gates and make themselves known.

"I'm afraid," he said, "that if they saw this thing flying low over the city, they might fire on it."

"With what?" I asked. "I thought you told me that you had no fire arms."

"We haven't," he replied, "but we have engines that throw

rocks or lighted torches for hundreds of feet into the air. They are upon the walls of the city and the decks of the ships anchored off shore. If one hit your propeller, you would be brought down."

"We shall land outside the city," I said, and this we did.

Japal is a very much better looking city than Mypos, and larger. There is a level plain stretching inland from it, and on this plain we landed about a hundred yards from one of the city gates. We could see the consternation our appearance caused the guard at the gate. Several warriors who had been standing outside, rushed in and slammed the gates closed. Others jammed the barbican, pointing and gesticulating.

Kandar and Artol dropped to the ground and walked toward the gate. Presently we could see them talking to the men in the barbican; then they turned and started back toward us. Immediately afterward the gates opened and several warriors rushed out; then Kandar and Artol commenced to run, the warriors pursuing them.

I realized that something was radically wrong. The crown prince of a country doesn't run away from his country's soldiers unless there *is* something radically wrong. I saw that the warriors were going to overtake Kandar and Artol before they could board the anotar, or at least bring them down with the spears they carried.

Of course I didn't know what the trouble was, but I saw that Kandar and Artol seemed to be in plenty. I had commenced to feel responsible for them. I think we always feel responsible for our friends. I know I do. So I decided to do something about it. My best weapon, under the circumstances, was the anotar. I gave her the gun and started toward the running men, and then I lifted her off the ground a little—just enough to clear Kandar's and Artol's heads—and dove straight for the warriors. I hadn't retracted my landing gear, and it and the pontoons simple mowed 'em down; then I rose, banked, and landed close to Kandar and Artol. They clambered into the after cockpit, and we were off.

"What happened?" I asked Kandar.

"There has been a revolution, led by a fellow named Gangor," he replied. "My father escaped. That is all I know. One of the warriors at the gate told me that much. He would have told me more if one of Gangor's officers hadn't come out and tried to arrest us."

"Wasn't it Gangor who arranged for your capture by the Myposans, Artol?" I asked.

"Yes," he replied. "Now I owe him double vengeance. I wish that I might have gotten into the city, even though I may never avenge what he did to me."

"You may some day," said Kandar.

"No," said Artol sadly; "he has but one life, and I must avenge my jong first."

"Where to now?" I asked Kandar. "We'll take you any place you'd like to go before we set out in search of Korva."

"I can think of only one place that my father may have escaped to," said Kandar. "Far back in the mountains lives a tribe of savage aborigines called Timals. My father once befriended Yat, their chief, and they are extremely loyal to him and to all other Japalians; though they refuse to own allegiance to any sovereign other than their own savage chieftain. I should like very much to go to the Timal country and see if my father is there."

The flight was uneventful. We passed over some wonderful game country and several mountain ranges, until we finally came to the Timal country, a high plateau surrounded by jagged peaks—a most inaccessible country and one easily defended against invasion.

Kandar pointed out a village in a canyon which opened out onto the plateau, and I dropped down and circled above it. The people stood in the single street looking up at us. They showed neither panic nor fear. There was something peculiar in their appearance, yet they seemed to be human beings. At first I couldn't make out what it was; but as we dropped lower, I saw that they had short tails and horns. They were armed with spears and knives, and some of the males were menacing us with the former when Kandar caught sight of his father and called to him.

"My brother, Doran, is here, too," Kandar told me. "He is standing beside my father."

"Ask your father if it's safe to land," I said.

He did so and received a negative answer. "Yat says you may come into the village, but not the strangers," Jantor shouted up to us.

"But I can't come in unless we are permitted to land the anotar," said Kandar. "Tell Yat that these people are friendly. One is Artol, a former member of your Guard; the others are

Carson of Venus and his mate, Duare of Vepaja. They rescued me from Gangor. Persuade Yat to let them land."

We saw Jantor turn then and speak to a large savage, but the latter kept shaking his head; then Jantor called to us again as we circled low above the village. "Yat says that strangers are not allowed in Timal—only I and the members of my family—and he doesn't like the looks of that ship that sails in the air. He says that it is not natural and that the people who ride in it cannot be natural—they might bring misfortune to his people. I can understand how he feels, for this is the first time that I ever saw human beings flying. Are you sure this Carson of Venus and his mate are human?"

"They are just as human as you or I," said Kandar. "Tell Yat that he really ought to let the ship land so that he can examine it. No one in Amtor ever saw such a thing before."

Well, eventually Yat gave permission for us to land; and I came down close to the village and taxied up to the end of the single street. I know that those ignorant savages must have been frightened as the anotar rolled toward them, but not one of them turned a hair or moved away a step. I stopped a few yards from Jantor and Yat, and immediately we were surrounded by bucks with couched spears. For a moment it looked serious. The Timals are a ferocious looking people. Their faces are hideously tattooed in many colors, and their horns only add to the ferocity of their appearance.

Yat strode boldly to the side of the ship and looked up at Duare and me. Jantor and Doran accompanied him. Kandar introduced us, and the old Timal chief examined us most carefully. Finally he turned to Jantor. "He is a man, even as you," he said, indicating me. " Do you wish us to be friends with him and his woman?"

"It would please me," said Jantor; "because they are the friends of my son."

Yat looked up at me. "Do you wish to be friends of the Timals and come among us in peace?" he asked.

"Yes," I replied.

"Then you may descend from that strange creature," he said. "You may remain here as long as you wish, the friends of Yat and his people. I have spoken, and my people have heard."

We climbed down, glad to stretch our legs again. The Timals gathered around, but at a respectful distance, and inspected us and the ship. They had much better manners than civilized people of the great cities of Earth, who, under like circumstances, would probably have torn our ship to pieces for souvenirs and stripped our clothes from us.

"They have received you in friendship," said Jantor, "and now you will find them kind and hospitable. They are a proud people who hold their honor most sacred. As long as you merit their friendship, they will be loyal to you; should you not merit it, they will destroy you."

"We shall try to merit it," I assured him.

TWENTY

Old Yat was tremendously interested in the anotar. He walked all around it, occasionally poking it with a finger. "It is not alive," he remarked to Jantor, "yet it flies like a bird."

"Would you like to get in it and see how I control it?" I asked.

For reply he crawled into the forward cockpit. I got in beside him and explained the controls to him. He asked several questions, and they were all intelligent questions. I could see that, despite horns and tail, Yat was a high type of reasoning human being.

"Would you like to go up in it?" I asked.

"Yes."

"Then tell your people to move away and not to come out on this level ground until I have taken off."

He did as I asked, and I came about and taxied down the valley onto the little plain. The wind was blowing right down the canyon; so my take-off was up hill, and we were going pretty fast practically up to the village before I left the ground. We skimmed over the heads of the watching Timals, and then I banked and climbed. I glanced at Yat. He showed no sign of nervousness; but just sat there as unconcerned as a frozen goldfish, looking all around at the scenery and peeking over the side of the cockpit at the panorama of landscape below.

"How do you like it?" I asked.

"Fine," he said.

"Tell me when you want to go back to your village."

"Go there," he said, and pointed.

I flew through a pass in the mountains as he had directed. Ahead and far below stretched a broad valley.

"Go there," he said, and pointed again. "Now, lower," he directed a moment later; and presently I saw a village beneath us. "Go low above that village."

I flew low above a thatched village. Women and children screamed and ran into their huts. A few warriors stood their ground and hurled spears at us. Yat leaned far over the side as I circled back at his request. This time I heard a warrior cry: "It is Yat, the Timal!"

Yat looked as happy as a gopher with a carrot. "Go home now," he directed. "Those were the enemies of my people." he said, after a while. "Now they will know what a great man is Yat, the Timal."

All the Timals of Yat's village were waiting when we returned. "I was sure glad to see you coming back," said Kandar. "These fellows were getting nervous. Some of them thought that you had stolen Yat."

Warriors gathered around their chief. "I have seen a new world," said Yat. "Like a bird I flew over the village of the Valley People. They saw me and knew me. Now they will know what great people the Timals are."

"You flew over the village of the Valley People!" exclaimed a warrior. "Why, that is two long marches away."

"I flew very fast," said Yat.

"I should like to fly in this bird ship," said a sub-chief, and then a dozen others voiced the same wish.

"No," said Yat; "that is for chiefs only."

He had now done something that no one else in his world had ever done. It set him apart from other men. It made him even a greater chieftain than he had been before.

We learned to like these Timals very much. They were very courteous to Duare, the women especially going out of their way to be kind to her. One would never have expected it in such primitive savages.

We rested there for a few days; and then I flew Jantor, Kandar, and Doran back to Japal to reconnoiter. As the anotar does not carry more than four comfortably, I left Duare and Artol behind. I knew that she would be safe with the Timals; and, anyway, I expected to be back before dark.

We circled low over Japal, causing quite a commotion in the streets. Jantor hoped that in some way he might get in touch with some of his friends and learn what was going on in the city. There was always the chance of a counter-revolution that would place him back on the throne; but either his friends were all dead or imprisoned or afraid to try to communicate with him, for he never saw one whom he could trust.

As we prepared to leave and return to Timal, I circled far out over the lake, gaining considerable altitude; and from this vantage point Jantor discovered a fleet of ships far down the lake.

"If it's not asking too much," he said to me, "I'd like to fly down there and see who that is."

I headed for the fleet, and presently we were circling above it—fifty ships of war packed with fighting men. Most of them were biremes, and there were several penteconters, open galleys with decks fore and aft and propelled by fifty oars as well as sails. Some of the biremes had a hundred oars on each side and carried several hundred warriors as well. All had their sails set, and were taking advantage of a gentle breeze.

"The Myposan war fleet," said Jantor, "and it's headed for Japal."

"Gangor is going to have his hands full," remarked Kandar.

"We must warn him," said Jantor.

"But he is your enemy," expostulated Doran.

"Japal is my country," replied Jantor. "No matter who is jong there it is my duty to warn him."

On the way back to Japal, Jantor wrote a message. We dropped down low over the palace grounds, Jantor making the sign of peace by raising his right hand. Almost immediately people commenced to come from the palace, and presently Jantor recognized Gangor and called to him.

"I have an important message for you," he said, and dropped the weighted note over the side. A warrior caught it before it reached the ground and took it to Gangor.

The fellow read it carefully and then motioned us to come lower, which I did, circling close above them.

"I appreciate your warning, Jantor," said Gangor when we were within easy ear shot. "I wish you would land. We shall need your help and advice in defending the city. I promise that you will not be harmed."

I looked at Jantor; so did Kandar and Doran. We waited for his curt refusal of the invitation.

"It is my duty," he said to us. "My country is in danger."

"Don't do it," counselled Kandar. "Gangor is not to be trusted."

"He would not dare harm me after making that promise," said Jantor; "too many warriors heard him, and they are not all dishonorable men."

"All those with him are traitors like himself," said Doran.

"My duty lies there," insisted Jantor. "Will you take me down, please?"

"If you insist, I'll land you outside the city," I said; "it is your right to risk your life at the hands of a scoundrel like Gangor; but I will not risk my ship and the safety of my mate."

I circled low above them again, and Kandar exacted a new promise from Gangor that his father would not be harmed and that he would be permitted to leave the city whenever he chose. Gangor agreed volubly—far too volubly, I thought.

"Bring that thing that you fly in right down here in the palace grounds," he said; "I'll have them cleared."

"Never mind," I said, "I shall land outside the inland gate."

"Very well," said Gangor, "and I myself will come out to meet you, Jantor, and escort you into the city."

"And don't bring too many warriors with you," I cautioned him, "and don't come within trident range of my ship. I shall take off immediately the jong has disembarked."

"Bring Kandar and Doran with you, Jantor," invited Gangor. "They will both be welcome, and I promise again that you shall all be perfectly safe the moment that you step foot within the walls of Japal."

"I shall feel better now that Doran and I are going along with you," said Kandar, as we rose and headed for the plain beyond the city.

"You are not going to accompany me," said Jantor. "You do not trust Gangor. Possibly you are right. If I die, the future of our country lies with you and Doran—the future of our dynasty. You must both live to bring men-children into the world. If all three of us placed ourselves in Gangor's power simultaneously, the temptation might prove too much for him to resist. I think that I alone shall be safe enough. Neither of you may accompany me."

"Come now, sir," exclaimed Kandar, "you must let us go with you."

"Yes," said Doran, "you must. We are your sons; what will

the people of Japal think of us if we let our father go alone into the hands of his greatest enemy?"

"You shall not accompany me," said Jantor, with finality. "It is a command," and that ended the matter.

I set the ship down three or four hundred yards from the inland gate, and presently Gangor came out of the city and approached us with a dozen warriors. They halted at plenty of distance from the ship; and Jantor, who had already dropped to the ground, advanced toward them.

"I wish we had never come here," said Kandar. "I can't help but feel that our father has made a grave mistake in trusting Gangor."

"He seems quite sure that Gangor will live up to his promise," I said. "You heard him ask me to wait and witness the battle and then come for him when it was over."

"Yes, said Doran, "but I don't share his faith. Gangor has always been notorious for his perfidy, but no one paid much attention to it because he was only captain of a merchant ship at the height of his fortunes. Who could have dreamed that he was to make himself jong of Japal!"

TWENTY-ONE

I couldn't help but have a great deal of respect for Jantor. He was doing a very courageous, albeit a very temerarious, thing. I watched him as he walked toward his enemies. His step was firm, his head high. He was every inch a jong.

I had taken off immediately he left us, and was circling about rather low. Jantor had approached to within a few steps of Gangor, when the latter suddenly raised his short, heavy spear and plunged it through the jong's heart.

Kandar and Doran cried out in horror. I opened the throttle and dove straight for the wretch; and as he saw me coming, he and his warriors turned and fled for the city. Low behind them, I turned my pistol on them. Several fell, but Gangor reached the city gate in safety.

Without a word I rose and flew over the city and out across the lake. For some time neither Kandar nor Doran spoke. Their faces were drawn and tense. My heart ached for them. Finally Kandar asked me where I was going.

"I am going to tell the Myposan fleet that Japal has been warned and is ready to annihilate them."

"Why?" he asked.

"It was your father's wish to save the city. Some day you will be jong there. Do you want it conquered by the fishmen?"

"You are right," he said.

It was late in the afternoon that I dropped down low over the leading Myposan galley, the largest of the biremes. They had evidently seen us from a distance, as the deck was crowded with warriors, all staring at us.

"Be careful," cautioned Kandar. "They are preparing a rock thrower. If they hit us, we're through."

I gave the peace sign then, and called down to them that I had a message for their commander. A big fellow whom I recalled having seen in Tyros' palace answered the peace sign and motioned for me to come closer.

"Tell them to take the rock out of that catapult," I shouted.

He nodded and gave the necessary order; and after they had unloaded the thing, I dropped down quite low. The anotar is quite maneuverable and can fly at very low speeds; so I had no difficulty in carrying on at least a broken conversation with the ship.

"Who commands the fleet?" I asked.

"Skabra, the vadjong," he replied.

"Do you know who I am?"

"Yes; the slave who killed Tyros," he replied.

"I should like to talk with Skabra, if she is not too mad at me," I said.

The fellow grinned. Their faces are hideous enough in repose; but when they grin, they are something to frighten grown-ups with. Their fish mouths spread across their faces, forcing their gills open. Their countless, sharp fish-like teeth are exposed behind their huge beards.

"Skabra is not angry," he said.

"Which is her ship?" I asked.

"This," he said.

"Well, tell her that Carson of Venus wishes to speak to her. Tell her I have very important news for her."

Just as I finished the sentence the old girl came on deck. God! but she's the beauty. She looks like a bloated cod fish.

"What do you want?" she demanded. "Do you want to murder me, too?"

83

"No," I shouted. "You were kind to my mate. I would not harm you. I have important news for you, but I can't talk this way. Get in a small boat and row off a little way. I'll come down and land on the water and talk with you."

"You must take me for a fool," she said. "I'd be at your mercy."

I had to keep circling the ship and shouting a few words at a time. It was no way in which to carry on a conversation.

"Very well," I said. "The word I have for you is very important, and I have given my word that I shall not harm you in any way. However, do as you see fit. I'll stand by a few minutes."

I could see them talking excitedly on the deck for a few minutes, and then I saw a boat being lowered with Skabra in it; so I came down a short distance from the ship and waited. Presently they came alongside. The old girl greeted me pleasantly. She didn't seem to harbor any ill will because I had killed her mate, nor was I surprised at that. You see I'd not only rid her of a most obnoxious husband; but I'd put her on the throne, where she'd rule until the horrid little amphibian monstrosity that was her son grew to maturity.

"The first thing I'd like to know," she said, "is how you escaped from Mypos."

I shook my head. "I might be a prisoner there again some time; so I'll keep that secret to myself."

"Perhaps you're wise," she said; "but if you do come again, you'll be treated well, as long as I'm vadjong. Now what is the important news you have for me?"

"Japal knows that your fleet is coming, and the city is fully prepared. I advise you to turn back."

"Why are you doing this?" she asked.

"For two reasons: You were kind to my mate, and the sons of Jantor are my friends. I do not wish to see Mypos and Japal at war."

She nodded. "I understand," she said, "but nevertheless I shall keep on and attack Japal. We need more slaves. Many of our galleys are undermanned. The creatures die like flies at the oars."

We talked a little longer; and then, finding that I could not persuade her to give up her plan, I taxied away and took off. As we approached Japal, we saw that the fleet was fully manned; but remaining close to the city. Kandar wanted to wait and learn the outcome of the battle. It was now late in the afternoon; so there was little likelihood that the engagement would take place before morning, as the biremes would move up slowly so as not to exhaust the men at the oars; they would need all their strength and energy for maneuvering during battle.

"They'll probably come up to within about a kob," Kandar said, "and lie to until dawn; thus the slaves will be well rested." A kob is two and a half of our Earthly miles.

I didn't like the idea very well, as I was anxious to return to Duare and get started on our search for Korva; but it meant so much to Kandar that I agreed to wait. He knew where there was a cove a short distance along the coast, and we flew there and anchored.

At dawn Kandar awakened me. "The Myposan fleet is moving in," he said. "I can hear the creaking of their oars."

I listened. Very faintly I could hear the complaining of the wooden oars against the wooden rowlocks. Even a greased oar is not entirely silent. We took off and headed for Japal, and almost immediately we saw the Myposan fleet coming in in three lines of fifteen or sixteen ships each. The fleet of Japal still lay close below the city wall.

When the first line of the Myposan fleet was within a hundred yards of the enemy fleet the engagement started. A ball of fire rose from the deck of one of the Japal ships, described a graceful arc, and landed on the deck of a Myposan bireme. The burning brand had been shot from a catapult. Immediately the engagement became general. Fire balls and rocks were hurled from both sides. Many fell into the water, but many found their marks. Three ships were on fire, and I could see men hauling buckets of water from the lake to fight the flames.

Still the Myposan fleet moved in. "They are going to grapple and board," said Doran.

Soon I saw why the Japal fleet hugged the shore, for now the batteries on the wall of the city opened up. These were heavier than the catapults of the ships; they threw larger fire balls and heavier rocks. The penteconters had moved up now between the big ships of the Myposans. They were much faster and more maneuverable. Their principal purpose, as far as I could see, was to harass the enemy by coming alongside and hurling short spears through the ports where the rowers sat chained to their benches. Disable enough oarsmen, and you have disabled the ship. A rock from a shore catapult dropped directly into the center of one of these pentecontars, killing two or three men instantly and crashing through the bottom of the ship, which immediately commenced to fill and sink. The survivors, leaping overboard, were speared from the deck of the Japal ship they had been attacking. I could hear the dying men screaming and cursing.

"That was a good shot," said Kandar.

By now, four of the attacking ships were burning, their crews taking to small boats, of which there were not half enough, while the slaves burned in their chains. Their screams were horrifying.

Other Myposan ships came alongside those of Japal, and there was hand-to-hand fighting on decks slippery with blood. It was a gruesome sight, but fascinating. I dropped lower to get a better view, as the smoke from burning ships was cutting down the visibility.

I dropped too low. A rock from a catapult struck my propeller, smashing it. Now, I was, indeed, in a bad fix.

TWENTY-TWO

My first thought, when I saw that my ship had been hit, was of Duare. Here I was, over a battle between two peoples who were my enemies. What chance had I of ever returning to Timal? What was to become of Duare? I cursed myself for my crass stupidity as I glided to a landing. I just had altitude enough to permit me to land about a mile along the shore from Japal. I hoped that in the heat and excitement of battle no one on the walls of the city had seen the accident or noticed where I had gone.

I had come down close beside a forest, and I immediately got Kandar and Doran to help me push the anotar into concealment among the trees. As I looked back toward the city, I saw that smoke from burning ships hid much of it from my view; and I hoped that it had also hidden my landing from the city.

Kandar and Doran were most sympathetic. They said that

86

the fault was all theirs. That if I had not been trying to help them, the accident would never have happened.

I told them that there was no use crying over spilled milk, and that what we had to do now was find some tools and some wood to make a new propeller. I removed what was left of the old one—one blade and the stub of the other.

As I was explaining to Kandar the tools I should need and the kind of wood, he became very much interested; and asked me many questions about the construction of a propeller, how to determine the correct pitch, and so forth. You would have thought that he was going to make one himself.

Getting the right wood was a simple matter. The same kind of trees from the wood of which I had made this propeller grew in the forest where we were, but getting tools was an entirely different matter.

"There are plenty in Japal," said Kandar. "We must find some way to get them. Doran and I have hundreds of friends in the city, if we could only reach them."

They racked their brains for some plan, but the whole thing looked utterly hopeless. Finally Doran hit upon something which at least contained the kernel of success—but a very small kernel.

"I know a man who makes knives," he said. "I know him very well, for he has done a lot of work for me. I also know that he is honest and loyal. He lives close to the wall, not far from the inland gate. If we could reach his house, we could get knives."

"But how can we reach his house?" demanded Kandar.

"By climbing the wall," said Doran.

Kandar laughed. "At its lowest point the wall is one ted high," he said. "I can't jump that high." A ted is 13.2 Earth feet.

"No one has to jump," explained Doran. "You stand on Carson's shoulders; I climb up and stand on yours—I am already over the wall."

"Suppose you got caught," I said. "Gangor would have you killed—no, I won't let you take that risk."

"There's practically no risk," said Doran. "We will do it after dark. Everyone will be tired after the battle; and anyway, the watch is never very good."

"How will you get back?" asked Kandar.

"My friend's house stands against the wall. The roof is only a vulat below the top of the wall. I shall go down through the door in his roof, get tools, come up, and—there you are!"

"It sounds simple," said Kandar.

"I think the risk is too great," I said.

"We shall do it," said Doran.

That night we approached the city after dark, Doran leading us to a point which he was sure was just outside the knife-maker's house. It was not far from the inland gate—too close, I thought, if the sentries kept any kind of watch at all.

Everything went splendidly. Kandar climbed on to my shoulders, and Doran scrambled up on to his. There we were, just like that, when a gruff voice behind us said, "Come down. You are prisoners. We are the guard."

I was holding onto Kandar's legs to support him, and before I could draw my pistol I was seized from behind. Kandar and Doran lost their balance and fell on top of me and half a dozen warriors. Most of us went down, but the fellow who had seized me never lost his hold.

When we had disentangled ourselves and gotten to our feet, I found that I had been disarmed. One of the warriors was displaying my pistol proudly.

"I saw him use this this morning," he said. "If I hadn't recognized him when I did and gotten it away from him he'd have killed us all."

"Be careful of it," I cautioned him; "it is apt to kill you."

"I shall be careful of it," he said, "and I shall keep it always. I shall be proud to show it to my children."

"Your children will never see it," said another. "Gangor will take it away from you."

We had been walking toward the inland gate while they were talking, and now we were admitted. Again I was a prisoner, but I thanked Heaven that Duare was not one also.

They shoved us into a room off the guardroom in the barbican, and left us there until morning. None of the warriors seemed to have recognized either Kandar or Doran, and I was hopeful that no one would.

Doran, who was quick witted, had told a cock-and-bull story about our having been out hunting; and, not getting back before the gates closed, we were trying to get into the city and go to our homes.

One member of the guard asked, "Why were you hunting when there was a battle?"

"A battle!" exclaimed Doran. "What battle? We have been gone for two days."

"The Myposans came in many ships," explained the fellow; "and there was a great battle, but we drove them off. We took many prisoners, but they got none."

"Fine," said Kandar. "I am sorry that we were not here."

About the middle of the morning an officer came and said that Gangor wanted to see the man who flew around in the air—the one who had killed so many of his warriors.

"That is I," I said, stepping forward.

"Who are these others?" he demanded.

"I don't know," I said. "They were returning from a hunting trip when I met them last night, and they asked me to help them get over the wall and into the city."

It seemed strange to me that an officer should not know either Kandar or Doran; but the former explained to me later that Gangor had evidently commissioned a lot of low born fellows, mostly sailors from ships he had sailed on; so it was not strange that they were not recognized.

"Well," said the officer, "I might as well take you all along; Gangor would probably like to see your friends, too."

The moment that we were ushered into Gangor's presence he recognized Kandar and Doran. "Ah!" he exclaimed, "the traitors. I saw you fighting against my ships yesterday."

"You saw nothing of the kind," I said.

"Shut up!" snapped Gangor. "You were fools to try to come into Japal. Why were you coming in? A-ha! I know. You were coming to assassinate me. For that you shall die. I condemn you all to death. Take them away. Later I shall decide how they shall die."

TWENTY-THREE

We were taken to a dungeon below the palace of the jong, into which Gangor had moved. It was a most unsanitary and unpleasant place. They chained us to the wall; our jailer, who did it, being unnecessarily rough with us. He wore the keys to the dungeon and our padlocks on a chain about his neck. He took the chain off to use the key when he fettered us; and he struck us each several times with it, just to satisfy his lust for cruelty. There could have been no other reason; as we offered no resistance, nor did we even speak to him. If I ever had murder in my heart, it was then; and for a long time I planned how I might kill him. It was then that an idea came to me.

After the fellow had left us, I noticed how dejected Doran appeared; and I told him to cheer up, that we had to die sometime. I didn't feel very cheerful myself. I kept thinking of Duare. She would never know what had happened to me; but she would guess that I was dead, for she would know that only death would keep me from returning to her.

"How can I be cheerful?" said Doran, "when it was my silly plan that brought us here to die."

"It is no more your fault than ours," said Kandar. "We had to take a chance. It was merely a misfortune, not a fault, which caused it to fail."

"I shall never forgive myself," insisted Doran.

We remained in that dungeon for a couple of weeks. A slave brought us food once a day; we saw no one else; and then, at last, our jailer returned. He was quite alone. I backed close to the wall as he came in.

"I just came to tell you," he said, "that you are to die the first thing in the morning. Your heads are to be cut off."

"It is that homely head of yours that should be cut off," I said. "What are you, anyway, a Myposan?"

I saw Kandar and Doran looking at me in astonishment.

"Shut up!" growled the jailer, "or I'll give you another taste of the chain."

"Get out of here!" I yelled at him. "You stink. Go take a bath before you come down here again among your betters."

The fellow was so mad that he couldn't speak; but he came for me, as I knew he would—he came with his chain swinging. It was what I had planned—it was happening just as I had hoped it would; and when he came within reach of me, I seized his throat in both my hands. He tried to scream for help; but I had his wind choked off, and he couldn't. But he was beating me all the time with his chain. I pushed him over closer to Kandar.

"Grab his chain," I said, "before he beats me to death."

Kandar got hold of it and held on, while I choked the brute. I thought of the blows that he had struck us so wantonly, and I gave his neck an extra twist. I have killed many men in self-defense or in line of duty; some I have been glad to kill, but usually it has made me sad to think that I must take a human life. Not so now, I enjoyed every second of it until his corpse hung limp in my grasp.

I snatched the chain from about its neck and let it slip to the floor; then I unlocked my padlock and freed myself. Quickly, I did the same for Kandar and Doran.

"At first," said Doran, "I couldn't understand why you wanted to enrage that fellow and get another beating for nothing, but the moment he stepped toward you I guessed what you had in mind. It was a very clever trick."

"Yes," I said, "but what now?"

"Maybe this is where we come in?" said Kandar. "We were both born and raised in this palace. We know more about it than the jong, our father, did."

"More than anyone in Japal," added Doran. "You know how little boys are. We explored every corner of the place."

"And you know a way out?" I asked.

"Yes," said Kandar, "But there's a hitch."

"What is it?" I asked.

"There is a secret passage leading from the palace out into the city. It ends in a building near the wall. In the cellar of that building another passage starts that leads outside the city."

"But where's the hitch?" I repeated.

"The hitch is," he said, "that the secret passage starts in the jong's own sleeping apartments, and the chances are that Gangor occupies them now."

"We'll have to wait until he is away," said Doran.

"Can we get to them without being apprehended?" I asked.

"We can try," said Kandar. "I think it can be done after dark."

"It is after dark now," I said.

"So we start," said Doran.

"And may our luck hold," added Kandar.

Kandar led the way along a dark corridor and up a flight of stairs at the top of which he cautiously opened a door and looked into the room beyond.

"All right," he whispered, "come on."

He led us into the palace kitchen, and through that and several pantries into a huge state diningroom. The jongs of Japal lived well. We followed Kandar to the end of the room

91

farthest from the main entrance, and here he showed us a little door hidden behind hangings.

"Where the jong used to escape when he became bored," he explained.

Beyond the door was a narrow corridor. "Go quietly," cautioned Kandar. "This corridor leads to the jong's sleeping apartments. We'll have a look in them and see if Gangor is there."

We crept along noiselessly through the dark little corridor until Kandar halted at a door. We pressed close behind him as he opened it a crack. The room beyond was in darkness.

"Gangor is probably drinking with some of his cronies," whispered Kandar, "and hasn't retired yet. We are in luck. Come on, follow me; but still go quietly."

We crept across that dark room, Doran touching Kandar to keep in contact and follow him, and I touching Doran. It seemed a perfectly enormous room to me, and traversing it that way in total darkness, I somehow lost my balance just enough to cause me to throw one foot out to regain my equilibrium. Well, I threw it in the wrong place at the wrong time. It hit a table or something and knocked it over. The thing fell with a crash that would have awakened the dead; and instantly there was a cry, and a light went on.

There was Gangor right in front of us sitting up on his sleeping couch, screaming for the guard. On a table at the side of the couch lay my pistol. Gangor had taken it away from the warrior of the guard all right. It would have been better for him had he not.

As I leaped forward and snatched it from the table, a dozen warriors burst into the apartment. "This way!" Kandar shouted to me, and the three of us backed away toward the secret entrance to the corridor leading from the palace. At least I thought that that was where he was leading us, but he wasn't. As he told me later, he had not wished to reveal the secret to Gangor and his warriors.

I menaced the advancing guardsmen with my pistol. "Stand back!" I ordered. "Don't come closer, or I'll kill you!"

"Kill them!" screamed Gangor. "Kill them all!"

A warrior rushed me. I pressed the trigger—but nothing happened. For the first time since I had had it, my r-ray pistol failed me—failed me when it was a question of life or death and even more; a question as to whether I was ever to return to Duare again.

But, unarmed as I was, there were other weapons at hand. Maybe they had not been designed as instruments of death, but they were to serve their purpose. I seized a bench and hurled it into the face of the advancing warrior. He went down; and immediately Kandar and Doran grasped the possibilities of the furnishings of the apartment, and seized upon the nearest things at hand.

Behind them a cluster of spears had been arranged upon the wall as a decoration. I saw them and dragged them down. Now we were armed! But the odds were against us—twelve against three; or rather eleven now, for the man I had hit with the bench lay where he had fallen, and Gangor only sat on his couch screaming for more guardsmen. I saw Kandar working his way toward him; and so Doran and I moved with him, keeping our backs against the wall.

Fencing with spears is quite an interesting experience; while thus engaged, one does not doze, I can assure you. It happened that the spear which had fallen to me was light and rather long, a fact which gave me an advantage that I was not long in realizing and seizing upon. I found that while I could not parry well with one hand, I could jab quite effectively; so picking up a light table to use as a shield, I succeeded so well that I jabbed an antagonist in the heart after parrying his thrust with my table.

Doran and Kandar had each killed a man, and now the remainder of them seemed less keen to push the assault. Kandar had worked around until he was close beside Gangor's couch; and as he jerked his spear from the heart of a dead guardsman, he wheeled and drove it through Gangor's body.

Gangor did not die immediately. He lay sprawled across his couch vomiting blood; and between paroxysms, screaming in agony. Jantor, jong of Japal, had been avenged.

Now more warriors were pushing into the chamber; and it looked pretty bad for us three, when there burst upon our ears the sound of gongs and trumpets. As if by magic, the fighting stopped, as we all listened.

93

TWENTY-FOUR

Beneath the sound of the gongs and trumpets, we could hear men shouting.

"It is the call to arms!" cried a warrior. "The city has been attacked."

"The Myposans have returned," said another. "Who will lead us? We have no jong."

"You have a jong," I cried. "Follow Kandar! He is your jong."

They hesitated for a moment; then a warrior said, "Kandar is jong. I will follow him. Who will come with me?"

Kandar, taking advantage of their indecision, started for the door; and Doran and I followed him. "Come!" commanded Kandar. "To the streets. To the defense of Japal!" Like sheep they followed him.

When he arrived in the palace grounds and the warriors there saw Kandar and Doran leading some of their fellows, they cheered; then Kandar took command, leading a strong party out into the city streets where fighting was in progress. It was then that I saw that it was not Myposans who had attacked Japal, but strange, repulsive looking warriors of a sickly greenish hue and entirely hairless—no hair on their heads, no whiskers, no eyebrows, no eyelashes—and right on the tops of their heads was a little knob of flesh. They fought with swords and long-handled hooks, holding the latter in their left hands. With these hooks they would catch an antagonist and draw him close; then cut or thrust at him with the sword. Oftentimes, the hook was enough if the point caught at the base of the brain. They were nasty weapons.

If my pistol had been serviceable they wouldn't have worried me much, but with only a spear I felt very much at a disadvantage. I had had no time to examine the pistol since I had recovered it, but now I stopped before getting into the thick of the fight and went over it carefully. Evidently some one had been tampering with it, probably in an effort to discover how it worked; and I was much relieved to see that they had merely changed an adjustment. In a few seconds I had remedied the trouble; and when I looked up I saw that I was just in time, or almost just in time. I wasn't quite sure which, for a big green devil was reaching for me with his hook.

I was in a most disadvantageous position, as I had rested my spear in the hollow of my left elbow with the butt on the ground while I worked on my pistol; and the hook had already passed over my shoulder to take me in the back of the neck. It was just the matter of a split second before I should be gaffed.

I did what was probably the best thing, but I did it quite mechanically—there was no time for conscious reasoning. I sprang toward my antagonist. Had I sprung away, the hook would have impaled me; but by springing toward him I confused him. At the same time I struck his sword aside with my left arm and sent a stream of r-rays through his heart. It was a close call.

Kandar and Doran were in the thick of the fight a little ahead of me. Kandar was closer, and he was hotly engaged with one of the invaders. He, too, had nothing but a spear; and I hurried to his aid. He had so far successfully knocked the gaff to one side every time his antagonist reached for him with it; and then he would have to parry a sword thrust; so he never got a chance to bring his spear into play as an offensive weapon. He was always on the defensive, and no duel or war was ever won that way.

I reached him just as a second enemy attacked him. The r-rays hissed from the muzzle of my gun, and both Kandar's antagonists went down; then I started right through the ranks of the enemy, spraying r-rays to the right and left and ahead, cutting a path wide enough to drive a combine through. I was having a glorious time. I felt as though I were winning a war all by myself.

Suddenly I realized that the invaders were fleeing before me and on both sides. I looked back. I could see nothing but these hideous warriors. They had closed in behind me, and I was being carried along with them. Presently I was tripped; and as I fell, I was seized on either side, my pistol was snatched from my hand, and I was hustled along with the defeated army.

Down the main street of Japal they dragged me and out through the inland gate, nor did their retreat end there; for Japal's fighting men followed them far out onto the plain, constantly harassing their rear. It was almost dark when they abandoned the pursuit and turned back toward the city. It was then that I became convinced that Kandar did not know I had been made prisoner. Had he, I am sure that he would never have given up the pursuit until I had been rescued.

A warrior on each side had been dragging me along up to this time; but now that the pursuit had ceased a halt was called; and while the creatures rested, a rope was tied about my neck; and when the march was resumed, I was led along like a cow to the slaughter.

I saw my pistol tucked into the loincloth of a warrior; and I kept my eyes on the fellow, hoping that I might find an opportunity to retrieve it. I knew that only as a forlorn hope could I use it if I had it; for my captors were so numerous that, though I might have killed many of them, eventually they would have overwhelmed me.

I was terribly depressed. Ill fortune seemed to dog my footsteps. Right on the threshold of freedom that would have permitted me to rejoin Duare immediately, my rash impetuosity had plunged me into a predicament which was probably as fraught with danger as any I had ever encountered. Why should I have tried to fight a battle practically single handed? I don't know. Probably I am overconfident in my own prowess, but I have reason to be. I have come through some mighty trying experiences and escaped hundreds of dangers.

Where were these strange, silent creatures taking me? What fate lay in store for me? I had not heard them speak a word since I had seen them. I wondered if they were alalus, lacking vocal organs.

One of them approached me as we resumed the march. He wore three gold armlets, and the haft of his gaff was circled by three golden rings. "What is your name?" he demanded in the universal language of Amtor.

So they were not alalus. "Carson of Venus," I replied.

"From what country come you?"

"The United States of America."

"I never heard of it," he said. "How far is it from Brokol?"

"I never heard of Brokol," I replied. "Where is that?"

He looked disgusted. "Every one has heard of Brokol," he said. "It is the greatest empire in Amtor. It lies forty kob from here on the other side of those mountains." That would be a hundred miles. I not only had to get myself captured, but now I had to walk a hundred miles!

"Then my country is ten million four hundred thousand kobs from Brokal," I said, doing some lightning mental calculating.

"There is nothing that far away from anything," he said, petulantly. "You are lying to me, and that will make it worse for you."

"I am not lying," I said. "That is the nearest my country ever gets to Brokol; sometimes it is farther away than that."

"You are the greatest liar I have ever heard of," he said. "How many people live in your country?"

"If I tell you, you won't believe me."

"Tell me anyway. It is probably a little country. Do you know how many people live in Brokol?"

"I'm afraid I could never guess."

"You are very right that you could never guess—there are fifty thousand people living in Brokol!" I guess he expected me to faint.

"Indeed?" I said.

"Yes, fifty thousand; and I am not lying to you. Now how many live in your little country? Tell me the truth."

"Somewhere around a hundred and thirty million."

"I told you to tell me the truth. There are not that many people in all Amtor."

"My country is not on Amtor."

I thought he was going to explode, he became so angry. "Are you trying to make a fool of me?" he demanded, turning a dark green.

"Not at all," I assured him. "There is no reason why I should lie to you. My country is in another world. If Amtor were not surrounded by clouds, you could see it at night shining like a tiny ball of fire."

"I said you were the greatest liar I had ever heard of," he said. "I now say that you are the greatest liar any one ever heard of; you are the greatest liar in the world."

I do not like to be called a liar, but what was I to do about it? Anyway, there was something of awe and respect in the way he said it that made it sound more like a compliment than an insult.

"I don't see why you should doubt me," I said. "The chances are that you have never heard of Vepaja, or Havatoo, or Korva, yet they are countries which really exist."

"Where are they?" he demanded.

"Right on Amtor," I said.

"If you can lead us to countries we have never heard of, you will probably not be sacrificed to Loto-El-Ho-Ganja; but you had better not lie to her or to Duma."

Loto-El-Ho-Ganja, literally translated into English, means most high more than woman. None of the various peoples of Amtor with whom I had come in contact had any religion, but this name and his mention of sacrifice in connection with it suggested that she might be a goddess.

"Is Loto-El-Ho-Ganja your vadjong?" I asked. Vadjong means queen.

"No," he said, "she is not a woman; she is more than a woman. She was not born of woman, nor did she ever hang from any plant."

"Does she look like a woman?" I asked.

"Yes," he replied, "but her beauty is so transcendent that mortal women appear as beasts by comparison."

"And Duma?" I asked. "Who is Duma?"

"Our jong—the richest and most powerful jong in Amtor. You will probably see him when we reach Brokol, and maybe Loto-El-Ho-Ganja, too. I think they will wish to see such a great liar, one whose hair and eyes, even, are lies."

"What do you mean by that?" I demanded.

"I mean that there can be no such thing as a man with yellow hair and gray eyes; therefore they must be a lie."

"Your powers of reasoning are amazing," I said.

He nodded in agreement, and then said, "I have talked enough," and walked away.

If these Brokols have anything to recommend them, it is their lack of garrulity. They talk when they have something to say; otherwise they remain silent, in which they differ greatly from most of my own species. I am always amazed, if not always amused, by the burst of feminine gabble which follows the lowering of a theater curtain for an intermission. There can't be that much important conversation in a lifetime.

TWENTY-FIVE

I must say that after my conversation with this chap, whose name I later learned was Ka-at (Kā'-at), I was really curious to reach Brokol and see a woman so beautiful that she made other women appear as beasts. If it hadn't been for my concern over Duare, I'd have looked forward to it as another rare adventure. One must die eventually, even though he has been inoculated with the longevity serum as have I; so if he has no one dependent upon him, he might as well crowd all of adventure and experience into his life that he can, even though he at times risks that life.

During the long marches to Brokol no one spoke to me again. They communicated with me and among themselves largely by signs. I sometimes wondered that their vocal cords did not atrophy. I had much time to think; and of course most of my thoughts revolved about Duare, but I also thought of the strange suggestions Ka-at had placed in my mind. I wondered what he meant when he said that Loto-El-Ho-Ganja had never hung from any plant. Why should anyone wish to hang from a plant? I am quite sure that the horse thieves they used to lynch in the days of our old West would not have chosen to hang from a tree or from anything else.

The Brokols carried nothing but their spears, swords, and a little bag of food; for we lived off the country as we went; so they covered quite a little ground every day. During the morning of the fifth day we climbed through a mountain pass, and from the summit I saw a city lying on a well watered tableland below.

The party halted at the summit; and, looking down upon the city, bowed three times from the waist. We were standing pretty close together, and the opportunity I had been awaiting came because of that. I was behind and touching the warrior who carried my pistol. As he bowed, I brushed against him; and when he straightened up, he did not have my pistol—it was hidden in my loincloth.

I didn't know when the opportunity to use it might come. I knew that I couldn't shoot my way out of a city full of enemies, but as a last resort I could sell my life dearly. Anyway, I was glad to have my weapon back again; somehow it gives me a feeling of security and superiority that I don't have without it; and that is strange; because before I came to Venus I never carried a weapon of any description.

The bowing at the summit of the pass, I learned later, was something of a religious ritual, Brokol being considered by them a holy city. In it was located the principal temple of Loto-El-Ho-Ganja. Here came the people of the lesser villages to worship and make offerings.

We continued the march immediately, and were soon at one of the gates of Brokol. I shall not bore you with the details of our entry into the city, but I may say that it was not a triumphal entry for Ka-at. He had been defeated, and he brought back no spoils and only a single prisoner. Ka-at was a yorkokor, or commander of a thousand men. Yorkokor means, literally, a thousand daggers; and is a military title corresponding with our colonel. The three gold armlets that he wore and the three golden rings which encircled the haft of his gaff were the insignia of his office.

I was taken to an open square or plaza in a poor part of the city and locked in a cage. There were a number of these cages, but only one other had an occupant. He was a human being like myself, and his cage was next to mine. We were not exactly on exhibit; but the plaza was not enclosed, and many Brokols came and gawped at us. Some of them poked us with sticks, and others threw stones at us. For the most part, however, they just looked and commented—a word or a short phrase. They were not given to loquacity.

One looked at me and said to his companion, "What is it?"

The other just shook his head.

"Yellow hair," said the first.

"Gray eyes," said the second.

They were running on terribly, for Brokols.

"You talk too much," the man in the next cage yelled at them.

One of them threw a rock at him, and then they both walked away.

"They hate to have anyone say they talk too much," confided my neighbor.

I nodded. I was suddenly sick at heart, as though I felt a premonition of tragedy. Somehow I connected it with Duare, and I didn't feel much like talking.

The fellow in the next cage shook his head sadly. "You don't look like a Brokol," he said, "but you talk like one. It is too bad. When I saw you coming I thought that I was going to have some one to talk with. I have been afraid that I was going to forget how to talk."

"I am sorry," I said. "I shall be glad to talk with you."

He brightened up. "My name is Jonda," he said.

"Mine is Carson."

"I am from Tonglap. Where are you from?"

"From Korva," I said. There was no use going through the futile explanation of where the United States of America was. No one on Venus could have understood it.

"I never heard of Korva," he said. "Tonglap is far away in that direction." He pointed toward the north. "I am a vookor in the army of Tonglap." Vookor really means one dagger, but is the title of an officer who commands one hundred men, a captain. Tonglap means big land.

The days dragged heavily, and I became much depressed. Here I was in a cage in a strange land, a prisoner of queer, half human creatures; my ship lay disabled at Japal; and Duare was far away in Timal. How long, I wondered, would those savage people remain friendly to her? I began to lose hope, for it seemed impossible that she and I ever would be reunited, that we should ever reach Korva.

Jonda had told me that at any moment one of us might be chosen as a human sacrifice to Loto-El-Ho-Ganja. "From remarks I have overheard," he said, "I think she either drinks the blood of the victim or bathes in it."

"I understand that she is very beautiful," I said. "Have you ever seen her?"

"No, and I don't want to. I understand that it isn't good for one's health to have Loto-El-Ho-Ganja take an interest in one. Let us hope that she never hears of us."

After a couple of weeks Jonda and I were taken from our cages and put to work cleaning up an oval field which had tiers of benches built around it. The benches were raised, the lower tier being some ten feet above the ground; so that the whole thing resembled a Spanish bull ring more than it did anything else. There were two main gates and a number of small doors in the wooden paling surrounding it.

I remarked to Jonda that it seemed strange to me that we

didn't see more slaves in the city. As far as I knew, there were only the two of us.

"I've never seen any others," he replied. "Duma, the jong, sent out that expedition under Ka-at to gather slaves; but he didn't do very well. He may have had his head lopped off for it by this time."

"Shut up!" snapped one of the warriors that were guarding us. "You talk too much. Work, don't talk."

While we were working, half a dozen warriors entered the arena and approached our guard. "The jong has sent for these two," said their leader.

One of our guard nodded, and asked, "And us?"

The leader of the warriors just nodded. No words wasted there.

They conducted us to the palace grounds and through what appeared to be a well kept orchard of small fruit trees. I could see what appeared to be some kind of fruit hanging from the branches, but only one or two to a tree. There were many guards about.

When we had come closer to the orchard, I was amazed to see that what I had thought was fruit were diminutive Brokols dangling in the air by stems attached to the tops of their heads. This suddenly explained many things, among them the knob on the tops of the heads of all the Brokols I had seen and Ka-at's statement that Loto-El-Ho-Ganja had never hung from a plant.

The little Brokols were perfectly formed. Most of them hung quietly, swaying in the breeze, with their eyes shut; but a few were very active, wriggling their arms and legs and making complaining sounds. It all reminded me of the first stirrings of a new born babe, yet there was something almost obscene about it. They were of all sizes, from those but an inch long to some that were fully fifteen inches in length.

Jonda pointed to one of these, and remarked, "Pretty nearly ripe and about to fall off."

"Shut up!" snapped one of our guard. That was practically the extent of the conversations we ever had with our captors.

TWENTY-SIX

We were taken into the presence of the jong, where we were told to bow four times. It is remarkable that from the depth of the African forest to the Court of Versailles, on Earth or Venus, there is a similarity in the trappings and the ritual surrounding kings.

The throne room of Duma was as elaborate as the culture and means of the Brokols could make it. There were battle scenes painted on the walls; there were dyed fabrics hanging at the windows and doorways; swords and spears and the heads of animals adorned the walls.

Duma sat upon a carved bench on a dais strewn with furs. He was a large man, as hairless and hideous as his subjects; and he was loaded with bracelets, armlets, and anklets of gold. A Brokol woman, the first I had seen, sat on a lower bench beside him. She, too, was weighted down with golden ornaments. She was Dua, the vadjong. This I learned later, as also that the jongs of Brokol were always named Duma; and the vadjongs, Dua.

"Which is the slave from Japal?" asked Duma, and then, "I see, it must be the one with yellow hair and gray eyes. Ka-at did not lie. Did you tell Ka-at that you came from a country ten million four hundred thousand kobs from Brokol, fellow?"

"Yes," I said.

"And did you tell him that there were a hundred and thirty million people in your country?"

"Correct."

"Ka-at did not lie," he repeated.

"Nor did I," I said.

"Shut up!" said Duma; "you talk too much. Could you lead an expedition to that country for the purpose of obtaining loot and slaves?"

"Of course not," I replied; "we could never reach it. Even I may never return to it."

"You are, even as Ka-at said, the greatest liar in the world," said Duma; then he turned his eyes upon Jonda. "And you," he said; "where are you from?"

"From Tonglap."

"How many people are there there?"

"I never counted them," replied Jonda, "but I may say that there are fully ten times as many as there are in Brokol."

"Another liar," said Duma. "Brokol is the largest country in the world. Can you lead my warriors to Tonglap, so that they may take prisoners and loot?"

"I can, but I won't," said Jonda. "I am no traitor."

"Shut up!" said Duma. "You talk too much." He spoke to an officer. "Take this one who is from Tonglap and put him back in his cage. Loto-El-Ho-Ganja wished to see the other one. She has never seen a man with yellow hair and gray eyes. She did not believe Ka-at any more than I did. She said, also, that she would be amused to hear the greatest liar in Amtor."

They led Jonda away, and then several men with plumes fastened to their heads surrounded me. They carried golden gaffs and very heavy short-swords with ornate hilts. Their leader looked at Duma, who nodded; and I was led from the throne room.

"When you enter the presence of Loto-El-Ho-Ganja, bow seven times," the leader instructed me, "and do not speak unless you are spoken to; then only answer questions. Ask none and make no gratuitous observations of your own."

Loto-El-Ho-Ganja has a throne room of her own in a temple that stands not far from the palace. As we approached it, I saw hundreds of people bringing offerings. Of course I could not see everything that they brought; but there were foods and ornaments and textiles. It evidently paid well to head the church of Brokol, as it does to head most churches and cults. Even in our own Christian countries it has not always proved unprofitable to emulate the simple ways of Christ and spread his humble teachings.

Loto-El-Ho-Ganja sat on a gorgeous golden throne that made Duma's bench look like a milkmaid's stool. She was surrounded by a number of men garbed like those who escorted me. They were her priests.

Loto-El-Ho-Ganja was not a bad looking girl. She was no Brokol, but a human being like me. She had jet black hair and eyes and a cream colored skin with just a tinge of olive, through which glowed a faint pink upon her cheeks. I'd say that if she were not beautiful, she was definitely arresting and interesting; and she looked alert and intelligent.

After I had bowed seven times she sat looking at me in silence for a long time. "What is your name?" she asked after a while. She had a lovely contralto voice. Listening to it, I could not imagine her drinking human blood or taking a bath in it.

"I am Carson kum Amtor, Tanjong kum Korva," I replied; which, in English, would be Carson of Venus, Prince of Korva.

"And where is Korva?"

"It is a country far to the south."

"How far?"

"I do not know exactly—several thousand kobs, however."

"Did you not tell Ka-at that your country lay ten million four hundred thousand kobs from Brokol?" she demanded. "Were you lying then or now?"

"I was not lying at all. The world from which I originally came is not Korva, and that other world is ten million four hundred thousand kobs from Brokol."

"By what name is it known?" she asked.

"The United States of America."

She wrinkled her brows in thought at that; and a strange, puzzled expression came into her eyes. She seemed to be straining to bring some forgotten memory from the deepest recesses of her mind, but presently she shook her head wearily.

"The United States of America," she repeated. "Would you tell me something about your country? I cannot see what you could expect to gain by lying to me."

"I shall be glad to tell you anything you wish to know," I replied, "and I can assure you that I shall not lie to you."

She arose from her throne and stepped down from the dais. "Come with me," she said, and then she turned to one of her priests. "I would examine this man alone. You may all leave."

"But, Loto-El-Ho-Ganja," objected the man, "it would be dangerous to leave you alone with this man. He is an enemy."

She drew herself up to her full height. "I am Loto-El-Ho-Ganja," she said. "I know all things. I have looked into this man's eyes; I have looked into his soul, and I know that he will not attempt to harm me."

The fellow still hesitated. "Such a thing has never been done," he said.

"You heard my command, Ro-ton," she said sharply. "Do you, my high priest, dare question my authority?"

He moved away at that, and the others followed him. Loto-El-Ho-Ganja led me across the room toward a small door. The throne room of this goddess, if that was what she was, was even more elaborate than that of Duma, the jong; but its wall decorations were gruesome—rows of human skulls with crossed bones beneath them; doubtless the skulls and bones of human sacrifices.

The small room to which she led me was furnished with a desk, several benches, and a couch. The benches and the couch were covered with furs and cushions. Loto-El-Ho-Ganja seated herself on a bench behind the desk. "Sit down," she said, and I seated myself on a bench opposite her.

She asked me about the same questions that Duma had, and I gave her the same answers that I had given him; then she asked me to explain how there could be another world so far from Venus, and I gave her a very sketchy explanation of the solar system.

"Sun, planets, moons," she said musingly, "moons and stars."

I had not mentioned stars. I wondered how she could have known the word.

"Before they brought me before you," I said, "I was told to speak only when I was spoken to, and to ask you no questions."

"You would like to ask me some questions?"

"Yes."

"You may," she said. "Ro-ton and the lesser priests would be shocked," she added, with a shrug and a smile.

"How did you know about stars?" I asked.

She looked surprised. "Stars! What do I know about stars? I am Loto-El-Ho-Ganja. That answers your question. I know many things. Sometimes I do not know how I know them. I do not know how I knew about stars. In the back of my mind are a million memories, but most of them are only vague and fragmentary. I try very hard to piece them together or to build them into recognizable wholes," she sighed, "but I never can."

"Of course you are not a Brokol," I said. "Tell me how you came to be here, a living goddess among alien people."

"I do not know," she said. "That is one of the things I can never recall. Once I found myself sitting on the temple throne. I did not even know the language of these people. They had to teach me it. While I was learning it, I learned that I was a goddess; and that I came from the fires that surround Amtor. My full title is Loto-El-Ho-Ganja Kum O Rāj," (literally Most High More Than Woman Of The Fire; or, for short, Fire Goddess) "but that is too long and is only used on state occasions and in rituals. Ro-ton and a few of the others I permit to call me just Loto in private." She pronounced it lo'to, and as it means Most High, it was still something of a title. "You," she added graciously, "may call me Loto while we are alone."

I felt that I was getting on pretty well, to be permitted to call a goddess by her first name. I hoped that she was going to like me so well that she wouldn't care to drink my blood, or even bathe in it.

"I shall call you Carson," she said. "Like so many other things that I cannot understand, I seemed to be drawn to you, from the moment I first saw you, by some mysterious bonds of propinquity. I think it was when you said 'United States of America.' That name seemed to strike a responsive chord within me. Why, I do not know. United States of America!" She whispered the words softly and slowly, almost caressingly; and there was that strange far-away look in her eyes.

TWENTY-SEVEN

Loto and I were getting on famously when there came a scratching at the door. "Enter!" said The Fire Goddess.

The door was opened, and Ro-ton stood scowling on the threshold.

"I thought I told you we were to be left alone," said the goddess with some asperity.

"I come from Duma," said Ro-ton. "He wishes to offer a sacrifice to Loto-El-Ho-Ganja," and he looked straight at me with a very nasty expression on his green face.

"If he insists, I shall accept his sacrifice," said Loto; "but I shall reserve the right to select the victim," and she looked so meaningly at Ro-ton that he turned a dark green, which faded

107

almost immediately to a sickly greenish white. "It will probably be one of those who disobey me."

Ro-ton faded from the scene, closing the door after him; while Loto tapped her sandalled toe upon the floor. "He aggravates me so," she said. "Whenever I demonstrate any liking for a person, he runs immediately to Duma and gets him to select that person as an offering. One of these days I am going to lose patience and select Ro-ton myself. That would be a great honor for Ro-ton, but I don't think he'd enjoy it."

"Is it true," I asked, "that you drink the blood of the sacrificial offerings?"

Her eyes flashed angrily. "You are presumptious!" she exclaimed. "You have taken advantage of my kindness to you to ask me to divulge one of the most sacred secrets of the temple."

I stood up. "I am sorry," I said. "Now I suppose I must go."

"Sit down!" she snapped. "I am the one to decide when you are to go. Have you no manners?"

"I have never before had the honor of being entertained by a goddess," I said; "so I do not know just how to act."

"You are not being entertained by a goddess," she said. "You are entertaining one. Goddesses do not entertain any one, especially slaves."

"I hope that I *am* entertaining you, Most High," I said.

"You are. Now tell me more about The United States of America. Has it many cities?"

"Thousands."

"Any as large as Brokal?"

"Most of them are larger. One has nearly seven million people."

"What is that city called?" she asked.

"New York."

"New York," she repeated. "New York. It seems just as though I had heard that name before."

Again we were interrupted by scratching on the door. It was a priest to announce that Duma, the jong, was coming to the temple to pay his respects to Loto-El-Ho-Ganja. Loto flushed angrily, but she said, "We will receive him. Summon the priests to the holy chamber." When the priest was gone, she turned again to me. "I cannot leave you here alone," she said; "so you will have to come with me."

We went out into the throne room. It was what she called

the holy chamber. Loto told me to stand over at one side; then she took her place on the throne. Priests were arriving. Ro-ton came. They made a barbarous spectacle in that skull decorated room, with their green skins and their plumes of office.

Soon I heard the sound of drums, first at a distance; then drawing nearer; and presently Duma entered, preceded by drummers and followed by fully a hundred officers. They stopped before the dais and bowed seven times; then Duma mounted the dais and sat on a low bench next to Loto-El-Ho-Ganja. Every one else in the room remained standing. You could have heard a pin drop, it was so quiet.

They went through a sort of stupid ritual for a while, Duma standing up every few seconds and bowing seven times. When that was over they commenced their conversation. I could hear every word.

"Ro-ton tells me that you have refused my sacrifice," said Duma. "That is something that has never before happened."

"I did not refuse it," replied Loto. "I simply said that I would select the victim."

"That is the same as refusing it," said Duma. "I wish to select my own offering."

"You may," said Loto, "but I have the right to refuse any offering that is not acceptable. You seem to forget that I am Loto-El-Ho-Ganja Kum O Raj."

"And you seem to forget that I am the jong of Brokol," snapped Duma.

"To a goddess, a jong is only another mortal," said Loto, icily. "Now, if you have no further matters to discuss, I permit you to withdraw."

I could see that Duma was furious. He turned dark green, and he fairly glared at Loto. "A jong has warriors," he said, angrily. "He can enforce his wishes."

"You threaten me?" demanded Loto.

"I demand that I be permitted to select my own offering." Duma was fairly shouting now.

"I told you that you might name your selection," said Loto.

"Very well," said Duma. "It is the slave, Carson, with whom you have been closeted alone for hours, defying the traditions of the temple."

"I decline your offering," said Loto.

Duma leaped to his feet. "Take that slave back to his cage," he shouted. "I'll attend to this woman later. Now I declare that she is no goddess, but that I, Duma, am a god. Let those who accept me as their god bow seven times."

That was the last I heard, as several warriors had seized me and hustled me out of the holy chamber.

They took me back to my cage and locked me in. Jonda was still in the adjoining cage; and when I told him what had happened, he said that I didn't have long to live now. "That's what comes of getting mixed up with goddesses and jongs," he added.

"They were going to kill me anyway," I reminded him. "At least this way nobody's going to drink my blood."

"Maybe Duma will," he suggested. "You say he's god now. If that is so, he can select you for his first sacrifice."

"I wonder if the people will stand for his ousting Loto-El-Ho-Ganja," I said.

"If a jong has plenty of warriors, his people will stand for anything," said Jonda.

"Loto-El-Ho-Ganja seemed all-powerful to me," I said. "The high priest and the jong did her homage and stepped around for her until Duma lost his temper."

"Look!" exclaimed Jonda, pointing. "Who is that they're bringing? I've never seen a human woman here before."

I looked and was shocked. "It is Loto-El-Ho-Ganja," I said.

"So Duma is a god now!" said Jonda.

Two warriors were escorting Loto-El-Ho-Ganja. They were not rough with her. Perhaps they felt that she might still be a goddess regardless of what Duma had proclaimed, and one doesn't willingly offend a goddess.

They were coming toward our cages; and presently they stopped in front of mine, unlocked the door, and pushed Loto in with me.

CHAPTER TWENTY-EIGHT

I have had many strange experiences in my adventurous life, but being locked up in a cage over night with a goddess was a new one. Loto appeared dazed. I imagine the shock of her fall from Olympus was terrific.

"What happened?" I asked.

"This is the end," she said. "Thank God, this is the end. I feel it."

She spoke in Amtorian, all but one word: God. *That she spoke in English!* There is no word for God in Amtorian. Most High More than Woman of The Fire is the nearest approach to the name of a deity that I have ever heard here. Where did she learn that one English word? I asked her; but she only looked more dazed than ever, and said that she did not know.

"Why is it the end, Loto?" I asked.

"He has condemned me to death," she said, and then she laughed. "I, who cannot die, am condemned to death. But he has condemned you, too—you and this other prisoner—and you *can* die. I wish that I might save you."

"You tried to, Loto," I reminded her. "Why did you do that? It has cost you your life."

"I liked you," she said. "I was drawn to you by some power I do not understand."

We three, Loto, Jonda, and I, condemned to death, talked together long into the night. They told me strange, almost unbelievable things about these green Brokol people. They told me that their blood was not red; but white, like the sap of some plants, and that they ate no meat, though they drank the blood of warm blooded animals.

I asked about the tiny Brokols I had seen hanging from trees, and they told me that the Brokol females laid small, nut-like eggs which were planted in the ground. These grew into trees; and, in a matter of years, bore the fruit I had seen hanging. When the little Brokols were ripe, they dropped from the trees, wild, untamed creatures that had to be captured and disciplined.

Each family usually had its own orchard of Brokol trees, the one I had seen, belonging to the royal family. Guypals, the great birds with which I had become familiar at Mypos, accounted for many little ripening Brokols, which accounted for the armed warriors guarding the royal orchard. Here was a race of people who not only had family trees, but family orchards.

When a woman planted an egg, she stuck a little marker in the ground beside it to identify it, just as our home gardeners place markers every spring in their gardens so that they will know which are beets and which tomatoes when they come up.

Because of guypals and insect pests the infant mortality of the Brokols is appallingly high, not one in a thousand reaching maturity. However, as the Brokols are polygamous and both the ground and the females extremely fertile, there is little danger that race suicide will exterminate them. I might mention that no dogs are allowed in the orchards.

During a lapse in the conversation, Loto suddenly exclaimed, "I did not drink human blood. While I was Loto-El-Ho-Ganja Kum O Raj, I could not tell you; but now that I have been deposed I am free to speak."

"Somehow, I could not believe that you did," I told her, "but I am glad to hear it from your own lips."

"No," she said, "it was Ro-ton, Duma, and a few of the more favored priests who got the blood to drink. It was only their craving for blood which ever induced them to sacrifice a human slave, as these were considered very valuable as workers. Most of the offerings were Brokols who had incurred the displeasure of Duma or Ro-ton, but they did not drink the blood of these. I did not even kill the victim; Ro-ton did that. I merely presided and repeated a chant; but the priests let the people think that I drank the blood, in order to impress them. It seems that the common people must be afraid of their goddess in order to be held under control."

"You and Carson speak of strange creatures of which I have never heard," said Jonda, the godless one.

"Let us talk of something else then," said Loto. "I should like to hear more about The United States of America, of New York—New York—New York—" She whispered the name slowly, drawing it out; and her eyes were dreamy and introspective. Suddenly she exclaimed, "Betty! Betty! Betty! I'm getting it!" She was terribly excited. "Call—call—Betty call. I almost have it! Oh, God, I almost have it! Brooklyn! Now I have it! Brooklyn!" Then she swooned.

I tried to revive her, but she didn't respond; so I had to let her lie there. I knew that she would regain consciousness eventually.

What she had said mystified me. What could she know about Brooklyn? I had mentioned New York, but never Brooklyn; yet I could not be mistaken—she had said Brooklyn plainly. And what did she mean by *call*, and who was Betty? When she came to, I intended to get an explanation, if I could. Could it be that there was another American on Venus, whom she had seen and talked with? If I had reached the Shepherd Star, another might have done so. Perhaps he had been a prisoner here, maybe an offering with whom she had talked before he died. I must find out! But what good it would do me, other than to satisfy my curiosity, I did not know; for was I not to die on the morrow?

Thinking these thoughts, I fell asleep.

It was morning when I awoke. I was alone. Loto was not in the cage, and the door was still securely locked!

TWENTY-NINE

I awoke Jonda, but he could give me no information. He was as much mystified as I. Something tells me that I shall never see Loto again and that I shall carry this unsolved mystery to the grave with me.

Shortly before noon Brokols commenced filing past our cages. They were going toward the "bull ring" that Jonda and I had once cleaned. Many of them stopped and looked at us, commenting, usually in a most uncomplimentary manner, upon our looks and antecedents.

Presently they came for us—a couple of dozen warriors. I wanted to use my pistol, but I decided to wait until we got in the arena and I could wreak greater havoc.

The warriors were much concerned and not a little upset by the absence of Loto. They saw that the lock of the door had not been tampered with. When they asked me how she had escaped, I could only say that I did not know. They took us to the arena, which was crowded with Brokols. It was very quiet, nothing like a Spanish bull ring or an American baseball game when they have a large audience. There was little conversation, no cheering, no shouting. When Duma entered with his family and entourage, the place was as quiet as a tomb.

Jonda and I were standing in the center of the arena with our guards, one of whom left us and went and spoke with Duma. Presently he returned and said that Duma wished me to come to him. Half the guards accompanied me.

"What became of the woman?" demanded Duma, overlooking the fact that I had not bowed to him either four times or once.

"That is a stupid question to ask me," I told him.

Duma turned the color of a green lime.

"You must know," I continued, "that if I did know, I wouldn't tell you. I don't know, but if I told you that, you would not believe me. No, I don't know; but I can guess."

"What do you guess?" he asked.

"I guess that you can't hold a goddess behind bars," I said, "and I also guess that she has gone to arrange punishment for you and Ro-ton for the way you have treated her. You were very stupid to treat the Most High More Than Woman of the Fire the way you did."

"It was Ro-ton's fault," said Duma.

Ro-ton was there and he looked very uncomfortable, and when Duma said again, "It was all Ro-ton's fault," he couldn't contain himself.

"You wanted to be the Most High More Than Man of the Fire," he blurted. "That was your idea, not mine. If she comes back, she'll know whose fault it was."

"Goddesses always do," I said. "You can never fool 'em."

"Take him away!" snapped Duma. "I do not like him."

"I think I hear her coming now," I said, looking up in the air.

Immediately Duma, Ro-ton, and all those around them looked up. It was a very tense moment, but no Loto-El-Ho-Ganja Kum O Raj appeared. However, I had upset their nervous equilibrium; which was all that I hoped to do; though it wouldn't have surprised me much if a girl who could have disappeared so completely and mysteriously as Loto had the night before had suddenly materialized carrying a flaming sword. However, she didn't; and I was haled back to the center of the arena.

Jonda bowed to me seven times. Jonda had a sense of humor, but the Brokols hadn't. There was a hissing noise, as though thousands of people had gasped simultaneously; and I guess that is exactly what happened; then the silence was deathly.

Duma shouted something that I could not understand, drums were beaten, and the warriors left us alone in the center of the arena.

"We are about to die," said Jonda. "Let's give a good account of ourselves."

Two warriors came out and handed us each a spear, or gaff, and a sword. "See that you put on a good show," said one of them.

"You are going to see one of the best shows ever put on in this arena," I told him.

When the warriors had retired to places of safety, one of the small doors in the arena wall was opened and six nobargans came out. The nobargans are hairy, manlike cannibals. They have no clothing nor ornaments; but they fight with slings, with which they hurl stones; and with the crudest kind of bows and arrows.

The derivation of the word nobargan may interest you. Broadly, it means a savage; literally, it means hairy men. In the singular it is nobargan. *Gan* is man; *bar* is hair. *No* is a contraction of *not,* meaning with; and is used as a prefix with the same value that the suffix *y* has in English. So *nobar* means hairy and *no-bargan,* hairy man. The prefix *kloo* forms the plural (hairy men) savages. I have preferred throughout this narrative to use the English form of plural as a rule, as the Amtorian is quite awkward; in this case, *kloonobargan.*

The nobargans came toward us, growling like wild beasts, from which they are not far removed. If they were proficient with their slings and bows, our gaffs and swords would offer no defense. We'd never be able to get close enough to use them.

I threw down my gaff and drew my pistol, carrying the sword in my left hand to use to fend off the missiles of the savages. Jonda wanted to barge ahead and get to close quarters, but I told him to wait—that I had a surprise for him, the nobargans, and the Brokols; so he dropped back at my side.

The savages were circling to surround us as I raised my pistol and dropped the first one; then all I had to do was pan, as the photographers say. One by one the creatures went down. Some missiles flew by our heads; and three of the beast-men had time to charge us, but I dropped them all before they reached us.

Utter silence followed, and endured for a moment; then I heard Duma raving like a madman. He had been cheated out of the sport he had expected. There had been no contest, and we had not been killed. He ordered warriors to come and take my pistol from me.

They came, but with no marked enthusiasm. I told them to stay back or I would kill them as I had killed the nobargans. Duma screamed at them to obey him. Of course there was nothing else for them to do; so they came on, and I dropped them just as I had the savages.

The Brokol audience sat in absolute silence. They are the quietest people! But Duma was not quiet. He fairly jumped up and down in his rage. He would have torn his hair, had he had any. Finally he ordered every armed man in the audience to enter the arena and get me, offering a splendid reward.

"Good work!" said Jonda. "Keep it up. After you have killed all the inhabitants of Brokol, we can go home."

"I can't kill 'em all," I said. "There are too many of them coming now. We'll be taken, but at a good price."

Thousands of armed men were jumping over the barrier and coming toward us. I can't say they were hurrying much. Everyone seemed to be quite willing to let some one else win the reward; but they were coming, nevertheless.

As they were closing in on us, I heard a familiar sound above me. But it could not be true! I looked up; and there, far overhead, circled an aeroplane. It could not be true, but it was. As far as I could see it, I could recognize that ship. It was the anotar—my anotar! Who had repaired it? Who was flying it? Who else could it be but Duare, the only other person in all this world who could fly an aeroplane.

"Look!" I cried, pointing up. "She comes! Loto-El-Ho-Ganja Kum O Raj comes for vengeance!"

Everybody looked up. Then they turned and looked at Duma and Ro-ton. I looked at them, too. They were beating it out of that arena as fast as they could go. I'll bet they're running yet.

The anotar was circling low now, and I was waving wildly to attract the attention of Duare, or whoever was in it. Presently Duare leaned out and waved.

I called to the Brokols to fall back out of the way or be killed by the bird ship coming with a new Loto-El-Ho-Ganja. I thought they might notice too soon that Duare was not the original Loto. They made room in a hurry, scrambling out of the arena and leaving the stadium as fast as they could go.

Duare landed in the arena—a beautiful landing—and a moment later I had her in my arms. I would have done the same thing had we been on the corner of 42nd and Broadway.

Doran was in the ship with her, and a moment later Jonda was in and I was at the controls with Duare at my side. We were both so full of questions that we almost burst, but eventually I learned that one of Kandar's first acts after he became jong of Japal was to send a strong body of warriors to Timal to bring Duare and Artol back to his court. He also, following my instructions, had had a new propeller made for the anotar. Knowing that I had been captured by the Brokols, they knew where to look for me; though they had little hope of reaching me in time.

We were flying at a couple of thousand feet altitude when I looked back at Jonda. He was gazing around and down, wide-eyed with excitement.

"What do you think of it?" I asked him.

"I don't believe it," he said. "I think Ka-at was right—you are the greatest liar in the world."

EDITOR'S NOTE:

Not that it has any bearing on this story, but just as an example of a remarkable coincidence, I want to reproduce here a news item that appeared in the daily press recently.

Brooklyn, Sept. 24. Special Correspondence. The body of Betty Callwell, who disappeared twenty-five years ago, was found in the alley back of her former home here early this morning. The preservation of the body was remarkable, as Miss Callwell must have been dead for twenty-five years. Friends who viewed the body insist that it did not look a day older than when she disappeared. The police fear foul play and are investigating.

THIRTY

When I was young I used to dream of living an adventurous life, and it may be that these youthful dreams more or less shape one's later life. Perhaps that is why I took up flying when I was old enough. It may account for the rocket ship I built for a trip to Mars—a trip that ended on Venus!

117

I had desired adventures; but recently I had had little else than misadventures, and I must admit that I was getting pretty well fed up on them; so, when Duare and Doran arrived in the nick of time over the arena in Brokol, while Jonda and I were facing the impossibility of withstanding the assault of several thousand warriors armed with swords and gaffs, and bore us off in the anotar, I made up my mind then and there that we were to have no more adventures or misadventures, but were heading south in our search for Korva just as quickly as possible.

Under ordinary circumstances I should have been glad to take Jonda to Tonglap, his homeland; but I was not going to risk Duare's safety any further; so, when Doran told Jonda that he would be welcome in Japal until he could find the means to return to Tonglap, I was more than pleased, since Japal was in the general direction we would have to travel to get to Korva, and Tonglap was not.

We were given a royal welcome in Japal, the anotar was stocked with food and water; and as quickly as we decently could, we bade our friends good-by and took off.

Duare and I had discussed our course and had come to the conclusion that if we flew in a southwesterly direction we would come pretty close to hitting the land mass known as Anlap, or Birdland, on which Korva is situated. This course took us down the length of the Lake of Japal for about five hundred miles and then out over a noellat gerloo, or mighty water, which is Amtorian for ocean.

"Isn't it restful!" sighed Duare.

"After what we've been through, almost anything would be restful," I replied. "This is almost too restful and too good to be true."

"I thought that I should never see you again, Carson. They told me some of the horrible customs of the Brokols—their drinking of human blood and all that. I was nearly frantic before I was able to take off in the anotar to search for you. Won't it be wonderful to get back to Korva, where we are loved?"

"And, for the first time since we met, have peace and security. My dear, if it's humanly possible, I think I shall never leave Korva again."

"Won't Taman and Jahara be amazed and delighted to see us again! Oh, Carson, I can hardly wait to get back."

"It's a long flight," I told her, "and after we reach Korva, we may have a long search before we can locate Sanara—it's a very little city in a very big country."

The ocean across which we were flying proved to be enormous, and it was a very lonely ocean. We saw a few ships at the lower end of the Lake of Japal and a few more close to the coast on the ocean; but after these, we saw nothing—just a vast expanse of gray sea, a sea that was never blue, for it had no blue sky to reflect; only the gray clouds that envelop Venus.

Amtorian shipping seldom sails out of sight of land, for all maps are wildly inaccurate; because of their belief that Amtor is a saucer shaped world floating on a sea of molten rock with what is really the nearer Pole as the periphery, or outer edge, of the saucer and the Equator at the center. You can readily see how this would distort everything. Then, too, the mariners have no celestial bodies to guide them. If they get out of sight of land, they are sunk, figuratively; and very likely to be sunk literally.

Duare and I were much better off, as I had built a compass in Havatoo; and I had roughly corrected the Amtorian maps from my knowlege of the true shape of the planet. Of course, my maps were pitifully inadequate; but they at least had some claim to verity.

We were getting pretty tired of that ocean, when Duare sighted land. I had been confident that Japal lay in the northern hemisphere; and from the distance we had travelled since leaving it, I was certain that we had crossed the Equator and were in the southern hemisphere, where Korva lies. Perhaps this was Korva that we were approaching! The thought filled us both with elation.

It was really a lovely land, although a barren rock would have looked lovely to us after the monotony of that long ocean crossing, during which we had seen nothing but water for a full week. As we neared the land, I dropped down for a closer view. A great river wound down a broad valley to empty into the sea almost directly beneath us. The valley was carpeted with the pale violet grass of Amtor, starred with blue and purple flowers. Little patches of forest dotted the valley. We could see their glossy, lacquerlike boles of red and azure and white, and their weird foliage of heliotrope, lavender, and violet moving to a gentle breeze.

119

There is something strangely beautiful about an Amtorian landscape, beautiful and unreal. Perhaps it is the soft, pastel shades, that make it look more like a work of art than a creation of Nature. Like a gorgeous sunset on Earth, it is something that could never be reproduced by man. I sometimes think that man's inability to reproduce the beauties of Nature has led to the abominable atrocities called modern art.

"Oh, how I'd like to get down there among those flowers!" exclaimed Duare.

"And get captured or killed by some of the weird creatures that roam your fantastic planet," I retorted. "No, young lady! As long as our food, our water, and our fuel hold out, we stay right up in the air, where we're safe, until we find the city of Sanara."

"So my planet is fantastic, is it?" demanded Duare, coming to the defense of her world like the Travel Bureau of Honolulu or the Los Angeles Chamber of Commerce. "I suppose your planet is perfect, with its crooked politicians, its constantly warring religious sects, its gangsters, and its funny clothes."

I laughed and kissed her. "I should never have told you so much," I said.

"From what you have told me, I gather that the best thing about your planet isn't there any more," she said.

"What's that?" I asked.

"You." So I kissed her again.

"Look!" I exclaimed presently; "there's a city!"

Sure enough, several miles up the river and close to it, there lay a city.

"It can't be Sanara, can it?" asked Duare, hopefully.

I shook my head. "No; it is not Sanara. The river near Sanara runs due east; this one runs due south. Furthermore, this city doesn't resemble Sanara in any respect."

"Let's have a closer look at it," suggested Duare.

I couldn't see any harm in that; so I headed for the city. It reminded me a little of Havatoo, except that it was entirely circular, while Havatoo is a half circle. There was a large central plaza, with avenues radiating from it like the spokes of a wheel; and there were other avenues forming concentric circles spaced equidistant from one another between the central plaza and the high outer wall of the city.

"It looks like two Havatoos stuck together," observed Duare.

"I wish it were Havatoo," I said.

"Why?" demanded Duare. "We just escaped from that city with our lives. I don't ever care to see it again. The very idea! I, the daughter of a thousand jongs, was not good enough to live in Havatoo; so they were going to destroy me!"

"That was a bit stupid," I admitted.

I dropped down close over the city. Everything about it was round—the central plaza was round, the buildings were all round, the whole city was round; and many of the buildings were capped with spheres.

Now people were running into the streets and the great central plaza and out upon their roofs, looking up at us. Many of them waved to us, and we replied.

"What an interesting city," said Duare. "I'd like to visit it. The people look very friendly, too."

"My dear," I replied, "you are becoming a veritable glutton for disaster."

"I wouldn't go down there for the world," said Duare. "I just said I'd *like* to visit it."

Just then my propeller flew off.

THIRTY-ONE

The propeller was the one that Kandar had made and fitted to the engine while I was a prisoner in Brokol. Evidently, he hadn't fitted it properly.

"I think you are going to get your wish, Duare," I said. "We haven't enough elevation to clear the city; so I guess I'll have to bring her down in that plaza."

As I spiralled to a landing, the people fled from the plaza giving me plenty of room; but the moment the anotar came to a stop, they swarmed out again forming a circle about it. They danced around the anotar, singing and laughing. Others, behind them, had gathered handfuls of flowers with which they showered us. The songs they sang were songs of welcome. Such a reception of strangers in an Amtorian city was without parallel in my experience; it was remarkable; it was amazing. And it certainly reassured us.

Presently three of them approached us; and the dancing

121

and singing stopped, as the others gathered around to listen. All were smiling. Somehow they reminded me of the acrobats I used to see on the old vaudeville circuits, with their set smiles —mugging, I think it was called.

One of the three bowed, and said, "Welcome to Voo-ad, if you come in peace." Voo-ad means First City.

"We landed because of an accident to our anotar," I replied; "but we come in peace and we are appreciative of your friendly reception."

"My name is Ata-voo-med-ro," he said. I say "he" because I couldn't tell whether the speaker was a man or a woman. Like all the others, he looked like both or neither; and as ata-voo-med-ro means A-One million three it gave me no clew to the speaker's sex.

"My mate is Duare of Vepaja," I replied, "and I am Carson of Venus."

"You are both very welcome here," he said, "and I hope that you will descend from that strange creature which flies through the air like a bird and come with me to pay your respects to Vik-vik-vik, our jong."

Just then I saw one of the people pick up my propeller and run off with it. I called Ata-voo-med-ro's attention to this, and asked him to have the prop brought back to me. It had fallen into a bed of flowers; so I hoped it had not been greatly injured.

"You shall have it when you need it," he assured me.

Duare and I climbed down from the anotar, and accompanied Ata-voo-med-ro and his two companions across the plaza toward one of the larger buildings which face it. A large crowd followed us to the door of this building, which proved to be the jong's palace.

There were neither old people nor children in the crowd, and they all looked more or less alike—plump and rather soft looking. Although they wore weapons—a sword and a dagger —they did not look like a race of fighters. Each of them wore a single, skirt-like garment, which I later discovered is not a garment at all; just a number of long pouches or pockets strapped about their waists and falling almost to their knees, but they are so close together that they resemble a pleated skirt. Running down the exact center of their face and body, both front and back, is a well defined reddish line that looks like a birth-mark.

As you know, the two halves of our faces and bodies are not identical. In these people the lack of identicalness is more marked, though not to the extent of being a deformity. Perhaps the fine red line bisecting their faces adds to the apparent difference between the two halves.

We were ushered into the presence of Vik-vik-vik, which in English means 999. He smiled at us most benignly, and said, "The Vooyorgans welcome you to Voo-ad," or, the First People welcome you to the First City.

He asked us many questions about the countries from which we came, and told us that we were to consider ourselves his guests during our stay in Voo-ad. I told him that I should like very much to make the necessary repairs on our anotar and depart as quickly as possible, if he would have the propeller returned to me.

"You see, we have been away from home for a long time; and we are anxious to return."

"I can very well understand that," he replied, "but we shall all be very much disappointed if you do not remain with us at least a couple of days. This portion of Anlap is almost a wilderness, and we have no neighbors who are friendly and very few visitors; so you can see that you would be doing us a great favor if you would remain a short time—we hear so little of the outside world of Amtor."

"We are really in Anlap?" I asked; "then perhaps you can tell us the general direction of Korva."

"I have heard of Korva," he replied, "but I do not know where it lies. Now please tell me that you will remain at least two days, as I wish to arrange a banquet and entertainment for you before you depart."

Under the circumstances the only decent thing we could do, in view of his generous hospitality, was to remain; so we told him it would be a pleasure to accept his invitation. He seemed genuinely pleased, and directed Ata-voo-med-ro to show us about the city and see that we wanted for nothing which might enhance the pleasure of our visit in Voo-ad.

Across from the jong's palace was a very large building— it must have been fully two hundred feet in diameter—that attracted our immediate attention when we left the palace with Ata-voo-med-ro. The building was an enormous dome at least a hundred feet high. It dwarfed everything around it. Naturally, it intrigued our curiosity; and I asked Ata-voo-med-ro what it was.

"You shall see it before you leave Voo-ad," he replied. "I shall leave it until the very last, as the supreme moment of your visit to our city. I can guarantee that you will find it extremely interesting."

He had led us about the city, showing us the shops, the flowers and shrubbery that grow in profusion, and calling our attention to the carvings on the buildings. He also took us into an art shop where the work of the best artists of Voo-ad was on exhibition. These people show remarkable aptitude in reproducing natural objects with almost photographic fidelity, but there was not the slightest indication of creative genius in any of the work we saw.

While all the people looked and dressed much alike, we saw many doing menial work; and I asked Ata-voo-med-ro if there were different castes among them.

"Oh, yes," he replied; "all the kloo-meds and above are servants; voo-meds who have no du are in the next higher class; they are the artisans; then come the voo-meds with a du—that is the class I am in. We are just below the nobles, who run from voo-yor-yorko to voo-med; royalty is always under yorko. There are other caste divisions, but it is all rather complicated and I am sure would not interest you."

Perhaps the above has not interested you; but in English it is a little more interesting, as it gives some meaning to their strange numerical names. What he said was that all the 2,000,000's and above were servants; the 1,000,000's with no prefix letter (du) were in the artisan class; then came his class, the 1,000,000's with a letter; the nobles run from 100,000 to 1,000,000; and royalty is always under 1000. Vik-vik-vik's 999 is always the jong's name or number.

These high numbers do not mean that there are that many people in Voo-ad; it is merely a naming system, and just another indication to me of their total lack of creative genius.

Duare and I spent two very dull days in Voo-ad, and in the afternoon of the second day we were summoned to attend the banquet being given by the jong. The table, built in the form of a hollow ring with people sitting on both sides of it, was in a circular room. There were about two hundred guests, all apparently of the same sex; for all were similarly garbed and looked more or less alike. They had plenty of hair on their heads, but none on their faces. There was a great deal of chattering and laughing, and those perpetual, frozen smiles when they were not laughing. I overheard a great deal of the conversation which elicited laughter, but could find nothing to laugh at.

Duare, who sat between Vik-vik-vik and me, remarked that some article of food she was eating was delicious, whereat Vik-vik-vik and others within hearing broke into laughter. It didn't make sense. I like to see people happy, but I also like to feel that it is because they have something to be happy about.

The food was really delicious, as were the wines; and the guests ate and drank what seemed to Duare and me enormous amounts. They seemed to derive far more pleasure and gratification from eating and drinking than the act warranted; some even swooned with rapture. I found it rather disgusting, and heartily wished that the banquet was over, so that Duare and I might take our leave. We both wanted a good night's rest, as we expected to leave the next day; and I still had the propeller to adjust—after it was returned to me. I asked the jong if he had arranged to have it returned to me immediately.

"You shall have it in plenty of time before you leave," he replied, with that kindly smile of his.

"We should like to leave as early tomorrow as possible," I said, glancing at Duare.

I was immediately concerned by her appearance; there was a startled, almost frightened look in her eyes. "Something is happening to me, Carson," she said.

I started to rise. A strange sensation pervaded me. I could not move. I was paralyzed from the neck down!

THIRTY-TWO

I looked around at the others at the table; they were still laughing and chattering—and they were moving their arms and bodies. They were not paralyzed—only Duare and I. I looked at Vik-vik-vik; he was staring at us intently.

"Here is a very choice fruit," he said, offering me something that looked like a cross between an avocado and a banana.

Of course I could not raise a hand to take it; then he offered it to Duare, who was equally helpless. Vik-vik-vik waited a moment, and then he threw the soft fruit in her face.

"So you spurn my hospitality!" he cried, and then he broke into loud laughter, attracting the attention of all the guests to us. "Even so," he continued; "even though you refuse to accept what I offer, you shall still be my guests. You shall be my guests forever!" At that, everybody laughed uproariously. "What a notable addition you two will make to our collection in the Museum of Natural History. I think we have no pairs whatsoever in the upper categories, and we certainly have no male with gray eyes and yellow hair."

"We have no female in this category, my jong," said Ata-voo-med-ro.

"Right you are," assented Vik-vik-vik. "We have a female nobargan, but I presume we may scarcely maintain that she is of the same species as this woman."

"What is the meaning of all this?" I demanded. "What have you done to us?"

"The results of what we have done should, I think, be quite obvious to you," replied Vik-vik-vik, still laughing.

"You have trapped us by pretended friendliness, so that you may kill us. I have known of many treacherous and despicable acts, but this would bring a blush of shame to even a nobargan."

"You are mistaken," replied the jong; "we have no intention of killing you; as specimens, you are far too valuable. In the interests of science and education you will be preserved forever, serving a much better purpose than you could be continuing you silly, carnal lives." He turned to Ata-voo-med-ro. "Have them taken away," he ordered.

Two stretchers were brought; and we were carried out of the banquet hall by eight of the 2,000,000 caste, four to a stretcher. Out of the palace they carried us and across the plaza to the enormous dome I have already described—the building that Ata-voo-med-ro had told us would be left until the very last, as the supreme moment of our visit to Voo-ad. When I thought of the fiendish hypocrisy of the creature, I could have gnashed my teeth—which was about all there was left for me to do.

Inside, the dome was one enormous room with platforms, arranged in concentric circles, upon which were specimens of many of the larger beasts and reptiles of Amtor, supported by props or scaffolding; while from the wall hung perhaps a couple of hundred human beings and nobargans in ingeniously devised slings which distributed their weight equally to all parts of their bodies.

Similar slings were adjusted to Duare and me, and we were hung upon the wall side by side in spaces beside which lettered plaques had already been affixed giving our names, the countries from which we came, our species, sex, and such other information as had evidently seemed to the Vooyorgans either educational or interesting. All this had been attended to while we were being entertained as honored guests!

The other specimens who were in a position to see us had watched our arrival and our "mounting" with interest. Others were quite evidently asleep, their chins resting upon their breasts. So we could sleep! Well, that would be something in the nature of a reprieve from the hideous fate which had overtaken us.

A group of Vooyorgons who had been in the building had gathered to watch us being hung in position; they read the placards describing us, and commented freely. They were most interested in Duare, who was possibly the first specimen of a female of our breed they had ever seen. I noticed one in particular who said nothing, but stood gazing at her as though entranced by her beauty. Watching him, I was suddenly impressed by the fact that the reddish median line was missing and that the two halves of his face were practically identical. This creature was, I presumed, what biologists term a sport. It differed, too, in other ways: it was not continuously smiling or laughing, nor did it keep up the incessant chatter of its fellows. (I find it difficult not to refer to these creatures as males. They all looked so exactly alike that it was impossible to determine which were men and which women, but the fact that they all carried swords and daggers has influenced me to refer to them as males.)

They had left us our weapons; and I noticed that all the other exhibits in sight still wore theirs, except that their spears, if they had any, were fastened to the wall beside them. These weapons, of course, enhanced the educational value of the specimens; and it was quite safe to leave them with creatures who were paralyzed from the neck down.

Vooyorgans were constantly entering the building and strol-

127

ling through the aisles to examine the exhibits. Sometimes they stopped to speak with a specimen; but as they usually poked fun at the poor helpless things, they were generally met with silence.

As darkness fell, the building was artificially illuminated; and great crowds of Vooyorgans came to look at us. They often stopped before us and laughed at us, making uncomplimentary and insulting remarks. These were the same people who had danced around us a couple of days before, showering us with flowers, welcoming us to their city.

After a couple of hours, the building was cleared and the lights dimmed; only a few guards remained. They were of the 1,000,000 caste, with letter, which includes what one might term the white collar class and the soldiers—if any of these plump, soft creatures could claim that honorable title.

Although the lights had been dimmed, it was still quite light enough to see quite plainly near the outer wall of the building, where we were hanging; as only the center lights had been completely extinguished.

About twenty guards had been left in the huge building; though why even that many, I do not know; there was certainly no likelihood that any of us would riot or escape; one can't do either successfully while animated only from the larynx up.

Several of them were discussing us and congratulating Vooad upon having acquired such valuable additions to her Museum of Natural History.

"I have always wanted to see a woman," said one. "These other specimens are always talking about their women. They differ somewhat from the males, don't they? Now, this one has an entirely different figure and a far more delicate face than the male; it also has much more hair on its head—more like we Vooyorgans."

"The gray eyes and yellow hair of the male make him an outstanding exhibit," said another. My eyes are a gray-blue, and sometimes look gray and at others blue. I guess it is hard to tell which color they really are, but my hair is *not* yellow; although Amtorians usually describe it as such, they having no word for blond.

One member of the guard standing in front of us was very quiet; it neither laughed nor gabbled. Suddenly it commenced to shiver, as though with ague; then it reeled drunkenly and fell to the floor, where it writhed as though in an epileptic fit, which I thought was what ailed it.

"Dan-voo-med is about to divide," remarked one of its fellows. A couple of others glanced at D-1,000,000 and sauntered off unconcernedly. "You'd better get a couple of stretchers," the first speaker called after them.

A companion looked down at Dan-voo-med, writhing, groaning, and struggling on the floor. "It is about time," it said. "Dan-voo-med was commencing to worry; *od* feared that *od* might be one of those unfortunate ones who die before they reproduce their kind," (*Od* is a neuter pronoun analogous to *it*.)

The creature's struggles were now become violent; its groans and screams filled the vast chamber, echoing and re-echoing from the domed ceiling; and then, to my horror, I saw that the creature was splitting apart along the reddish median line I have described—right down the center of its head and body.

With a last, violent convulsion, the two halves rolled apart. There was no blood. Each half was protected by a thin, palpitating membrane, through which the internal organs were clearly observable. Almost immediately two stretchers were brought and the two halves were placed upon them and carried away. That both were still alive was evident, as I saw their limbs move.

Poor Duare was as white as a ghost, and almost nauseated by the revolting thing that we had witnessed. "Oh, Carson!" she cried; "what manner of horrid creatures are these?"

Before I could reply, a voice from my other side exclaimed, "Carson! Carson Napier! Is it really you?"

THIRTY-THREE

I turned to look. The voice came from a man hanging on the wall beside me. I recognized him immediately. "Ero Shan!" I cried.

"And Duare is here, too," he said; "my poor friends! When did they bring you here?"

"This afternoon," I told him.

"I have been asleep," he said; "I try to sleep as much as I can; it is one way of passing away a lifetime hanging on a wall;" he laughed, a little wryly. "But what ill luck brings you here?"

I told him briefly, and then asked how he had ever come to leave beautiful Havatoo and get into such a predicament as this.

"After you and Duare escaped from Havatoo," he commenced, "the Sanjong (rulers of Havatoo) commissioned me to attempt to build an aeroplane from your plans. I discovered that some of the essential features you must have carried in your head, for they were not on your drawings."

"That is too bad," I said; "they were not on the drawings that I left in Havatoo; because I had become accustomed to keeping the final drawings in the anotar after it had neared completion. I really don't know why I did so."

"Well, I finally achieved an anotar that would fly," he continued; "though I nearly killed myself half a dozen times in the attempt. Some of the best minds in Havatoo were working with me, and finally we designed and built a plane that would really fly. I was never so delighted with anything in my life; I wanted to be up all the time, and I kept going farther and farther from Havatoo. I flew Nalte to Andoo to see her parents and her people, and what a sensation the anotar was there!"

"Oh, tell us about Nalte," exclaimed Duare. "How is she?"

"She was well and happy the last time I saw her," said Ero Shan; "I hope she still is."

"Possibly well; but not happy, with you gone," said Duare.

"And to think that we shall never see one another again," he said, sadly; "but then," he exclaimed more brightly, "I have you two now: what is your misfortune is my good luck, though I'd forfeit it to have you safely out of here."

"Go on with your story," I urged; "tell us how you got into this fix—an exhibit in a museum of natural history!"

"Well, I had flown some distance from Havatoo one day into an unexplored district to the southwest, when I ran into the worst storm I have ever encountered in my life; it was of a violence that beggars description and was accompanied by clouds of hot steam."

"The same storm that drove us north to Mypos," I suggested. "The Sun broke through rifts in the cloud envelopes, causing terrific winds, and making the ocean boil."

"It must have been the same storm," agreed Ero Shan. "Anyway, it carried me across a sea to this land; and when I was

130

close to Voo-ad, my engine quit; and I had to come down. People came running from the city—"

"And danced around you and threw flowers at you," I interrupted.

Ero Shan laughed. "And fooled me completely. Did Vik-vik-vik give a banquet for you?" he asked.

"This afternoon," I said. "We seem to come to grief wherever we go—even in beautiful Havatoo."

"I must tell you," said Ero Shan; "after you two escaped, the Sanjong reviewed their findings on Duare and discovered that they had erred in condemning her to death. You are both now free to return to Havatoo."

"That is splendid!" I exclaimed, laughing. "Won't you please tell Vik-vik-vik?"

"At least," said Duare, "if we can retain our sense of humor we shall not be entirely miserable—if I could only forget the horrible thing we just witnessed while you were asleep."

"What was that?" asked Ero Shan.

"One of these creatures had an epileptic fit, and fell apart," I explained. "Have you ever seen anything like that?"

"Often," he said.

"The halves seemed to be still alive when they carried them away," said Duare.

"They were," Ero Shan told her. "You see, these creatures are amoebic neuters; and their dividing is the physiological phenomenon of reproduction. There are neither males nor females among them; but more or less periodically, usually after enjoying an orgy of eating and drinking, they divide into two parts, like the amoeba and other of the Rhizopada. Each of these parts grows another half during a period of several months, and the process continues. Eventually, the older halves wear out and die; sometimes immediately after division and sometimes while still attached, in which case the dead half merely falls away, and the remaining half is carted off to make itself whole. I understand that this division occurs about nine times during the life of a half.

"They are without sentiments of love, friendship, or any of the finer characteristics of normal human beings; and because they cannot create their kind, they have no creative genius in art or letters; they can copy beautifully, but are without imagination, except of the lowest order.

"Their reception of you was typical. Being weaklings,

131

averse to physical combat, they use hypocrisy as a weapon. Their singing, their dancing, their flower throwing are all instruments of deception; while they were feting you, they were having your placards lettered; duplicity is their outstanding characteristic."

"Is there no escape?" asked Duare.

"There is a man near me who comes from a city called Amlot, somewhere in Anlap, who tells me he has been here fully a hundred years and that in all that time no one has escaped."

"Oh, why couldn't they have killed us!" exclaimed Duare; "it would have been much kinder."

"The Vooyorgans are not kind," Ero Shan reminded her.

We slept. A new day came, bringing its string of sightseers. The creature that had shown an interest in Duare came early, and stood staring at her. For hours it loitered about her, always staring at her—whether in admiration or dislike, I could not tell. Unlike the others, it did not smile. Finally it came close and touched her leg.

"Get away from there!" I shouted.

It shrank back, startled; then it looked at me, and said, "I would not harm the woman."

"Who are you, anyway?" I demanded, "and why are you hanging around my mate? She is not for you; no woman is for you."

The creature sighed; it really looked unhappy. "I am Vik-yor," it said. "I am not like my fellows. I am different. I do not know why. I do not enjoy what they enjoy—eating and drinking until they fall apart. I shall never fall apart; I shall never divide; I am no good to myself nor to anyone else. If I could be always with such as she, I would be happy."

After a while Vik-yor went away. His name, or number, indicated that he was of the royal caste. "How did he happen?" I asked Ero Shan.

"He is a sport," he explained; "they occur occasionally, especially in the older, or royal caste. This one may have been part of a division of Vik-vik-vik; when it grew its other half, it was identical with the original half, and there was no line of demarcation between the two halves—no line of cleavage. I suppose that, like the first amoebae which must have had a tendency to develop into some higher form of life, these creatures show the same tendency by not dividing; possibly it is a step toward a form of human being like ourselves."

"It will take several million years and nothing short of a miracle," said Duare.

"The fact that he is so definitely attracted to you," said Ero Shan, "would indicate that he is groping for something better and nobler than just being an amoeba. Why don't you encourage him a little?—I mean be kind to him. A friend here might be a very valuable asset."

Duare shuddered. "They are all so repulsive to me," she said. "I am always expecting them to fall apart."

"Vik-yor can't fall apart," Ero Shan reminded her.

"Well, that is at least something in his favor. Perhaps I'll try what you suggest, Ero Shan. It can't do any harm. I might even try being what Carson calls a vamp and make Vik-yor fall in love with me," she said, laughing.

"I think he already has," I said.

"Jealous?" demanded Duare.

"Of an amoeba? Scarcely."

"I think he is a male amoeba," teased Duare; "he has already learned to paw."

THIRTY-FOUR

Well, Vik-yor kept coming to the museum every day; and now we all tried to be decent to him. His devotion to Duare was almost doglike, and she quite startled me by encouraging him. It didn't seem possible that Duare of Vepaja, the daughter of a thousand jongs, who had been brought up to consider herself as near a goddess as the Vepajans know, could try to arouse the love of such a creature as Vik-yor.

I joked her about it. "If I were only an amoeba," I said, "you would not have scorned my love for so long as you did; you would have sought after me and made love to me yourself."

"Don't be horrid," said Duare; "to win our freedom, I would make love to a Myposan."

"Do you think you are going to win our freedom?" I asked.

"I am going to try," she said.

"But what good would freedom do three people paralyzed from the neck down?"

"There is freedom in death," she said.

"You mean you are going to try to get Vik-yor to kill us?" I demanded.

"As a last resort," she replied; "wouldn't that be better than life here?—the man from Amolt has been here a hundred years!"

"But Vik-yor would never kill you," said Ero Shan.

"He wouldn't know he was killing me."

"How do you plan on doing it?" I asked.

"I am going to teach Vik-yor how to use your r-ray pistol," she explained, "and tell him that if he will put it against our hearts and squeeze the trigger, we'll all join him outside and run away, as that will liberate our other selves from the flesh that now holds them."

"What makes you think he wants to run away with you?" I demanded.

"I have learned much about men since I left my father's palace in Vepaja."

"But Vik-yor is not a man," I argued.

"He's getting there," said Duare with a twinkle in her eye.

"He's just a damn rhizopod," I growled; "and I don't like him."

The next day, when he came around, Duare really went to work on him. "I should think you would be bored to death here in Voo-ad," she said; "you are so different from all the others."

Vik-yor really smiled. "Do you think I am?" he asked.

"Certainly I do," cooed Duare. "You should be out in the world where there are things to see and things to do—where there are life and action and beautiful women."

"The most beautiful woman in the world is here," said Vik-yor, getting bold. "Oh, Duare, you are the most beautiful thing I ever saw!"

"And paralyzed from the neck down," said Duare. "Now, if I were not paralyzed and we were free, we could all go out into the world in our anotar and have a wonderful time."

"Do you mean that you would take me?" he asked.

"Of course," said Duare.

"Could I be with you always?" he demanded. It was a good thing for Vik-yor that I was paralyzed.

"You could be with me as much as possible," said Duare.

Vik-yor looked at her for a long time—one of those devouring, possessive looks that send husbands to the upper dresser drawer looking for the family gun.

Vik-yor came close to Duare. "I can free you," he whispered, but I heard him.

"How?" demanded the practical Duare.

"There is an antidote for the poison that paralyzed you," explained Vik-yor. "It is necessary that this be kept on hand; for sometimes, when they have drunk too much wine, our own people make a mistake and drink the poison intended for a potential exhibit. A single drop on the tongue neutralizes the poison in the nerve centers."

"When will you bring it?" asked Duare, "and how can you give it to us and free us without the guards knowing?"

"I shall come at night and bring poisoned wine to the guards," explained Vik-yor; "then I can free you, and we can escape from the city."

"We shall all be very grateful," said Duare, "and we will take you with us."

"I shall free only you," said Vik-yor; "these others mean nothing to me; and I do not wish your mate along, anyway."

For an amoeba, Vik-yor seemed to be doing quite well along evolutionary lines; he was by now at least a louse. What the future held for him, I could not predict—unless I became rid of my paralysis; then, I was sure, my prophetic powers would approach the miraculous. So it didn't want me along!

To that proposition of Vik-yor, Duare shook her head. "I will not go without Carson of Venus and Ero Shan," she said.

"I will not free them," replied Vik-yor; "I do not like him;" he nodded in my direction. "He does not like me. I think he would like to kill me, and I am afraid of him."

"Would you kill Vik-yor, if you were free, Carson?"

"Not if he behaves himself," I replied.

"You see!" said Duare; "Carson says that he will not kill you if you behave yourself."

"I will not free him," replied Vik-yor, stubbornly. Evidently he didn't intend to behave himself.

"Very well," said Duare, "there is nothing more to be said on the subject; but if you will not do that much for me, you needn't come and talk to me any more. Please go away."

Vik-yor hung around for a while trying to get Duare to talk

to him; but she wouldn't say a word, and finally he walked away and left the building.

"That is that," I said "our little scheme has failed; the triangle is disrupted; your boy friend has gone off in a huff, and you will not see him again."

"You don't know your amoebae," retorted Duare; "it will be back."

"I have a plan, Duare," I said. "It would be better for one of us to escape, than for all of us to remain here forever. You have that opportunity, and there is no reason why Ero Shan and I should keep you from taking advantage of it."

"Never!" said Duare. "I will never go without you and Ero Shan."

"Listen," I said; "let Vik-yor free you; then take my r-ray pistol. I think you know enough about the construction of the anotar to replace the propeller with Vik-yor's help. If you can't get away without him, you can always use the pistol on him if you find it necessary. Fly to Sanara; I am positive that it lies almost due south of us. Once there, I am sure that Taman will send an expedition to rescue Ero Shan and me."

"That is the best plan yet," said Ero Shan.

"I don't like the idea of going off and leaving you two," demurred Duare.

"It is our only chance," I told her; "but if Vik-yor doesn't come back, we'll not have even this chance."

"Vik-yor will come back," said Duare. It's amazing how well women know males—even male amoebae—for Vik-yor did come back. It was a couple of days before he came—two days of agonizing uncertainty. I could almost have hugged him when I saw him sidling in our direction. He was pretending to be deeply interested in some other exhibits. I don't know why I keep calling it *he*; but I suppose that when you know something has fallen in love with your wife, you just naturally don't think of it as *it*.

Anyway, it finally reached us. Paying no attention to Ero Shan or me, it hesitated before Duare. "Oh, you're back, Vik-yor!" she exclaimed; "I am *so* glad to see you. You've changed your mind, haven't you? You're going to let us all go away with you, out into that beautiful world I have told you about."

"No," said Vik-yor. "I will take you, but not the others; and if you will not come willingly, I intend to poison these two at the same time that I poison the guards; then you'll have to come with me alone, or be killed; for when Vik-vik-vik discovers that the effects of the poison have worn off, he will have you destroyed."

"Go with him, Duare," I said; "never mind us."

Vik-yor looked at me in surprise. "Maybe I have been mistaken in you," it said.

"You certainly have," Duare assured it. "Carson is a very nice person, and we really should have him along in case we get into trouble; he's an excellent swordsman."

"No!" snapped Vik-yor. "I know why you want him along; you like him better than you do me. That is why I was going to poison him anyway before we left, but now I may change my mind."

"You'd better," exclaimed Duare, vehemently, "for if you harm him in any way, I'll kill you! Do you understand that? I'll go with you, but only on condition that no harm comes to Carson of Venus or Ero Shan."

"Very well," agreed Vik-yor. "I want you to like me; so I'll do all that I can to please you—except take these two with us."

"Is the anotar all right?" she asked him. "Have the people damaged it in any way?"

"It is all right," replied Vik-yor; "it stands in the plaza just where you left it."

"And the part that fell off—do you know where that is?"

"Yes, and I can get it any time I wish; all I have to do is take poisoned wine to the home of the one who found it."

"When will you come for me?" asked Duare.

"Tonight," replied Vik-yor.

THIRTY-FIVE

"Your boy friend is the de' Medici of the amoebae," I remarked after Vik-yor had left us.

"It is horrible!" exclaimed Duare. "I shall feel like a murderess myself."

"You will be an accessory before the fact," I twitted her, "and so, equally guilty."

"Please don't joke about it," she begged.

"I am sorry," I said, "but to me these creatures are not

human; poisoning them would be the same to me as spraying oil on a stagnant pond to kill off mosquito larvae."

"Yes," added Ero Shan; "don't let it depress you; think of what they have done to us; they deserve no consideration nor pity from us."

"I suppose you are right," admitted Duare; "but, right or wrong, I'm going through with it."

The remainder of that day dragged on like a bad dream in clay up to its knees. When no sightseers or guards were near us, we went over our plans again and again. I urged on Duare the advisability of attempting to make at least a crude map of the country she would cover while searching for Sanara. She could estimate distances rather closely by the ground speed of the anotar, and her compass would give her her direction at all times. By noting all outstanding landmarks on her map, she would be able to turn over to Taman some very valuable data for the rescue expedition.

Of course we had no idea of the distance to Sanara. Anlap, the land mass on which it was located, might be a relatively small island, or it might be a continent: I was inclined to think that it was the latter; Sanara might be three thousand or five thousand miles from Voo-ad. Even were it close, it might take Duare a long time to find it; you can't land any old place on Amtor and ask directions, even when there is any one to ask. Duare would have to find Sanara and recognize it before she would dare land. She might be a year finding it; she might never find it. As she would have to come down occasionally for food and water, there would always be the risk of her being captured or killed—and then there was Vik-yor! I certainly was going to be in for a lot of worrying—maybe for years; maybe for the rest of my life—worry and vain regret.

At long last night fell. More hours passed, and Vik-yor did not come. Only the guards remained in the museum—the guards and the living dead. A basto bellowed. How the dickens they ever got some of the big beasts they had on exhibit, I'll never know. A basto stands fully six feet tall at the shoulder and weighs twelve hundred pounds or more. Singing and dancing around one of them and throwing flowers at it wouldn't get you anything but a goring; then it would eat you.

The bellowing of the basto started off the rest of the lower animals, including the nobargans, which growl and roar like beasts. We were treated to a diapason of savage discord for fully an hour; then they stopped as unaccountably as they had started.

"Your boy friend must have got cold feet," I remarked to Duare.

"Why would cold feet keep him from coming?" she wanted to know.

"I keep forgetting that you're not from the land of the free and the home of the brave."

"Where's that?" asked Ero Shan.

"It is bounded on the north by Canada, on the south by the Rio Grande, on the east by the Atlantic Ocean, and on the west by the Pacific."

"That must be in deepest Strabol," said Ero Shan, "for I never heard of one of those places."

"Here comes Vik-yor!" exclaimed Duare, excitedly.

"Your gigolo comes!" I said, rather nastily I'm afraid.

"What is a gigolo?" asked Duare.

"A form of life lower than an amoeba."

"I am afraid that you do not like Vik-yor, my darling," said Duare.

"I am glad that there was a comma in your voice at the right place," I said.

"Don't be silly," said Duare.

I am inclined to believe that every one as much in love as I am with Duare waxes silly occasionally. Of course, I knew that Duare loved me; I knew that I could trust her to the ends of the world—but! That is a funny thing about love—that *but*. The thought that that pussy, amoebic neuter was in love with her, or as nearly so as the thing could understand love, and that it was going to be with her for an indefinite time, while I hung on a wall, dead from the neck down, got my goat. If you are a man and if you are in love, you will know just how I felt.

Vik-yor was carrying a jug. Knowing what was in the jug would have given me a strange sensation, if I could have felt any sensations; but I did feel disgust for the sneaking thing that would take the life of its own fellows.

He came up to Duare. "Is all arranged?" she asked—"the anotar? the propeller?"

"Yes," it replied; "and we are very fortunate, for tonight

139

Vik-vik-vik is giving a banquet; and every one will be so drunk that we can get away without being detected."

"You have the antidote?"

It withdrew a small vial from one of its pocket pouches and held it up to her. "This is it."

"Give me some right away," begged Duare.

"Not yet; I must remove the guards first;" then he raised the jug to his lips and pretended to drink.

One of the guards drew near. "Oh," said the guard, "you are Vik-yor! I thought some one had come in that was not permitted after closing hours. We are always glad to see royalty interested in the exhibits."

"Would you like some wine?" asked Vik-yor.

"Yes; very much," replied the guard.

"Call all your fellows, then," said Vik-yor, "and we will all drink together."

Pretty soon, all the guards were gathered there, drinking out of Vik-yor's jug. It was a horrible experience—hanging there watching wholesale murder being done. I had to ease my conscience by thinking how they had used similar duplicity to lure us to a fate even worse than death; and that, anyway, they were being given a pleasant ending; for soon they were all as drunk as hoot owls and laughing, dancing, and singing; then, one by one, they toppled over, dead. There were twenty of them, and they all died practically at our feet.

Vik-yor was proud as a peacock. "Don't you think I'm clever?" it asked Duare. "They never guessed that I was poisoning them; even Vik-vik-vik could do no better."

"You are quite remarkable," said Duare; "now give me the antidote."

Vik-yor fished down first into one pouch and then into another. "What did I do with it?" the creature kept repeating.

Duare was getting more and more frightened and nervous. "Didn't you bring it?" she demanded. "Or was that something else you showed me?"

"I had it," said Vik-yor. "What in the world did I do with it?"

In spite of myself, I could scarcely keep from hoping that he would never find it. To be separated from Duare under circumstances such as these was unthinkable; death would have been preferable. I had a premonition that if she went away with Vik-yor I should never see her again. I commenced to regret that I had ever been a party to this mad enterprise.

"Look in the one behind," urged Duare; "you have looked in all the others."

Vik-yor pulled its belt around until it could reach into the pouch that had been hanging down behind. "Here it is!" it cried. "My belt must have slipped around while I was dancing with the guards. I knew I had it; because I showed it to you. I couldn't imagine what had become of it."

"Quick! Give me some!" demanded Duare.

Vik-yor turned the vial upside down and shook it; then he removed the stopper and told Duare to stick out her tongue, which he touched several times with the stopper. I watched, spellbound. Ero Shan was craning his neck to see Duare.

Presently she gasped. "It's happening!" she said. "I can feel life coming to my body. Oh, Carson, if only you could come with me!"

Vik-yor was watching Duare intently. It reminded me of a big cat watching a mouse—a fat, obscene cat. Presently it stepped up to her and cut her down. It had to support her for a moment; and when I saw its arm about her, it seemed to me that she was being defiled. Almost immediately, however, she was able to stand alone; and then she moved away from him and came to me. She couldn't reach my lips; I was hung too high on the wall, but she kissed my hand again and again. I could look down and see her doing it, but I could not feel it.

Vik-yor came up behind her and laid a hand on her shoulder. "Quit that!" it said.

Duare reached up and removed my r-ray pistol from its holster. I thought she was going to use it on Vik-yor, but she didn't. "Why don't you?" I asked her, looking meaningly at Vik-yor.

"Not yet," she replied.

"Come!" ordered Vik-yor.

"You'd better take the holster, too," I said. She came and got it; and again she clung to my hand, kissing it. This time Vik-yor jerked her away roughly.

"You may not guess it, Vik-yor," I said, "but some day you are going to die for what you think you are going to do and what you have done and even for what you never will do; and I am going to kill you."

The thing just laughed at me, as it dragged Duare away. She was turning her dear face back toward me all the time. "Goodby, my darling!" she called to me, and then Vik-yor spoke.

"You will never see her again," it taunted me. "She is mine now, all mine."

'The thing lies!" cried Duare, then: "Goodby, my darling, until I come back to you!"

"Goodby!" I called, and then she was lost to sight behind a great gantor, that elephantine beast of burden such as I had seen in Korva.

I glanced at Ero Shan. There were tears in his eyes.

THIRTY-SIX

Vik-yor and Duare had not had time to leave the building before there came a great noise from the entrance—laughing and chattering and the scuffling of many feet; and presently I saw at least a hundred people lurch and stagger into view. It was Vik-vik-vik and the banquet guests, and most of them were quite drunk.

At sight of the guards strewn about the floor, Vik-vik-vik became violent and abusive. "The lazy beasts!" cried the jong, and went up and kicked one of them. It was then that they discovered that the guards were dead.

"They are all dead!" said one of the creatures. "Who could have killed them?"

"Never mind that now," said Vik-vik-vik; "I'll find out later. First, I want to get the woman I came for. Come, Ata-voo-med-ro! Where is the antidote? We'll have her back to life and take her to the banquet. She's going to live in the palace with Vik-vik-vik. Other jongs have a vadjong; why shouldn't I?"

"You should!" cried some sycophant.

Vik-vik-vik and Ata-voo-med-ro searched the wall where Duare should have been. "She's gone!" exclaimed the latter.

The jong looked at me and demanded, "Where is she, creature?"

"How should I know?" I replied. "She has been gone a long time."

"How did she get away? Who took her?" demanded Vik-vik-vik.

"I do not know," I replied. "I had been asleep; when I awoke, she was gone."

Vik-vik-vik turned to the guests. "Search for her! Search the whole city! Hurry!" Then it said to Ata-voo-med-ro, "Summon all those who were on guard here today," and Ata-voo-med-ro scampered out after the others.

The jong looked searchingly at Ero Shan. "Did you see her go?"

"Yes," replied Ero Shan.

"Who took her?"

"A man."

"What man?" demanded the jong.

"Well it wasn't anyone you know, for the only men in Voo-ad are hanging on these walls."

"Who was it, then?"

"I never saw him before," said Ero Shan; "he had wings like an angan, but he was not an angan; he was a man—a human man. He flew in and looked at the guards, and they all fell dead; then he cut the woman down and flew away with her. He said that he was coming back to look at you and all the rest of the Vooyorgans; so pretty soon you will all be dead—unless you liberate all the human beings in here. That was just what he said."

"Nonsense!" said Vik-vik-vik; "you are lying to me," but he looked worried.

Just then I heard the b-r-r-r of an r-ray pistol from the direction of the plaza, and there were screams and shouts mingled with it.

"What was that?" demanded the jong.

"It sounds like the man who came for the woman," said Ero Shan. "When he thought, his brain made a noise like that. I guess that is what killed the guards."

Vik-vik-vik left then, and he left on the run—probably for his palace.

"That was Duare!" I said to Ero Shan. "They caught her; she didn't have time enough."

"They haven't got her yet," said Ero Shan, as the humming of the pistol came to our ears again, mingled with the shouts and screams of the Vooyorgans.

"The whole population of the city must be out there, from

the noise they're making. I wonder if Duare can fight them all off."

"They're not very keen on fighting, I should say," replied Ero Shan. "I think she has an excellent chance, if they don't succeed in damaging the anotar."

"Or if Vik-yor doesn't turn yellow."

"He couldn't be any yellower."

The noise in the plaza continued for some time, punctuated by occasional bursts of r-ray fire. When I heard these, I knew that Duare still lived and that they hadn't recaptured her yet; but between bursts I was nearly frantic with apprehension.

After a while the noise died down; there was no more shouting and the r-rays ceased to hum. What had happened? What had been the outcome of Duare's courageous attempt to escape? Had they recaptured her? Had they killed her? Had she really gotten away? Was I ever to know the answer to even one of these questions?

Ero Shan spoke to me, breaking the thread of my lugubrious reverie. "Perhaps we should never have let her go," he said.

"I am glad she went," I replied. "I would rather that she were dead than eternally condemned to this hideous existence."

"And of course," suggested Ero Shan, taking a brighter view of the situation, "there is always the chance that she may succeed; and that some day your friend Taman, Jong of Korva, may march on Voo-ad and release us."

"But suppose," I countered, still prone to look upon the dark side because of my fear and sorrow concerning Duare; "suppose that Taman does come; will we be much better off? We shall still be paralyzed."

"Oh, come!" exclaimed Ero Shan; "don't be so gloomy. When Taman takes Voo-ad, he can force the jong to furnish him with the antidote."

"You speak as though it were already an accomplished fact," I said, smiling. "That is the way we should feel. I am sorry that I have been so depressed; I'll buck up from now on. By the way, what was the purpose of that cock-and-bull story you told Vik-vik-vik—about the man who flew in and flew away with Duare?"

Ero Shan laughed. "If you can put fear into the hearts of

your enemies, you already have an advantage over them—especially if it is fear of the supernatural; that is something they can't combat. Killing you doesn't help any; they feel that it will only increase their danger. Then, too, I wanted to disabuse his mind of any suspicion he may have had that you or I were in any way responsible. Had he believed that, the reasonable thing for him to have done would have been to have had us destroyed, lest we free ourselves and others."

I scarcely slept all that night, wondering about Duare. I tried to question the new guards when they came on duty; but they just told me to shut up, and they kept as far away from Ero Shan and me as they could after they had removed the dead bodies of their fellows.

Long day after long day dragged slowly by, and still we heard no faintest word concerning Duare. The guards would not talk to us, neither would those who came to see the exhibits; it was evident that they had received orders, undoubtedly from the jong.

Had Duare escaped? If she had, she was off somewhere alone with Vik-yor. That thought added nothing to my peace of mind. I killed Vik-yor in some dozens of different and most satisfying ways during those long hours. I also killed Ata-voo-med-ro and Vik-vik-vik, nor did I stop there; I indulged in a perfect orgy of murder—the vain, wishful imaginings of impotency. However, it was very pleasurable imagining; and there are few pleasures in which one may indulge while hanging against a wall, dead from the neck down.

THIRTY-SEVEN

Vik-yor and Duare had not reached the exit when Vik-vik-vik and the banquet guests burst into the museum. "Quick! Hide!" whispered Vik-yor, dragging Duare back behind the body of the gantor. "The drunken fools!" muttered Vik-yor. "They have upset all my plans; now we may not get away at all."

"They have passed," said Duare, presently; "now we may go on."

Vik-yor hesitated. "They may come back," he said.

145

"If they discover that I am gone, they'll make a search," said Duare; "then you will be caught."

"And killed," said Vik-yor, trembling. "But I won't be killed! I won't be here; they'll just find you; they won't know that I had anything to do with setting you free. You stay here; I'm going to join them and pretend that I was at the banquet, too."

"You're going to do nothing of the sort," snapped Duare; "you're going out into the plaza and help me fix the anotar; you're going through with this thing."

"I am not," insisted Vik-yor. "Vik-vik-vik would have me killed if he knew I had set you free."

"If you don't come along with me," warned Duare, "he will know."

"How will he know?"

"I'll tell him!"

"No, you won't," snarled Vik-yor, and drew a dagger.

Duare whipped out the r-ray pistol. "Put that dagger back, or I'll kill you," she threatened.

Vik-yor hesitated. It knew nothing about an r-ray pistol, but it was an arrant coward, and Duare's tone of voice alone would have been enough to frighten it. It started to return the dagger to its sheath.

"No!" said Duare; "give it to me—and your sword, too; you're not to be trusted."

Reluctantly, Vik-yor handed over the weapons. "Suppose they attack us now?" it asked.

"You can hide behind me," said Duare. "Come, now! We're going to the plaza." She had to poke the muzzle of the pistol in the middle of the thing's back in order to force it toward the exit. A moment later they were in the plaza. It was deserted at this time of night, and they crossed to the anotar in safety.

The propeller lay beneath it, and a hasty examination showed that it was undamaged; then she examined the flange, shrunk to the end of the crank shaft, to which it had been bolted. The bolts were there and undamaged—the nuts must have vibrated off almost simultaneously; Kandar had evidently neglected to use either lock washers or cotter keys.

These Duare found among the spare parts in the cockpit of the anotar, together with the necessary nuts. Climbing forward on the wing, she told Vik-yor to hand up the propeller and then to come up himself and give her a hand. Together, they fitted

146

the propeller over the bolts; and Duare started the nuts by hand; then she applied the wrench, a heavy tool that she had difficulty in handling in the awkward position in which she had to work.

She had two nuts securely set and cottered when the guests came rushing from the museum in search of her. "There she is!" cried one, discovering her almost immediately; and then they all came running toward the anotar. Vik-yor scrambled into the cockpit and hid. Duare switched the wrench to her left hand and drew her pistol.

"Keep away!" she called, "or I'll let you have it."

Perhaps they didn't know what she was going to let them have; so they came on. The r-rays hummed from the muzzle of the weapon, and the leaders crumpled to the pavement. That stopped the others, at least for the time; and Duare continued to tighten the remaining nuts.

Vik-yor peeked from the cockpit; it saw the dead and heard the screams of the wounded. Things looked pretty safe to it; so it crept out and came to Duare's side. Duare was working feverishly. She had thought everything out far in advance of either Carson or Ero Shan. Perhaps discovery by these Vooyorgans would make it more difficult than she had hoped, but she was still determined to go on with it—and flying away from Voo-ad without Carson and Ero Shan was no part of it.

The thing that she had planned on doing, after she and Vik-yor had repaired the anotar, was to force him to give up the vial of antidote, even if she had to kill him to get it, and then to go back into the museum and free Carson and Ero Shan. Discovery by the Vooyorgans had greatly complicated matters, but it had not compelled Duare to give up the plan.

More creatures were now rushing into the plaza, and the anotar was surrounded. Again Duare was forced to stop her work and turn a stream of r-rays upon those who menaced her most closely, and again the others fell back. This time Vik-yor did not hide. Feeling safe under the protecion of Duare, it remained and watched her using the pistol on its people. The thing intrigued it greatly and gave it ideas, one of which it put into practice almost immediately after Duare returned the pistol to its holster and went to work on the last remaining nut. While the girl's attention was centered on her work, Vik-yor stole up behind her and stealthily removed the pistol from its holster.

The first intimation Duare had that the weapon had been taken from her was the sudden b-r-r-r of r-rays. She wheeled about in astonishment to see Vik-yor pumping r-rays indiscriminately into the crowd surrounding the anotar. Many of the creatures were falling, dead and wounded; and the others were fleeing for the safety of near-by buildings.

"Give me that!" snapped Duare.

Vik-yor turned it on her. "Finish the work!" it said. "I want to get out of here."

"You fool!" cried Duare. "Turn that thing the other way; if you kill me, you'll never get away. Give it back to me!"

"No," said Vik-yor, sullenly. "I shall keep it. Your only chance of getting away yourself is to do as I say. Do you think I'll give this thing back to you, so that you can kill me? I am not such a fool."

Duare returned to her work; she could wait. She gave the last nut its final turn and hammered in the cotter key; then she turned back to Vik-yor. "Get into the cockpit," she said; "we are ready to go."

Vik-yor climbed into the cockpit, and Duare took her place at the controls. The engine started; the propeller spun; the anotar moved. Duare taxied down wind to the far end of the plaza; then she came about into the wind. Hundreds of pairs of eyes watched her from windows and doorways, but no one ventured out to detain her—Vik-yor had been too unrestrained in firing practice.

The anotar gained speed; it rose gracefully into the air; and, turning south, disappeared into the night.

Vik-yor was terrified; it trembled and yammered in a frenzy of fear. "We shall fall!" it jibbered. "We shall fall!"

"Be quiet!" snapped the girl.

"Take me down! Let me out!"

Duare would have gladly done so had she had possession of the vial of antidote and her pistol. She did not reply, but elevated the nose of the anotar and rose higher. Vik-yor was cowering beside her, covering its eyes with its hands.

"Are you coming down?" it asked.

"Just a moment," said Duare; "don't look now." She climbed to five thousand feet. Wisps of cloud from the inner envelope whipped against the windshield; in the weird light of the Amtorian night, the ground was barely visible—it appeared much farther away than it really was.

Duare cut the engine and glided. "You may get out now," she said.

Vik-yor uncovered its eyes and looked over the side of the cockpit; and then, with a scream, it shrank back. It was trembling so that it could scarcely speak. It glanced up and saw the clouds close above, and it screamed again.

"Quit screaming!" ordered Duare.

"You would have killed me," Vik-yor managed to say at last; "you would have let me get out way up here."

"Give me the antidote and my pistol, and I'll take you down and let you get out," offered Duare.

The creature looked over the side again; this time for much longer. "We do not fall," it said. Finding that the anotar remained aloft, it slowly regained a little composure, if not courage.

"Well," said Duare, "if you want to go down and get out, give me the vial and the pistol."

"You'll take me down, and I'll keep them both," said Vik-yor.

"What makes you think so?" demanded Duare.

"This," said Vik-yor, shoving the pistol against the girl's side; "take me down, or I'll kill you!"

Duare laughed at him. "And then what would happen to you?" she demanded. "Do you think this anotar flies itself? If I left these controls for a minute, the ship would dive nose first to the ground so fast that it would bury itself and you."

"You are lying," said Vik-yor. "It would come down by itself."

"That's just what I told you—it would come down by itself all right, but there would be nothing left of the anotar or us. Don't you believe me?"

"No; you are lying."

"All right; I'll show you;" and with that, Duare put the ship into a spin.

Above the roar of the wind, rose the shrieks of Vik-yor. Duare levelled off at five hundred feet. "Now, do you think I was lying?" she asked. Her voice was firm and level, betraying no slightest indication of the terror that had gripped her for the last two thousand feet of that long dive. Only twice before had she brought the anotar out of a spin, and then Car-

149

son had been beside her at the other controls. This time, up to the last moment, she had thought that she was not going to bring it out.

"Don't ever do that again!" wailed Vik-yor. "We might have been killed."

"Will you give me the vial and the pistol now?" asked Duare.

"No," replied Vik-yor.

THIRTY-EIGHT

By the time morning came, and Vik-yor could look down and see the world passing slowly beneath them, it had lost much of its fear of the strange situation in which it found itself. It now had almost complete confidence in Duare's ability to keep the thing up in the air, and with returning confidence it commenced to think of other things than the hazards of flying.

"You kept pressing your lips to his hands," it said. "Why did you do that?"

Duare's thoughts were far away. "Eh?" she said. "Oh, because I love him."

"What is love?" asked Vik-yor.

"You would not understand; it cannot be explained to one who cannot know love. It is what one feels for one's mate."

"Did he like to have you press your lips to his hand?"

"I am sure he did; I certainly hope so."

Vik-yor held out a hand. "Do it to me," it directed.

Duare struck the hand away, and shuddered. "You disgust me," she said.

"You belong to me," said Vik-yor. "You are going to teach me what love is."

"Don't talk about love to me," snapped Duare; "you defile the very name."

"Why don't you like me?" asked Vik-yor.

"It is not alone because you are not a human being," replied the girl; "I have liked many of the lower animals. It is because you are cruel and cowardly; because you made me come away and leave my mate in that horrible place; because you haven't

150

one of the finer characteristics of a man; because you are not a man. Have I answered your question?"

Vik-yor shrugged. "Well," it said, "It doesn't make much difference whether you like me or not. The thing is that I like you; what you like or don't like affects you, not me. Of course, if you liked me, it might be much more pleasant. Anyway, you belong to me. I can look at you; I can touch you. As long as I live you will be always with me. I never liked anyone before. I didn't know that there was such a thing as liking another creature. We Vooyorgans don't like anyone; nor do we dislike anyone. A person is with us today and gone tomorrow—it makes no difference to us. Before I commenced to change, I used to divide like the others. Even after being with one of my halves for years, I never missed it after we divided; nor did I ever have any feeling whatever for the new half that grew. Once I was half of Vik-vik-vik, the jong; I was the left half. It is the right half that retains the name and identity. I have always been a left half until now; now I am a whole; I am like you and Carson and Ero Shan—I am a man! After studying the ways of other forms of life, some of the wise ones among us think that our right halves are analogous to the females of other species, and the left halves to the males; so, you see, I have always been a male."

"I am not interested," said Duare.

"But I am," said Vik-yor. "It makes no difference whether you are interested or not, if I am. I like to talk about myself."

"I can almost believe that you are a man," said Duare.

Vik-yor was silent for some time. It was occupied by gazing at this new world over which it was flying like a bird. Duare was trying to plan some way of getting hold of the vial and the pistol; her whole life, now, revolved about that one desire.

"I am hungry," said Vik-yor.

"So am I," agreed Duare, "but I don't dare land unless I have my pistol; we might be attacked."

"I can kill things with it," said Vik-yor. "Didn't you see me last night? I must have killed fifty."

"Firing into a crowd of hundreds is not the same as firing at a charging basto," said Duare; "where there were so many, you couldn't miss them all."

"Perhaps not," said Vik-yor, "but I shall keep the pistol. If you had it, you would kill me. What are you doing?" Duare was spiralling down above a large lake. "Look out!" cried Vik-yor. "We shall be drowned, if you go into the water."

"All right," said Duare; "it is better to drown than starve to death. Will you give me the pistol?"

"No," said Vik-yor; "I would rather drown." As a matter of fact, it had suddenly concluded that this was just another attempt of the woman to frighten it into giving up the pistol. Vik-yor was far from being a fool. However, it was thoroughly shaken when Duare failed to bring the anotar up and it settled upon the surface of the lake; for Vik-yor could not swim.

Duare took a drinking vessel from one of the compartments; and, going out upon the wing, dipped up some water. She took a long, satisfying drink; then she lay down on the wing and washed her hands and face.

"Give me some water," said Vik-yor, when she arose.

Duare dumped the remaining water from the vessel, and came back into the cockpit.

"Didn't you hear me?" demanded Vik-yor. "I told you to give me some water."

"I heard you," said Duare, starting the engine.

"Well, go and get me some," ordered the Vooyorgan.

"When you give me my pistol," said Duare, taxiing for a take off.

"I will not give you the pistol," said Vik-yor.

"All right," said Duare, as she swept down the lake for the take off. "That was very good water, and we may not find fresh water again for days."

Vik-yor said nothing, but it was doing a lot of thinking: maybe having a woman was not such a good thing after all; if it could learn to fly this thing, it could kill the woman and—well, what? That stumped Vik-yor. It couldn't go back to Voo-ad after what it had done, for Vik-vik-vik would surely have it killed; it couldn't live in this savage world full of terrible beasts and men.

Vik-yor was not the first to get hold of something and then not be able to let go—the Vooyorgan was certainly in a fix; possibly as bad a fix as any amoeba had been in since the dawn of life on Amtor.

Duare continued to fly south, as she couldn't carry out the plan she had in mind until she recovered the r-ray pistol. In the meantime she might find Sanara, in which event she would be among friends who would take the pistol away from Vik-yor. Presently there loomed ahead an obstacle that barred further flight toward the south—a forest that induced within her a little surge of nostalgia. Only in her native Vepaja had she ever seen another such forest. The tops of its trees were lost in the inner cloud envelope five thousand feet above the ground; the enormous boles of some of its giants were a thousand feet in diameter. In Vepaja the homes of her people were carved in living trees a thousand feet above the floor of the forest. One could not fly above such a forest, and threading one's way through its mazes was hazardous in the extreme. Carson might have ventured it, were it necessary; but not Duare. She turned toward the east, seeking a way around it.

She was becoming very hungry, but these mighty forests bore their fruits too high. The forest extended for perhaps a hundred miles, ending at the foot of a mountain range which presented an equally insurmountable obstacle to further south-ward flight, as its towering peaks were lost in the eternal clouds. Down its canyons roared mountain torrents, fed by the perpetual rains that fell upon its upper slopes. The torrents joined to form rivers which cut the alluvial plain that stretched eastward as far as the eye could reach, and these rivers united to swell a mighty waterway that rolled on toward the horizon and some distant, nameless sea.

Nowhere in all this vast and lonely wilderness had Duare seen a sign of human habitation; but there were grazing herds and prowling carnivores, and forests of small trees where edible fruits and nuts might be expected to abound.

It might be all right to try to starve Vik-yor into submission, thought Duare, did that not also presuppose her own starva-tion; so the Vooyorgan won a moral victory, and Duare searched for a safe landing place near a forest. A herd of grazing herbivores galloped away as she dropped down and circled to reconnoiter before landing. Seeing no sign of dan-gerous beast, Duare brought the ship down close to the forest.

"What are you going to do?" demanded Vik-yor.

"Find something to eat," replied Duare.

"Bring me something, too," ordered the Vooyorgan.

"If you eat," said Duare, "you will get it yourself."

"I do not wish to go into the forest; some dangerous beast might attack me."

"Then you'll go hungry."

"I am starving," said Vik-yor.

Duare climbed from the cockpit and dropped to the ground. She would have felt safer had she had the pistol, but she had learned that it was useless to ask for it.

"Wait for me!" called Vik-yor. Hunger had finally bested its cowardice, and it was climbing from the anotar. Duare did not wait, but continued on toward the forest. Vik-yor ran after her, and when it caught up with her it was out of breath. "Why don't you wait for me?" it demanded. "You belong to me; you should do as I tell you."

Duare looked at it disgustedly. "I belong to a *man,*" she said.

"I am a man," said Vik-yor.

"You wouldn't be a man in thirty million years; I am surprised that you even had nerve enough to crawl out of a stagnant pool."

They had entered the forest; and Duare was looking up at the trees in search of food, when Vik-yor suddenly dashed past her and scrambled up a tree; then a hideous roar shattered the silence of the wood. Duare wheeled about. A tharban was creeping toward her. Vik-yor had seen it, and fled without warning her. He was now safely ensconced in a nearby tree, shaking as with palsy.

THIRTY-NINE

The tharban might be described as the Amtorian lion, although it does not bear much resemblance to *Felis leo* except that it is a ferocious carnivore. It is much larger; its tawny coat is striped lengthwise with dark brown markings; its enormous jaws, splitting half the length of its head, are armed with sixteen or eighteen large fangs and its feet are equipped with three heavily taloned toes; it has a black mane, much like that of a horse; long, pointed ears, and the tail of a lion. It also has a most abominable disposition and an insatiable appetite.

For Duare, the situation was not overly auspicious. Though there were trees all around her, she could not possibly climb to safety before the creature could overhaul her.

"Shoot it!" she called to Vik-yor.

The Vooyorgan drew the pistol; but his hand shook so that

he could not aim, and the r-rays buzzed futilely in many directions other than the right one.

"Look out!" cried Duare; "you'll hit me!"

The tharban appeared to be enjoying the situation, for it continued to creep slowly upon the prey which it knew could not escape.

"Throw the pistol down to me!" cried Duare.

"No!" shouted Vik-yor; "I won't give it to you—I told you I wouldn't."

"Fool!" screamed Duare. She faced the terrible creature with only a sword—a tin whistle would have been almost equally as effective. She was about to die, and Carson would never know. He would hang there on that wall until death released him, the longevity serum with which he had been inoculated in Vepaja, a curse rather than a blessing.

Suddenly the tharban halted in its tracks and voiced a thunderous roar; the very ground seemed to tremble to it. Duare realized that the creature was looking at something beyond and behind her, and she cast a quick glance in that direction. The sight that met her eyes appalled her. Slinking upon her from behind was a creature as large and as terrible as the tharban. Its body closely resembled that of a Bengal tiger; in the center of its forehead was a single eye on a short antenna; from the shoulders, just anterior to the forelegs, grew two enormous chelae; and its jaws were as terribly armed as those of the tharban.

This creature, Duare knew well; for they haunt the forests of Vepaja from the ground to the highest branches where life may be found, and they prey upon all forms of life. By the advent of this terrible beast, Duare's situation was altered only to the extent of the probability of which one reached her first; and they were about equidistant from her.

Answering the tharban's roar, came the scream of the tongzan. Now the tharban charged, fearing its prey would be stolen by the other. The same fear must have motivated the tongzan simultaneously, for it charged, too. And Duare, between these two engines of destruction, seemed about to be torn to shreds. Vik-yor, safe in a tree, watched the events unfolding beneath it with thoughts only of itself. With Duare dead, it could no longer travel in the anotar; it would be earthbound, prey to some hideous creature such as those two which were about to rend and devour Duare. Vik-yor felt very sorry for itself, and cursed the hour that it had looked upon a woman or thought that it might emulate a man.

As the two beasts rushed for her, Duare threw herself to the ground; and the creatures met above her. She felt their pads and talons upon her body; their roars and screams resounded in her ears as they battled above her. Presently one of them gave back a few feet, uncovering her; and then Duare rolled cautiously aside. Now she could see them; so engrossed were they in their duel that they paid no attention to her. The tongzan had already lost its single eye and most of its face; but it held to the thargan with one mighty chela, drawing it closer to those terrible jaws and cutting and rending it with its other chela.

Duare moved cautiously to a near-by tree and clambered to safety; she had been careful to select a small tree, lest the tongzan's mate should come, for they cannot climb a tree of small diameter. From the safety of her sanctuary, she watched the bloody duel below. The tharban had inflicted hideous punishment on the tongzan, which was literally torn to ribbons from its muzzle back to its shoulders, nor was the tharban in much better shape. It, too, was torn and bleeding; and one foot had been completely severed by a giant chela, which was now groping for its throat while its mate held the huge tharban in a viselike, unbreakable grip.

The blinded tongzan screamed continually, and the tharban roared; the forest reverberated to the hideous din. Vikyor still clung to its tree, shaking from terror. Duare, in an adjoining tree, viewed it with contempt—the thing that aspired to be a man. She glanced down at the battling carnivores; the tongzan was clawing the tharban to ribbons with the talons of both its powerful front feet, and the blindly groping chela was finding the throat. At last, spreading wide, it found its goal; and then those mighty nippers closed; and the tharban's head rolled upon the ground, severed as cleanly as by a guillotine.

For a moment the victor stood over its fallen antagonist, and then it commenced to devour it. Blind, horribly mutilated, still its insatiable maw must be filled. Blood flowed from its countless wounds in veritable torrents, yet it ate and ate until it sank lifeless upon the bloody remains of its repast—dead from loss of blood.

Directly above her, Duare discovered a bunch of grape-like

156

fruit; and soon she, too, was satisfying her hunger; while Vik-yor eyed her enviously. "Bring me some of that," it said.

"Get your own," advised Duare.

"There is no fruit in this tree."

Duare paid no more attention to him; looking around, she discovered a tree that bore nuts which she recognized as both delicious and nutritious. She climbed down from her tree and swarmed up another; here she gathered nuts and ate them. She filled her pouch with them and descended.

"I am going," she called Vik-yor; "if you wish to come with me you have better get down out of that tree." She would have gladly gone off and left it, but for the pistol; which she must have to carry out her plan.

"I am afraid," cried Vik-yor, "another of those creatures might come along."

Duare continued on toward the anotar. Suddenly she stopped and called back to Vik-yor; "Stay where you are! Hide! I'll come back for you later—if they don't get you." She had seen a dozen men sneaking toward the anotar; they were short, squat, hairy men; and they carried spears. Duare broke into a run, and so did the warriors—it was a race for the anotar. Duare had a slight advantage—she was nearer the anotar than they, and she was fleeter of foot.

One of the warriors outdistanced his fellows, but Duare reached the plane first and clambered into the cockpit just as the warrior arrived. As he clambered onto the wing in pursuit of her, the engine started and the propeller whirred. The ship taxied along the rough ground, and the warrior had all he could do to keep from being thrown off. It rose and zoomed upward. The man clutched the edge of the cockpit; he looked down, preparing to jump; he had had enough; but when he saw the ground so far below, he shut his eyes and seized the edge of the cockpit with both hands.

Duare banked; and the man's body slid its full length along the wing, while he clung frantically to his hold. He screamed. Duare banked again, more steeply, trying to shake him off; but he hung on with a grip of death; then, as she flattened out, he clambered into the cockpit beside her.

For a moment he just sat there, panting, limp as a dishrag; too terrified to move. Duare fastened her safety belt and climbed. The man looked over the side, and drew a crude dagger from his belt. He stuck the point of it against Duare's side. "Take me down," he commanded in a coarse guttural. "If you don't, I'll kill you."

"And this thing will fall, and you'll be killed," warned Duare. "You'd better take that knife out of my side if you want me to take you down."

He pulled the knife back a couple of inches. "Hurry!" he said; "take me down."

"Will you promise to let me go, if I take you down?" asked the girl.

"No; you belong to me. I take you back to the village."

"You're making a mistake," said Duare. "If you promise to let me go, I'll take you down. If you don't—"

"What?" asked the man. "I'm going to keep you. What do you think you would do if I don't promise to let you go?"

"I'll show you!" said Duare, with a trace of venom in her voice. "You asked for it, and you're going to get it."

"What did I ask for?" demanded the man.

"This!" said Duare, and looped the anotar.

Screaming, the man plunged to his doom. He fell not far from his companions, who came over and examined the splash and the hole his body had made in the ground.

"There is not much left of Djup," said one.

"The thing is coming back," said another, looking up into the sky.

"If it comes close, we can kill it with our spears," said a third; "we have killed big birds before."

"We cannot kill it," said the first warrior, "because it is not alive. I am going into the forest, where it cannot follow us," and as he started on a run for the forest, the others followed him.

Duare tried to head them off; but fear gripped them, they would not turn aside; they ran into the forest at the very point at which Duare had emerged. They saw the dead bodies of the tharban and the tongzan, and sat down and commenced to eat. They ate like beasts, tearing the meat from the carcasses in great chunks and growling ceaselessly.

Vik-yor sat in the tree above them, paralyzed with fear. Oh, why had it ever left Voo-ad? What in the world had made it think that it wanted a woman? Now, it hated her. It was all her fault. It did not know it, but it was learning fast that there is always a woman at the bottom of everything—especially trouble.

One of the warriors looked up and pointed. "What is that?" he asked his fellows. It was Vik-yor's foot carelessly protruding below some foliage.

"It is a foot," said another.

"There must be a man at the end of it,"

"Or a woman! I am going up to see."

The shaking of the tree caused Vik-yor to look down. When it saw one of the hairy warriors ascending, it screamed and started up the bole. The warrior pursued; and, being a better climber than Vik-yor, soon overhauled it. Vik-yor forgot about the r-ray pistol that was hidden in one of its pocket pouches. With it, it could have routed fifty hairy warriors.

The warrior seized Vik-yor by one of its ankles and dragged it down. Vik-yor would have fallen to the ground, had the warrior not supported it. Hanging to its captive's hair, the warrior descended.

FORTY

Duare cruised about near the forest, waiting for either the warriors or Vik-yor to come out; she would not abandon the pistol. Had she known what was going on in the wood, her hopes would have been crushed.

Vik-yor, trembling and almost too weak to stand, was surrounded by its captors, who were discussing it. "We have just eaten," said one; "we can take this back to the women and children." He pinched Vik-yor. "It is tender; perhaps we can find something else for the women and children. I am sure that I could eat some of this tonight."

"Why not eat it here?" demanded another. "The women and children will make a loud noise if we don't give them some."

"It is mine," said the warrior who had climbed the tree after Vik-yor. "I am going to take it back to the village." He tied a leather thong about Vik-yor's neck, and dragged the creature along behind him. The other warriors followed.

When they came out into the open, Duare saw them and flew closer. There was Vik-yor! How was she ever to recover the pistol now? The warriors looked up at the anotar and discussed it. Some of them thought that they should go back into the forest; but when Duare circled high above them and gave no indication that she was going to swoop down on them, they lost their fear and kept on toward their village.

The village lay on the bank of a river not far from where Vik-yor had been captured. It was not a village easily seen from the air, as it consisted of a few poor, grass shelters scarcely three feet high, the village blending into the tall grasses among which it was built.

Before they reached the village, Duare circled very low above the little party and begged Vik-yor to drop the pistol, thinking that she could dive and frighten the warriors away from it before they could recover it; but Vik-yor, with the stubbornness of the ignorant, refused.

At last they reached the village, where a couple of dozen filthy women and children ran out to meet them. They tried to lay hands on Vik-yor, as they screamed for meat; and Duare, circling low again, heard them and realized that Vik-yor might soon be lost to her and the pistol along with him.

Banking low above them, she called out, "Look out! I'm coming down to kill you!" Then she dove for them. She knew that she was taking long chances, for they were sure to hurl their spears; and one lucky hit might cause her to crash—but she must have that pistol!

In a shower of spears, she came down on them, her landing gear lowered with which to rake them. It was too much for them; they turned and ran; so did Vik-yor, whose life was endangered as much as were the lives of the others. Fortunately, Vik-yor ran in the opposite direction from that taken by the savages; and Duare landed beside him.

"Get in!" she cried. "Hurry! Here they come!"

Sure enough, they were coming after their meat—a half dozen women in the lead—but they were too slow. Duare easily outdistanced them, and a moment later the anotar rose into the air and flew away.

"If I had had that pistol," said Duare, "none of these things would have happened. Now give it to me, so that we won't have to go through things like that again."

"No," said Vik-yor sullenly.

"I suppose you'd rather be killed by a wild beast or eaten by savages than give me that pistol so that I can protect us."

"I shall not be eaten by savages nor killed by wild beasts," said Vik-yor. "I am going back to Voo-ad; nothing that Vik-vik-vik can do to me would be as bad as what I've gone through. Take me back to Voo-ad at once."

"And be hung up on a wall again! Do you think I'm crazy? But I'll tell you what I will do: If you'll give me the pistol and vial, I'll take you back; and I'll get word to Vik-vik-vik that I made you take me away."

The Vooyorgan shook its head. "No," it said. "With the pistol that kills so easily, I might be able to make Vik-vik-vik see reason. If I go back without it, I shall be killed. I have been watching you fly this thing; I can fly it. If you will not take me back to Voo-ad, I shall kill you and fly back by myself. Perhaps that would be the better way after all. Think what an impression I would make if I flew into Voo-ad all alone. I think that then I might kill Vik-vik-vik and become jong. The more I think of it, the better I like the idea; what do you think of it?"

"I can't say that it appeals to me to any great extent," replied Duare. "In the first place I don't like the idea of being killed; in the second place, you couldn't fly the anotar. You might get it off the ground, but you'd be sure to crack up. Of course you'd kill yourself, but that wouldn't compensate for the loss of the anotar."

"You are trying to discourage me," said Vik-yor, "but you can't fool me," It stuck the muzzle of the pistol against the girl's side. "Take the thing down to the ground," it ordered.

Duare was certain that the creature intended to kill her as soon as the anotar landed and then try to fly it itself. The only way in which she might thwart this plan was to keep the anotar in the air.

"I told you to take it down," snapped Vik-yor when it became apparent that the plane was losing no altitude.

"If I do you'll kill me," said Duare.

"If you don't, I'll kill you," returned Vik-yor. "I have these other things you call controls; I just shoot you and then commence flying it myself. The reason I told you to take me down was so I could let you out, and then practice a little while by myself. Then, if I should find that I do not like it, I would take you in again."

"There will be nothing for me to get into, after you have practiced for a couple of minutes."

"You needn't try to make me change my mind by frightening

me," said Vik-yor. "I have made up my mind, and once my mind is made up—"

"Yes," said Duare; "I have noticed that. Very well," she added, "take that pistol out of my ribs and I will take you down."

Vik-yor replaced the pistol in one of its pocket pouches, and watched every move that Duare made as she brought the anotar to a landing. "Now get out," it said.

"You are headed into the wind," said Duare; "keep going straight ahead, and don't try to climb too fast;" then she stepped to the wing, and dropped to the ground.

Vik-yor opened the throttle wide; and the anotar leaped forward, swerving to the right. Duare held her breath, as the ship bounced and leaped erratically; she gasped as one wing grazed the ground; then the anotar leaped into the air. Duare could hear Vik-yor's screams of terror—they were almost worth the loss of the anotar.

The creature had managed to level off, but the ship was rolling first on one side and then on the other; it described circles; it started into a dive; and then the nose was suddenly jerked up, and it zoomed aloft. Finally it rolled completely over; and Vik-yor was flying upside down, its screams filling the welkin with horrific noise.

Each moment, Duare expected to see the ship crash; that would not have surprised her; but when Vik-yor completed a half loop and leveled off barely a few feet from the ground, she *was* surprised. The ship was headed for the river, near which it had taken off. In its terror, the Vooyorgan was clawing at everything on the instrument board, including the ignition switch—and the motor stopped.

The ship sailed gracefully up the river a few feet above the water, until, losing momentum, it pancaked to a safe landing, its pilot hanging half conscious in its safety belt. Duare could scarcely believe that that mad flight had not ended in tragedy, that the anotar was still whole; yet there it was, floating serenely down the river as though it had not just been through as harrowing an experience as may come to a well behaved aeroplane in a lifetime.

The girl ran to the river bank, praying that the current would bring the anotar to shore—it seemed to be drifting closer in. Finding that it had not been killed, Vik-yor was on the verge of hysterics with relief. It yammered and gibbered with delight.

"Didn't I tell you I could fly it?" it shrieked.

A shift in the current was now drifting the anotar toward the center of the river; soon it would be past Duare. She looked into the deep flowing water. What ravenous monsters might lurk beneath that placid surface! To lose the anotar, was to forfeit her life and Carson's as well. It was that last thought that sent her into the midst of the hidden dangers of the flood. Striking out boldly, she swam strongly toward the anotar. A slimy body brushed against her leg. She expected great faws to close upon her next, but nothing happened. She closed in upon the anotar; she seized a pontoon and climbed to the wing; she was safe!

Vik-yor had found her store of nuts and was devouring them greedily. She did not care; all she cared about was that the anotar was unharmed and that she was aboard it.

FORTY-ONE

Duare started the motor, that she might keep the anotar under control; but she let it continue to drift down the river. Finally she found that for which she was looking—a little island with a patch of backwater at its lower end. She brought the anotar into this quiet water and dropped anchor.

Vik-yor paid no attention to what was going on; it was still gobbling nuts like a famished squirrel. Duare reached for a nut, but Vik-yor struck her hand away and pushed the nuts out of her reach. Duare watched it in amazement; it scarcely hesitated long enough to chew the tough meat of the nuts; it even had to gasp for breath. Soon it commenced to laugh, and then it would stop long enough to sing; only to commence again a moment later.

"Wine!" it cried; "if I only had wine! But there is water." It looked around and saw that the anotar was swinging idly against the shore of a small island. "What are we doing here?" it demanded.

"We are going to remain here overnight," said Duare. "I am tired."

"I am going ashore," said Vik-yor. "You won't go off and leave me; because I have the vial and the pistol." It commenced to laugh and sing, as it gathered up all of the remaining nuts and carried them ashore; then it lay down on its belly and drank from the river.

It continued to eat and drink until Duare thought that it must burst; and the more it ate and drank, the more hysterical it became. In final and complete ecstasy, it rolled upon the ground, screaming and laughing; then it lay still, panting. It lay there for about fifteen minutes; then it rose slowly to its feet, completely enervated.

It took a few steps toward the anotar, its eyes glassy and staring; it shuddered and fell to the ground, writhing in convulsions; it screamed. "I am dividing!" it cried; "and I can't divide!"

Duare watched it in the throes of its futile contortions until it died.

Duare went ashore and took the vial and the pistol from the thing's pocket pouches; then she weighed anchor and started the motor. The anotar rose like a great bird and circled, while Duare got her bearings. The subdued light of the young night gave good visibility; at midnight it would be darkest, for then the Sun would be shining upon the opposite side of the outer cloud envelope, and the refracted light would be at its lowest intensity. By midnight, Duare could be back at Voo-ad.

She set her course toward the north. The great mountain range was upon her left, mysterious and a little frightening in the half light; then came the mighty forest, dark and forbidding. What a different world this was without Carson! Now it was a world filled with loneliness and menace, a gloomy, terrifying world. With him, it would have been just as dark, but it would have been thrilling and interesting.

But now she was flying back to him! Would she find him still alive? Would her bold plan of rescue be crowned with success? These were the questions to which the night and the hours held the answers.

FORTY-TWO

Ero Shan awakened, and looked around. The Museum of Natural History was deserted except for a few sleepy guards and the sad and hopeless array of exhibits.

"Awake, Carson?" he asked.

"Yes," I replied; "I have slept only fitfully. I cannot rid my mind of the fear that something terrible has happened to Duare. Think of her out there in the night alone with that sub-human creature, and it had the pistol. I heard the guards saying that Vik-yor killed many of its own people with my pistol. It must have taken it from Duare, and it was her only guarantee of safety."

"Don't worry," counselled Ero Shan; "it won't help. Do you believe in the prophetic qualities of dreams?"

"No."

Ero Shan laughed. "Well, neither do I; but I just had a pleasant dream. It may not have been prophetic, but it was cheering. I dreamed that we were all back in Havatoo, and that Nalte was giving a wonderful dinner for us. All the members of the Sanjong were there, and they were heaping praise on Duare."

"I had a dream, too," I said. "I saw the anotar crash, and I saw Duare's broken body lying dead beside it."

"It is well that you don't believe in dreams," said Ero Shan.

"I don't believe in dreams," I almost shouted, "but why did I have to dream such a thing as that!"

A guard came up. It carried a little switch, with which it hit me across the face. "Be quiet!" it snapped; then, from behind the great gantor at my left, came the b-r-r-r of an r-ray pistol; and the guard which had struck me slumped to the floor.

Other guards came running up, as a figure stepped into view from behind the gantor.

"Duare!" I cried.

The guards started for her; but she came on straight toward them, the deadly rays humming from the muzzle of her weapon. As four or five went down, the others turned and fled, shouting an alarm.

Duare rushed to me, the vial in her hand. Quickly she touched my tongue several times with the stopper; then she turned to minister to Ero Shan. Even before the antidote had taken full effect, she cut us both down.

I felt life returning; I could move my legs, my arms. Warriors were rushing into the building, alarmed by the shouts of the guards. Duare turned to meet them as Ero Shan and I staggered to our feet. Duare only turned to make sure that we could follow her; then she started for the doorway, and Ero Shan and I were at her heels with drawn swords.

The Vooyorgans went down before those rays of death like wheat before a scythe, and the living turned and ran from the building. Spears were hurled; but fortunately they missed us, and at last we stood in the plaza, where we saw a crowd making for the anotar—a rage-filled mob bent upon destroying it.

"Quick!" cried Duare; "to the anotar!"

It was an invitation that we did not need—we were already half way to it. The Vooyorgans were swarming over the ship by the time we reached it. Whether they had done any irreparable damage or not, we could not tell. They were more determined than I had imagined they would be; but they were a poor match against Ero Shan's sword and mine, and none against the r-ray pistol that Duare handled like a veteran. Soon, those that survived had fled to the safety of the nearest buildings; and we stood in complete command of the situation.

"Give me the vial, Duare," I said.

"What do you want of it?" she asked as she handed it to me.

"Those other poor devils in there," I said, nodding toward the museum.

"Yes," she said; "I had intended freeing them, too; but when the creatures put up such resistance. I couldn't take the time, especially with the anotar in danger. But how can you do it? We should not separate, and we don't dare leave the anotar."

"Taxi it right up to the entrance," I said, "so that it blocks it completely. You with the pistol and Ero Shan with his sword can hold that position while I go in and free the exhibits."

It took me a full half hour to free the human beings. They were all warriors, and they all had their arms—and were they Hell-bent on revenge! Those that I freed first helped me cut down the others, and by the time we were all through, a couple of hundred well armed warriors were ready to march out into the plaza.

I won't try to tell you of their gratitude; several hard bitten fighting men, with faces and bodies covered with scars, broke down and wept. They wanted to follow me to the ends of the world, if I wished them to; and if the anotar would have held them, I'd have taken them all, for with them I could have conquered a world.

We taxied the anotar from the entrance and let them out. When they found they couldn't come with me, they said goodby and started for the palace of Vik-vik-vik; and as we rose silently above Voo-ad, we heard screams and curses coming from the building.

I asked Duare what had become of Vik-yor. She told me, and then she said, "The poor creature not only could not multiply, but it could not divide."

A short time later Ero Shan pointed back. The sky was red with flames. The warriors I had released had fired Voo-ad.

"They will welcome no more visitors with flowers and song," said Ero Shan.

"And Vik-vik-vik will give no more of his delightful banquets," added Duare.

Into the night and the south we flew, and once again Duare and I were safe and together. Once again we were taking up our search for the city of Sanara, which is in the Empire of Korva in the land of Anlap.

FORTY-THREE

Anlap is a considerable land mass lying in the southern hemisphere of Venus. A portion of it lies in the south temperate zone, but it extends toward the north far into Strabol, the torrid zone. Practically all of this part of Anlap is totally unexplored and uncharted, its northern boundary being indicated on Amtorian maps by dotted lines.

When Duare, Ero Shan, and I escaped from Voo-ad in the anotar we flew directly south, for there I believed lay Korva, the empire ruled by my friend Taman.

How far away lay Sanara, the Korvan seaport which Taman

had made capital of the empire since the overthrow of the Zani revolutionists, we had no idea. Duare had flown a considerable distance in this direction while preparing to effect the escape of Ero Shan and myself from Voo-ad, and she had told me that farther progress south had seemed effectually blocked by forests of tremendous height and a great mountain range, the tops of both of which were eternally hidden in the innermost of the two great cloud envelopes which surround Venus, protecting her from the terrific heat of the sun. We were to learn later that Anlap is roughly divided into three parts by this mountain range and another one much farther to the south. Both of these mighty ranges run in an east-west direction and between them is an enormous, well-watered plateau, comprising vast plains of almost level land.

I would have been glad to have returned Ero Shan to his native city of Havatoo, had Duare's safety not been my first and almost only consideration; and I may say that I also longed for that peace and safety and relaxation which Sanara seemed to offer and which I had enjoyed for only a few brief intervals since that fateful day that my rocket ship had sped into the void from desolate Guadalupe on my projected trip to Mars which had ended on Venus.

Ero Shan and I had discussed the matter and he had been most insistent that we fly directly to Sanara and thus ensure the safety of Duare before giving any thought to his return to Havatoo; but I had assured him that once there, I would assist him in building another anotar in which he could return home.

After we reached the mountains I turned east, searching for a break in them where I might continue our southward journey, for it would have been suicidal to attempt to fly blind through the lower cloud envelope without the slightest knowledge of the height to which the mountain range rose. But I will not bore you with an account of that tedious search. Suffice it to say that the lower cloud envelope does not always maintain the same altitude, but seems to billow upward and downward sometimes as much as five thousand feet; and it was at one of those times that it was at its highest that I discerned the summits of some relatively low peaks beyond which there seemed to be open country.

I was flying just below the inner cloud envelope at the time and I immediately turned south and, with throttle wide, sped across those jagged peaks which, since creation, no man, doubtless, had ever looked upon before.

Speed was of the utmost importance now, as we must get through before the cloud envelope billowed down and enveloped us.

"Well," said Duare, with a sigh of relief, as the vast plain which I have previously mentioned opened out below us, "we got through, and that augurs well, I think, for the future; but this doesn't look much like the country surrounding Sanara, does it?"

"It doesn't look at all like it," I replied, "and as far as I can see there is no sign of an ocean."

"It may not look like Korva," said Ero Shan, "but it is certainly a beautiful country."

And indeed it was. As far as the eye could reach in every direction the plain was almost level, with only a few low, scattered hills and forests and rivers breaking the monotony of its vast, pastel-shaded expanse.

"Look," said Duare, "there is something moving down there."

Far ahead I could see what appeared to be a procession of little dots, moving slowly parallel with a great river. "It might be game," said Ero Shan, "and we could use some meat."

Whatever they were, they were moving with such exact military precision that I doubted very much that it was game; however, I decided to fly over them, drop down, and investigate. As we came closer and could see them better they resolved themselves into the most amazing things that any of us ever had seen. There were about twenty enormous man-made things crawling over the plain. In front of them, on their flanks, and bringing up the rear, were a number of smaller replicas of the leviathans.

"What in the world are they?" demanded Duare.

"The whole thing looks to me like a battle fleet on land," I replied. "It's the most amazing sight I have ever seen; and I am going to drop down and have a closer look at it."

"Be careful," cautioned Duare. "Don't forget that thing you call a jinx, which you say has been 'camping on our trail' for so long."

"I know you are perfectly right, my dear," I replied, "and I won't go too close, but I'd like to see just what those things are."

I circled above the Brobdingnagian caravan and dropped down to about a thousand feet above it; and this closer view revealed that its individual units were far more amazing and extraordinary than they had appeared at a distance. The largest units were between seven hundred and eight hundred feet long, with a beam of over a hundred feet; and they rose to a height of at least thirty feet above the ground, with lighter superstructures rising another thirty feet or more above what I am constrained to call the upper decks, as they resembled nothing so much as dreadnaughts. Flags and pennons flew from their superstructures and from their bows and sterns; and they fairly bristled with armament.

The smaller units were of different design and might be compared to cruisers and destroyers, while the big ones were certainly land dreadnaughts, or, I might say, superdreadnaughts. The upper decks and the superstructures were crowded with men looking up at us. They watched us for a moment and then suddenly disappeared belowdecks; and I realized instantly that they had been called to their stations.

That didn't look good to me and I started to climb to get away from there as quickly as possible; and simultaneously I heard the humming of t-ray guns. They were firing at us with that deadly Amtorian t-ray which destroys all matter.

With throttle wide I climbed, zig-zagging in an attempt to avoid their fire, upbraiding myself for being such a stupid fool as to have taken this unnecessary chance; and then a moment later, as I was congratulating myself upon having made good our escape, the nose of the anotar disappeared, together with the propeller.

"The jinx is still with us," said Duare.

FORTY-FOUR

As I came down in a long glide the firing ceased and a couple of the smaller units detached themselves from the column and came slithering across the plain toward us at terrific speed. They were right there when we landed and their guns were trained on us. I stood up in the cockpit and raised my hands in sign of peace. A door in the side of the contraption opened and six men dropped to the ground and came toward us. All but one were armed with r-ray pistols and rifles; the exception, who led them, evidently being an officer. Their costumes consisted of loinclothes, sandals, and helmets, the helmets being the only unusual departure from the almost universal Amtorian costume of men. They were a rather grim-looking lot, with square jaws and set, unsmiling faces. They were rather handsome in a sinister sort of way. They came and stopped beside the anotar, looking up at us.

"Get down," said the officer.

Ero Shan and I dropped to the ground, and I helped Duare down. "Why did you shoot us down?" I demanded.

"Perhaps Danlot the lotokor will tell you," replied the officer, "I am taking you to him."

They herded us into the belly of the strange craft from which they had come. There must have been between two and three hundred men aboard this three hundred foot neolantar, as I later learned they called it. On this lower deck were the sleeping quarters, galley and mess rooms, as well as room for the storage of provisions and ammunition. On the next deck were batteries of guns that fired through ports on both sides and at the blunt and rounded bow and stern. The upper deck to which we were finally taken was also heavily armed, having guns in revolving turrets forward and aft, lighter guns on top of the turrets, and batteries forward and aft over which the turret guns could fire. The superstructure rose for the center of this upper deck. The upper deck of the superstructure was what, I suppose, one might call the bridge, while below that were the cabins of the officers.

All these ships are called lantars, which is a contraction of the two words "lap" and "notar," lap meaning land and notar meaning ship. The big dreadnaught is called a tonglantar, or big land ship; the cruiser a kolander, or fast land ship; the destroyer a neolantar, or small land ship. I call them superdreadnaughts, cruisers and destroyers because these are what they most resemble in our navies on Earth.

We were taken to one of the superdreadnaughts, which proved to be the flagship of the fleet. This craft was simply tremendous, being seven hundred and fifty feet long with a hundred and sixteen foot beam. The upper deck was thirty feet above the ground and the superstructure rose thirty feet above that. It was dressed with ensigns, banners, and pennons; but otherwise it was a very grim and efficient-looking fighting machine. Forward, on the upper deck, was a group of officers; and to these we were escorted.

Danlot, the lotokor who commanded the fleet, was a hard-bitten, stern-looking man. "Who are you, and what were you doing coming over the fleet of Falsa in that thing?" he demanded. He was scrutinizing us all most intently and suspiciously as he spoke.

"We have been lost for many months," I said, "and we were trying to find our way home."

"Where is that?" he asked.

"Korva," I replied.

"Never heard of it," said Danlot. "Where is it?"

"I am not quite sure myself," I replied; "but it is somewhere south of here, on the southern coast of Anlap."

"This is Anlap," he said, "but the sea is to the east, and there is no Korva there. To the south are mountains that cannot be crossed. What is that thing you were flying through the air in; and what makes it stay up?"

"It is an anotar," I said; and then I explained the principle of it to him briefly.

"Who built it?" he asked.

"I did."

"Where have you just flown from?"

"From a city called Voo-ad, north of the mountains," I replied.

"Never heard of it," said Danlot. "You have been lying to me and you are a poor liar. You say you are coming from a place that no one ever heard of and going to a place that no one ever heard of. Do you expect me to believe that? I'll tell you what you are—you are Pangan spies, all of you." At that I laughed. "What are you laughing at?" he demanded.

"Because your statement is absolutely ridiculous on the face of it," I replied. "If we had been spies, we would never have come down to be shot at."

"The Pangans are all fools," snapped Danlot.

"I might agree with you that I am a fool," I said, "but I am no Pangan. I never even heard of a Pangan before. I had no idea what country I am in now."

"I still say that you are spies," he insisted; "and as such you will be destroyed."

"My mate," I said, indicating Duare, "was formerly the jangong of Vepaja; and my friend Ero Shan is a soldier-

172

biologist of Havatoo; and I am Carson of Venus, a tanjong of Korva. If you are civilized people, you will treat us as befits our rank."

"I have heard of Havatoo," said Danlot. "It lies over three thousand miles east of here, across the ocean. Many years ago a ship was wrecked on the Falsa coast. It was a ship from a land called Thora; and on board it was a man from Havatoo, who was a prisoner of the Thorists. These Thorists were a bad lot and we killed them all, but the man from Havatoo was a very learned man. He still lives with us in Onar. Perhaps I shall let you live until we return to Onar."

"What was the name of this man from Havatoo?" asked Ero Shan.

"Korgan Kantum Ambat," replied Danlot.

"I knew him well," said Ero Shan. "He disappeared mysteriously many years ago. He was a very learned man; a soldier-physicist."

"He told me that he fell off the quay into the river one night," said Danlot, "was swept over the falls below the city and miraculously escaped with his life. He managed to climb onto a floating log below the falls, and was carried down to the ocean, where he was captured by the Thorist ship. As there was no way in which he could return to Havatoo, he has remained here."

After this Danlot's attitude toward us softened. He told me that they were on their way to the Pangan city of Hor. He didn't like the idea of taking us into battle with him; he said we would be in the way, especially Duare.

"If I could spare a ship," he said, "I would send you back to Onar. There are absolutely no quarters for women on these lantars."

"I can double up with my klookor," said the officer who had brought us, "and the woman may have my cabin." A klookor is a lieutenant.

"Very good, Vantor," said Danlot; "you may take the woman back with you."

I did not like that and I said so, but Vantor said there was no room for me aboard his ship and Danlot cut me short peremptorily, reminding me that we were prisoners. I saw the shadow of a sarcastic smile curl Vantor's lips as he led Duare away, and I was filled with foreboding as I saw her leave the flagship and enter the destroyer. Immediately after this the fleet got under way again.

Danlot quartered me with a young sublieutenant or rokor and Ero Shan with another, with the understanding that we would have to sleep while these men were on duty, and give up the cabins to them when they returned to their quarters. Otherwise we had the run of the ship; and I was rather surprised at that, but it convinced me that Danlot no longer felt that we were Pangan spies.

About an hour after we got under way I saw something dead ahead coming across the plain toward us at a terrific rate of speed, and when it got closer I saw that it was a diminutive lantar. It came alongside the flagship, which was still moving forward and did not diminish its speed, and an officer came aboard from it and went immediately to Danlot; and almost immediately thereafter the flags and pennons on all the ships were struck, with the exception of the ensign, and an additional flag was raised below the ensign on the staff which topped the superstructure. It was a red flag, with crossed swords in black—the battle flag of Falsa. Now the fleet fanned out, with destroyers in three lines far ahead, followed by three lines of cruisers, and the battleships in rear at the apex of the triangle. From the front and either flank little scout ships came racing in and took their positions on either side of the ships to which they were attached.

The men of the flagship were all at their stations. The great fleet moved steadily forward in perfect formation. It was battle formation all right and I knew that a battle must be impending, but I could see no enemy; and as no one was paying any attention to me, I went up to the bridge to get a better view of what was going on and to see if I could locate an enemy. There were officers and signalmen there, sending and receiving messages. There were four t-ray guns mounted on the bridge, each with its complement of three gunners; so that the bridge, while large, was pretty well crowded, and certainly no place for a sightseer, and I was surprised that they permitted me to remain; but I later learned that it was on Danlot's orders that I was given free run of the ship, on the theory that if I were a spy, I would eventually convict myself by some overt act.

"Have you ever been in a battle between lantar fleets?" one of the officers asked me.

"No," I replied; "I never saw a lantar until today."

"If I were you, then, I'd go below," he said. "This is the most dangerous place on the ship. In all probability more than half of us will be killed before the battle is over."

As he ceased speaking I heard a whistling sound that rose to a long drawn out shriek and ended in a terrific detonation, as a bomb exploded a couple of hundred yards ahead of the flagship.

Instantly the big guns of the battleship spoke in unison.

The battle was on.

FORTY-FIVE

The very largest guns of the battleship hurl shells weighing a thousand pounds to a distance of about fifteen miles, while smaller bore guns hurl five hundred pound shells from twenty to twenty-five miles. These guns are used when the enemy is below the horizon, as the t-ray and the r-ray describe no curve in their flight. Moving as they do always in a straight line, the target must be visible to the gunner.

The leading destroyers and cruisers were now out of sight, bearing down on the enemy to get their terribly destructive t-ray guns into action. Enemy shells were bursting all about us; and our battleships were firing salvo after salvo.

Presently the battleships leaped forward at accelerated speed, rolling and bumping over the uneven ground so that the sensation was much the same as being on the deck of an ocean-going ship in a heavy sea; yet the firing never ceased.

I saw a direct hit on the superstructure of the next ship in line. Every man on the bridge of that ship must have been killed instantly. Though it seemed to me like a man without eyes, it kept its place in line and continued firing; its commander and his staff operating it from an armoured control room in the bowels of the ship from radio instructions received from the flagship. While handicapped, it was still able to fight.

"You see what I meant," said the officer who had advised me to go below, nodding in the direction of the wreck of the superstructure.

"I see," I said, "but it is far more interesting here than it would be below."

"You will find it still more interesting when we close with the enemy," he said.

We could now see our cruisers and some of the destroyers ahead. They were closely engaged with enemy craft and at last we saw the big battleships of the enemy coming up over the curve of the planet; and in another half hour we were in the thick of it. The little scout ships were buzzing around like mosquitos, and they and the destroyers were launching wheeled torpedos at the enemy ships, while enemy ships of the same classes were attacking us similarly.

The booming of the big guns had given place to the hissing of t-rays, which are capable of destroying nearly all forms of matter.

These ships have two forms of protection, heavy armorplate against shells, over which lies a thin protective coating which is impervious to t-rays, but which can be dissolved by a certain chemical. And now that the two fleets were in close contact, another form of gun was brought into action, which fired shells containing this acid, and when a direct hit was made you could see a great blotch on the side of the hit ship where the t-ray protective material had been dissolved, and the armorplate beneath was exposed. Immediately the ship was vulnerable to t-rays on this spot and the t-ray guns of opposing ships were at once trained on it; and it became the strategy of such a ship to continually maneuver so that this vulnerable spot was not presented to the enemy.

As we approached the vortex of the battle I discovered that one of its most interesting phases centered about the little wheeled torpedos. Mounted on a tricycle undercarriage, they are self-propelling, and are supposed to move in a straight line toward the target at which they are aimed when they are launched, thus naturally a rough terrain will deflect them; and they are really highly effective only at very close range. Their purpose is to disable the heavy, endless belts upon which the lantars run after the manner of our own caterpillar tractors and tanks. One of the functions of the little scout ships is to destroy enemy torpedos as well as to launch their own; and this they do with small t-ray guns. To me, these would be the most interesting ships to command. They are amazingly fast and maneuverable and the busiest things I ever saw, darting to launch a torpedo, zig-zagging out again at terrific speed

176

to avoid t-ray fire, or chasing an enemy torpedo to put it out of commission.

The flagship was in the thick of the battle now, and I soon found more interesting things than the little scout ships close at hand, for we were engaged in a duel with the men on the superstructure of an enemy warship close off our starboard side. Six of our men were already dead and one of our guns had been put out of action. A chemical shell had hit its shield, removing the protective coating and exposing it to the deadly t-ray fire of the enemy. The t-rays opened a big hole in it, and the gunners dropped one by one. Two men were dragging another shield to the gun and I gave them a hand. We held it in front of us to protect us from enemy fire, but in getting it into position my companions exposed themselves, and both were killed.

I looked around to see if someone was coming to command the gun, but I found that everyone else on the bridge had been killed, with the exception of the crews of the other guns, one of which was now being fired by the only remaining officer. So I took my place on the seat at the gun's breech and glued my eye to the little periscope which barely topped the shield. I was entirely protected from everything but shellfire until another chemical shell should strike my shield.

Through the periscope I could plainly see the bridge of the enemy ship, and I could see that they were not much better off than we. The deck was littered with dead, and it was evident that two of their guns were out of commission. Below me the two ships were hurling broadsides of chemical shells and t-rays into one another's hulls. There was a gaping hole in the side of the enemy ship, but our t-rays had not yet reached a vital spot.

Now I turned the periscope back on the enemy bridge and saw a foot protruding beneath the shield of the gun directly opposite me. I set my sights on the foot and blew it off. I heard the fellow scream and then I saw him roll to the deck. He should have held onto himself better, for now his head was exposed, and a couple of seconds later that followed his foot. The gun, however, kept on firing. There might be two more gunners behind that shield.

The t-ray travels in a straight path, not much greater in diameter than an ordinary lead pencil. The two bursts that I had fired from the gun had convinced me that it was an extremely accurate weapon. Naturally, the rolling and the bumping of the two ships as they forged along side by side made almost any hit more or less of an accident. No matter how much a ship rolls, there is an instant at each end of its roll when it is static, and it was at this instant that I had fired my two bursts. Now I determined to try for another lucky shot, and sought to train my gun on the tiny opening in the muzzle of the enemy gun that was facing me. If I could strike that tiny target, the gun would be permanently disabled. Following that little target with my sight was nerve-racking. I fired a dozen bursts without accomplishing anything and then for a fraction of a second the two ships seemed to stand perfectly still simultaneously. My sight was directly on the opening in the muzzle of the enemy gun as I pressed the button which liberates the t-ray. I could see the gun quiver as the t-rays bored completely through it, and I knew that I had made a direct hit and that that gun would fire no more.

Only one gun was now in action on the enemy bridge, and I could see two of its gunners lying dead outside the shield; so I was pretty sure that it was manned by only one man and that the surviving gunner or gunners of the piece I had hit would try to reach the remaining gun and reinforce its crew; so I turned my piece on the space between the two guns and waited. Sure enough, both gunners started to dart across simultaneously and I got them both.

Looking around for new worlds to conquer, I turned my periscope on other parts of the enemy battleship. It had taken a terrific beating, but most of its guns were still in action. I saw a point, very low down on the hull, where a chemical shell had burst. It was on the armored apron that protects the running gear. I turned my piece on that spot and pressed the button. It was impossible to hold it there constantly because of the movement of the two ships, but I had the satisfaction of seeing a hole appear in the armor; and I kept on plugging away at it until there was a hole there as big as a man's head, exposing the great metal track upon which the monster traveled. The track was moving so fast that the t-rays were spread over a considerable surface, with the result that no immediate effects were observable; but presently I saw the tracks crumple beneath the giant wheels, and jam. Instantly the battleship swung toward us with the blocking of its wheels on the port side, while the starboard side was still in motion.

We veered away at full speed just in time to avoid a collision; and then, as the enemy ship came to a stop, we left her to the mercy of the destroyers and scout ships that swarmed around her like hyenas and jackals.

For the first time since I had manned the gun I had an opportunity to look about me and I saw that the enemy fleet was in full flight, with our destroyers and cruisers harrassing it. Astern as far as eye could see the plain was dotted with disabled ships of both sides, and I could see hand to hand fighting on the ground as the Falsans sought to take prisoners.

Night was falling and the flagship was signaling the fleet to return to formation. As far as I was concerned, the battle was over; and as I looked around the bridge I could appreciate why the officer had suggested that I go below. He and I and two gunners were the only survivors of the engagement. As I stood up and surveyed the carnage, he came over and spoke to me.

"You fought that gun well," he said.

"Not much like a Pangan spy, do you think?" I said, smiling.

"No, nor not much like a man who has never seen a lantar before," he said.

"I have seen other ships, and fought them too, but they sailed on oceans and not on land."

"You will get plenty more fighting tomorrow," he remarked. "We should reach Hor by early afternoon, and then there will really be fighting."

"What is this war all about?" I asked.

"It's a matter of grazing land for the herds," he replied. "Panga wants it all. So we have been fighting over it for the last ten years, and while we have been fighting, the men of Hangor have stolen nearly all of their herds and the men of Maltor have stolen nearly all of ours."

"Doesn't either side ever win any decisive battles?" I asked.

"Our fleet always defeats theirs," he replied. "But so far we have been unable to take the city of Hor; that would decide the war."

"And then what?" I asked.

He shrugged. "Your guess is as good as mine," he said, "but the chances are we will go to war with Maltor to recover our stolen herds."

After the battle a couple of hospital ships and a transport

179

came up from the rear. The transport brought replacements and the hospital ships took the wounded aboard. Most of the night was devoted to making repairs and there was little sleep.

When morning broke I saw two very strange looking craft that had come up during the night. They were heavily armored, enormous monstrosities, with cone-shaped prows that came to a point about fifteen feet above the ground. Each had four very heavy guns pointing straight ahead just in rear of the cones. The muzzle of each gun was flush with the surface of the armorplate, the guns themselves being hidden in the interior of the hull. There was one on either side, one above, and one below the prow; lighter, protective t-ray guns, fired from ports along the sides and at the stern. The hulls were cylindrical in shape and the whole ship looked like an enormous torpedo. I could not see what their purpose could be, for it was evident that their maneuverability would be very poor.

Shortly after daylight we got under way, and soon thereafter Danlot sent for me.

"Your conduct during yesterday's action has been reported to me," he said. "Your action was highly commendable and I would like to show my appreciation in some way."

"You can do that," I replied, "by permitting me to rejoin my mate."

"That was another matter I wished to speak to you about," he said. "Your mate is missing."

"Missing!" I exclaimed. "What do you mean? Was she killed during yesterday's action?"

"No," he replied. "Vantor's body was found in his cabin this morning. He had been stabbed through the heart, and your mate was not on the ship when they searched it for her."

FORTY-SIX

Duare gone! Out there somewhere alone and on foot in this strange land.

"You must let me go and look for her," I said.

Danlot shook his head. "You could accomplish nothing,"

he said. "I have sent two scouting lantars to search the country for her."

"That is kind of you," I said.

He looked at me in surprise. "Evidently you do not understand," he said. "Your mate has murdered one of our officers, or at least the evidence indicates as much and she must be brought to justice."

I was appalled. "You cannot mean that!" I exclaimed. "it is quite obvious why she had to kill him. It is evident that he deserved to be killed."

"We do not look at such matters that way," replied Danlot. "Vantor was a good officer, with years of training. He was extremely valuable to Falsa, much more valuable than forty women. And now," he said, as though the incident were closed as far as I was concerned, "what can I do for you to show my appreciation of what you did yesterday?"

It took all the willpower I possessed not to tell him what I thought of his justice and his valuation of Duare, but I realized that if I were ever to help her I must not antagonize him; also there was budding in my mind the germ of an idea. "Ero Shan and I would like to help man one of the little fast scouting ships," I said. "They seem to offer a far greater field of action than any of the others."

He looked at me a moment before he replied, and then he said, "You like to fight, don't you?"

"When there is anything to fight for," I replied.

"What have you got to fight for here?" he asked. "You are not a Falsan, and you can certainly have no quarrel with the Pangans, if what you have told me about yourself is true, as you never even heard of them until yesterday."

"I should like to have the opportunity of winning in some measure the confidence and gratitude of Falsa," I replied. "It might temper the judgment of the court when my mate is brought to trial."

"You must hold your women in high esteem in your country," he said.

"We do," I replied; "in the highest esteem. A woman's honor there would be worth the lives of forty Vantors."

"We are different," he said. "We consider women as necessary evils, and little more than that. I have paid more for a good zorat than most women bring. But to get back to your request—I am going to grant it. As you will be here the rest of

181

your lives, you and your friend might as well learn to serve Falsa in some useful way."

"Why do you say that we will be here the rest of our lives?" I asked.

"Because you will," he replied. "It is absolutely impossible to cross the mountains which hem Anlap on the north and south. To the east is an ocean and you have no ship. To the west is an unknown land which no man has ever explored. And furthermore, I don't think that you would be permitted to leave. You would know too many of our military secrets, and if by chance you could reach some other country, by the same token those people could reach us; and we have enough trouble with the Pangans without having men from some strange country making war upon us."

After my interview with Danlot I sought out Ero Shan. "You don't know it," I said, "but you want to come with me and help man one of the fast little scouting ships."

"I don't know what you're talking about," he said.

"I know you don't, because I only just now got permission from Danlot for you and me to serve aboard one of the little ships."

"That's all right with me," he said, "but just why do you want to do that?"

I told him about Duare then and that, as service on one of the scouting ships would permit us to range much farther than the main fleet, we might by chance find her, which we never could do aboard a big battleship.

"And then what would you do?" he asked. "The officer in command of the scouting ship would bring Duare back for trial, and you couldn't do anything about it."

"I think we could," I said. "We would have learned how to operate the ship and we have our r-ray pistols—and there would be only five men to dispose of."

Ero Shan nodded. "I see possibilities in that idea," he said with a smile.

While we were still talking, an officer came up and told us that we had been ordered aboard the Athgan 975, which lay alongside the battleship. We immediately went to the lower deck and out through the door there, where we found the Athgan 975 awaiting us. The word "Athgan" means scout, and it is a compound of ath, meaning look, and gan, meaning man, which gives "look-man," or scout.

The commander of the 975 was a rokor, or sublieutenant, named Ganjo. He didn't seem very enthusiastic about having a couple of green men detailed to his ship. He asked us what we could do, and I told him that we were both gunners; so he set Ero Shan at a gun in the stern and me at one in the bow, which pleased me because it permitted me to sit beside the driver—I don't know what else to call him, possibly pilot would be better.

There were seven men aboard the ship in addition to rokor—the pilot, four gunners, and two torpedomen. The gunners each had two guns, one firing chemical shells and the t-rays. The guns were double-barreled affairs, the t-ray barrel being on top of the chemical shell barrel, and clamped to it rigidly, so that only one set of sights was necessary. The guns protruded beyond the hull of the ship about three quarters of their length, and could swing forty-five degrees in any direction. The port and starboard guns and the gun in the stern had a similar range of action. There was a torpedo tube on each side of the ship, so, with our great speed and maneuverability, we were a very dangerous little buggy. From the start I watched every movement that the pilot made and it was not long before I was confident that I could pilot the 975 myself and I was most anxious to try it.

The squadron to which the 975 was attached raced far ahead of the fleet, and I soon realized why the Falsans wore helmets, for, notwithstanding that we were strapped to our seats with safety belts, we were banged around considerably, as the little ship raced with terrific speed over all sorts of terrain.

Before noon we came in sight of a large city which I knew must be Hor. Up to this time we had not seen anything of an enemy fleet, but now their scout ships and destroyers came racing from one of the city's gates. They far outnumbered us, and as we were merely a scouting force, our squadron commander ordered us to retire. We kept just out of effective range, and one of the athgans was detached and sent back to the main fleet to report to Danlot. We hung around waiting for the main body of the enemy fleet to come out, but they didn't show themselves; and in the early afternoon our fleet put in an appearance, but it heralded itself long before it arrived, sending salvos of shells over our heads which burst inside the city; and the big guns of the city answered from the city walls.

Hor was rather an imposing-looking metropolis of considerable extent, and with tall buildings showing beyond its lofty wall. It was a huge fortress, which looked absolutely impregnable; nor in ten years had Falsa been able to reduce it.

As we were watching the effect of the shell fire, I saw a direct hit by a thousand pound shell on one of the taller buildings. There was a terrific detonation and the building simply fell apart. We could hear the crash way out on the plain, and we saw the dust rise high above the city wall. The Pangans replied with a terrific bombardment, which demolished two of our dreadnaughts.

And now the fleet moved closer and I saw the two mighty monstrosities moving up. I asked the pilot what they were.

"Something new that's never been used before," he replied; "but if they work, the Pangans are in for the surprise of their lives."

Just then three gates flew open and the whole Pangan fleet came out, firing. It seemed to me that it was a very stupid maneuver, for they were all bunched at the gates and offered a splendid target, and I said as much to the pilot.

"You never can tell what the Pangans are going to do," he said. "Their jong probably got mad when that building was demolished and ordered the whole fleet out to punish us. Only about half their fleet was in the battle yesterday; so we will be in for some pretty hot fighting now. Here come the gantors!" he exclaimed. "Now we'll see them in action."

The two huge, torpedo-shaped ships were advancing at considerable speed, with a flock of protecting destroyers on either side. A huge Pangan battleship was coming to meet them, firing every gun that she could bring to bear; but the gantors, as the pilot had nicknamed them after an elephantine Amtorian beast of burden, came roaring on. The battleship, evidently sensing that she was going to be rammed, turned to run back, coming broadside to the nearer gantor, which suddenly leaped forward at terrific speed.

There was no hope for the battleship. The sharp, deadly, armoured point of the gantor struck it amidships fifteen feet above the ground and rammed into it for fifty feet, firing its bow guns and its forward port and starboard guns, raking the whole interior of the battleship.

As it hung there a moment, finishing its work of destruction, the other gantor passed it, and you may rest assured the remainder of the Pangan fleet gave it a wide berth, opening up a broad path for it; and though there was no ship in front of it, it kept on straight toward the city.

The first gantor in the meantime backed out of the stricken battleship and, apparently unscathed, followed its companion. I saw now that each of them was headed for a gate, and I instantly recognized the real purpose for which they had been constructed. We followed close behind one of them with several other athgans. Behind us came a column of battleships.

"If we get inside the city," said our rokor, "we are to take the first left-hand avenue. It leads to the barracks. That is the objective of our squadron. Shoot anyone who offers resistance."

The gates of Hor are of wood covered with armorplate, but when the gantor hit them, they crashed down upon the avenue beyond, and the gantors went over them and we followed, turning into the first avenue at the left.

Through the gates behind us the great battleships had rolled. On toward the center of the city they moved. We could hear the sound of the battle that was being carried into the heart of Hor as we made our way toward the barracks. This building, or series of buildings, we found along one side of an enormous parade ground.

The Pangans were certainly unprepared for anything of this sort. There was not a single gun ready to receive us, the men who rushed from the barracks having only their r-ray pistols and rifles, which were utterly useless against our armored athgan.

The battle went on in the city until almost dark. Falsan athgans ranged the avenues, striking terror to the hearts of her citizens, while the battleships massed in the great square before the jong's palace and dealt death and destruction until the jong surrendered. But in the meantime the main body of the Pangan fleet had escaped through the rear gates of the city. However, Hor had been taken and the ten year war was supposedly over.

During the fighting in the city we had suffered three casualties on the 975. The pilot had been killed by a chance r-ray shot through an open port, as had our rokor, and the man at the port gun. I was now piloting the athgan, and as the pilot is supposed to rank directly beneath the rokor, I assumed command of the ship. The only reason I got away with it was because there was no superior officer to know about it and the three remaining Falsans were simple warriors who could have been commanded by anyone with initiative.

FORTY-SEVEN

I waited in the plaza for some time, expecting instructions from my squadron commander, but I got none. Pangans, mostly girls, were moving about the plaza freely; and presently I saw a number of Falsan warriors with them, and it was evident that the men had been drinking. About this time three Pangan girls came to the 975 and offered us liquor in small jugs. Ero Shan and I refused, but the three Falsans on board accepted it enthusiastically, and after a few drinks they became hilarious; and, remarking something to the effect that to the victors belong the spoils, they left the ship and went off arm in arm with the Pangan girls.

Ero Shan and I were now alone on the ship. We discussed our situation and what we might do under the circumstances.

"Now that we have complete possession of the 975," I said, "we might as well take advantage of it and go out and search for Duare."

"We stand about one chance in a million of finding her," he replied, "but I'm for that millionth chance if you are."

"Well, we certainly can't find her in the City of Hor," I said; "so we might as well go out and scour the country in the vicinity of the place where she disappeared."

"You realize, of course, what the penalty will be for stealing a ship and deserting when we are finally picked up."

"Oh, we're not deserting," I said, "we're looking for our squadron commander."

Ero Shan laughed. "It's all right if you can get away with it," he said.

I headed the 975 back along the avenue down which we had come from the gate at which we had entered the city. Along the entire route we encountered crowds of drunken warriors, singing and dancing with Pangan girls.

"The Pangans seem to be a most hospitable people," remarked Ero Shan.

"The Falsans say that they are fools," I said, "but I should say that it is the Falsans who are the fools right now."

When we reached the gate, which still lay where the great gantor had thrown it, we found it heavily guarded by Falsan warriors, who halted us. There were no girls here, and these men had not been drinking. An officer approached and asked where we thought we were going.

"I am looking for my squadron commander," I replied. "I can't find him in the city and I thought possibly the squadron might have formed outside of Hor."

"You will probably find him up around the central plaza," said the officer. "Most of the fleet is there and none of our fleet is outside the city."

Disappointed, I turned back and took the main avenue which led toward the center of the city and the jong's palace; and as we proceeded, evidence of the hospitality of the Pangans multiplied, the visible effects of which had degenerated into nothing less than a drunken orgy. One thing that was particularly noticeable was the absence of Pangan men from the avenues, and the fact that few, if any, of the Pangan girls appeared to be under the influence of liquor.

In the central plaza, before the jong's palace, pandemonium reigned. A great many ships of our fleet were there, packed in without military order, their decks filled with Pangan girls and drunken Falsan warriors.

For the purpose of carrying out the fiction that I was looking for my squadron commander, I made inquiries from a warrior attached to the flagship, a man whom I knew would recognize and remember me.

"Squadron commander," he repeated. "He is probably in the palace. The jong is giving a banquet for the officers of our fleet," He handed me a jug. "Have a drink," he invited. "It is good liquor, the best I ever tasted. These Pangans are really wonderful people, treating us this way now that, after ten years, we have won the war and conquered Hor. Have a drink."

"No, thanks," I said. "I have got to get into the palace and find my squadron commander." And we moved off in the direction of the great gates of the jong's palace.

"Do you really mean that you want to get in there?" asked Ero Shan.

"I certainly do," I said. "I think Danlot should know that

187

his entire force is drunk. You come with me, Ero Shan. Whatever happens, we will stick together."

The guard at the palace gate halted us. "I have an important message for the lotokor Danlot," I said.

The man sized us up. Except for our helmets, we wore no regulation article of the Falsan uniform. The fellow hesitated and then he called an officer, to whom I repeated my statement.

"Certainly," he said; "come right in. You will find your commanding officer in the banquet hall."

The corridors of the palace, and apartments into which we could see as we made our way toward the banquet hall, were filled with drunken Falsan officers and sober Pangans. At the entrance to the banquet hall we were halted again, and once again I repeated the statement that I had a message for Danlot. While we were waiting for an officer whom the sentry had summoned, we had an opportunity to take in the scenes in the banquet hall. Long tables filled the room, at which were seated all the higher officers of the Falsan navy, practically all of whom were obviously under the influence of liquor; and beside each drunken Falsan sat a sober Pangan. On a raised platform at the far end of the room, at a smaller table, sat Hajan, jong of Panga, with the highest officers of his realm and the ranking officers of the Falsan navy. Danlot sat on the jong's right. He was slumped in his chair, his chin resting on his breast. He seemed to be asleep.

"I don't like the looks of this," I said to Ero Shan in a whisper.

"Neither do I," he replied. "I think we should get out of here. It would be a waste of time delivering your message to Danlot."

"I'm afraid it's too late anyway," I said. I had scarcely ceased speaking, and we still stood looking into the banquet hall, when Hajan the jong rose and drew his sword. It was evidently a prearranged signal, for simultaneously every Pangan officer in the banquet hall followed the example of his jong, and every Pangan sword was pointed at the breast of a Falsan. Trumpets sounded, and other trumpets carried the call to arms down every corridor of the palace and out into the city.

I snatched off Ero Shan's helmet and my own and tossed them on the floor. He looked at me in sudden surprise and then smiled, for he realized that now no one could identify us as Falsans, and that for the time being we might be overlooked, possibly long enough to permit us to escape.

A few of the Falsan officers resisted and were killed, but most of them were disarmed and made prisoners. In the confusion we made our way out of the palace and through the gates with a number of Pangan officers.

As we reached the plaza we saw Pangan troops pouring in from every avenue, while Pangan girls were pouring from every ship and fleeing to safety.

The fighting in the plaza was soon over, as it was in other parts of the city, for the drunken, disorganized Falsans could put up little or no resistance since most of them had been surreptitiously disarmed by the Pangan girls.

Within an hour the Falsans had been herded into the plaza before the barracks, and were being held there under guard. Most of them lay asleep on the sward in drunken stupors. A few of those who had been on guard at the gates escaped on foot out into the night. The Pangans had taken thousands of prisoners and the entire Falsan land fleet. It looked to me as though the ten-year-old war was over.

"The Pangans were not such fools after all," I said to Ero Shan.

We were standing near the 975, looking at it longingly and wondering how we could get out of the city with it, when an officer came up behind me and tapped me on the shoulder.

"Who are you two?" he demanded as I turned around to face him.

"We were prisoners of the Falsans," I replied, "but after the men who were guarding us got drunk, we escaped." Then I had an inspiration. "We are both gunners," I said, "and I am a pilot. We would like to enlist in the service of your jong."

The officer scratched his head. "You don't look like Falsans," he admitted, "but you're not Pangans; so I'll put you under arrest until morning, and then the proper authorities can decide what is to be done to you." He summoned some soldiers then and told them to lock us up until morning and then to bring us to his headquarters. From his insignia I saw that he held a rank similar to that of colonel. Nowhere that I have been on Venus have I found any differentiation between Army and Navy, and the ranks that I have translated into military titles a Navy man would probably have translated into Navy titles. I like the system, for it certainly simplifies matters

189

of precedence and rank, and makes for a unified fighting force comprising all branches of every service.

Ero Shan and I were taken to a guardhouse and locked up; and there ended a day of action, excitement, successes, and reversals; and with it the blasting of my hopes to steal the 975 and prosecute my search for Duare.

FORTY-EIGHT

The following morning no one came to take us to the officer who had arrested us until after noon, and as we were conducted through the city we saw columns of dejected Falsans marching through the gates of Hor out onto the plains beyond. Our guard told us that Danlot and several other high Falsan officers were being held as hostages until the signing of a peace treaty satisfactory to Panga. In the meantime the remainder of the Falsans were being permitted to depart for home, taking with them two ships loaded with provisions. They were faced with a march of some two thousand miles, with only humiliation and vain regret as their constant companions. Yesterday they had been a victorious army; today they were defeated and disarmed, their entire grand fleet captured by the Pangans.

"I do not envy the next girl who offers one of those men a drink," remarked Ero Shan.

We were taken to the headquarters of Banat, the Yorkokor who had caused our arrest; and he accompanied us to a still higher officer, a lotokor, or general; unless you are a Navy man, in which event you may call him an admiral. Banat explained the circumstances of our arrest, and repeated the statement that I had made to him at the time.

"Where are you from, if you are not from Falsa?" demanded the general. "Perhaps you are from Hangor or Maltor."

"Ero Shan is from Havatoo," I explained, "and I am from Korva, which lies beyond the mountain range to the south."

"There is nothing beyond that mountain range," said the general. "That is the end of the world. Were you to cross those mountains, you would fall into the sea of molten rock upon which Amtor floats."

"There are many countries beyond those mountains," I replied; "and I have lived in several of them ever since I first came to Amtor."

"Since you first came to Amtor!" exclaimed the general. "What do you mean by that? You must have been born on Amtor, and you couldn't have lived anywhere before you were born."

"I was not born on Amtor," I replied. "I was born in a world, which at its nearest approach to Amtor is 26,000,000 miles away."

"The man is mad," said the general. "There is no other world but Amtor."

"I am not so mad," I replied, "but that I can fight a gun and pilot a ship; and I would like the chance to do that for Panga until I can resume my search for my mate."

"Your mate? Where is she?"

"She, too, was captured by the Falsans when our anotar was shot down, but she escaped from them the night before they attacked Hor."

"What is an anotar?" he asked.

"It is a ship that flies in the air," I replied. "Ero Shan, my mate, and I were trying to reach Korva in it when the Falsans shot us down."

"A ship that flies in the air!" snorted the general. "First you tell me that you are from another world, and now you tell me that you ride around in a ship that flies in the air. Are you trying to insult my intelligence?"

"Possibly his last statement is true," said Banat. "I was talking with some of the Falsan officers at the jong's banquet last night, and they told me of this marvelous invention which they had shot down, in which two men and woman were riding through the sky."

"They were drunk," snapped the general.

"They told me this before they had started to drink," replied Banat. "I am sure that in this matter the man is speaking the truth."

"Well, if you want to assume the responsibility for them," said the general, "you may have them and assign them to such duties as you wish."

After we left the general I told Banat that I was more familiar with the small scout ships than with any others, and that I had been a prisoner on the 975, which was in the plaza before the palace and that I was perfectly capable of piloting it.

191

Banat took us to his own home, which seemed strange to me until I discovered that he was tremendously interested in what I had told him about another world than Amtor. He questioned me at length and showed a very intelligent interest in my explanation of our solar system.

"You mean to say that Amtor is a round ball flying around the thing you call the Sun?" he demanded. "And that it turns all the way around every day? Why don't we fall off when it's upside down? There's something, my friend, that you will have hard work explaining."

So then I had to explain gravity to him, and I think he grasped in a vague sort of way, but anyway he was terribly impressed with my knowledge, and he admitted that what I had told him explained many things that had hitherto puzzled him; the one that impressed him most being an explanation of the transition from night to day, which occurred with regularity every so many hours.

"Another thing that has always puzzled me," he said, "is how Amtor could float on a sea of molten rock without itself melting."

The upshot of our conversation was that he became so sufficiently impressed with my experience and erudition that he agreed to let me pilot the 975 and have Ero Shan aboard as a gunner.

Ero Shan and I devoted the next few days to getting the 975 in shipshape condition and erasing all signs of the battle through which she had passed. For this purpose Banat had detailed a number of Pangan mechanics, and as he had attached no officer to the 975, I was in charge of the work.

About ten days after our arrival in Hor, Banat told me that we were ordered out with a fleet that was to take the field the next day against the City of Hangor, whose men had been conducting raids against the Pangan herds all during their war with Falsa. It was to be a punitive expedition in which the captured Falsan land fleet was to be used. Hangor, he told me, lay on the coast, about five hundred miles east of Hor; and that it was founded hundreds of years ago by outlaws from Hor and from Onar, the capital of Falsa, who had become roving bandits. He said that they were a bad lot, and now that the war with Falsa was over, the Pangans would devote themselves to the destruction of Hangor. He assigned six men to complete the crew of the 975, and again he failed to appoint any officer, with the result that I went out in command. It seemed a loose and careless way of doing things, but I was to learn that that was one of the failings of the Pangans. They are at heart not a military people, and they often act impulsively and without due deliberation.

I noticed that as we moved toward Hangor there was nowhere near the efficiency displayed that had been apparent when the fleet had been in the possession of the Falsans. The ships must have been strung out over a distance of twenty miles. No scout ships were sent ahead, nor were there any flankers. Even when the fleet was within fifty miles of Hangor it was still not in battle formation, nor were the men on the ships at their stations.

We were paralleling a range of low hills at the time, when suddenly a fleet of fast cruisers and scout ships debouched from a ravine, and before the commander of the Pangan fleet knew what was happening, his force had been cut in two. Chemical shells and t-trays were striking the big ships from all directions, and the little scouts were launching their wheeled torpedos as they ranged up and down our lines, almost without opposition.

The tactics of the Hangors was entirely different in some respects from that of the Falsans. Their fast cruisers ranged up alongside of our big ships, and as they were getting into position, fighting men poured up from the lower decks until the upper decks were filled; and then they poured over our rails and, with r-guns and swords, fell upon our officers and crews from the bridges to the lower decks; and all the while their wicked little scout ships raised havoc up and down the line.

I got into a dogfight with three of them and was holding my own all right till one of their torpedos smashed my starboard track. That was the end of me as far as fighting was concerned; and when they saw that I was out of commission, they streaked off to continue harrassing the remainder of our fleet.

Within half an hour of the first attack many of our ships were disabled and the remainder were in full flight, many of them being pursued by fast cruisers and the little scouts.

"Here's where we change navies," said Ero Shan.

"It's all right with me if they'll have us," I replied; "and almost any navy would be better than the Pangans'. I never saw such glaring inefficiency and stupidity in my life."

"No wonder the Falsans said they were fools," remarked Ero Shan.

"While nobody is paying any attention to us," I said to Ero Shan, "let's make a break for those hills."

"An excellent idea," he said; and then he turned to the Pangan members of our crew. "How about it?" he asked.

"They'd only catch us," said one of the men; "and they'd kill us for trying to escape."

"All right," I said, "do as you please. Come on, Ero Shan," and we jumped from the 975 and started for the hills.

FORTY-NINE

We reached the hills apparently without being observed, but after going up the canyon a short distance we clambered up its side until we reached an elevation from which we could look out over the plains. We could see the 975 and standing beside it the Pangan crew waiting to be made prisoners. In all directions we could see the Pangan ships racing to escape, and the fast cruisers and the scout ships of the Hangors clinging to them relentlessly. Many Pangan ships were out of commission and others had been captured in battle. It was a complete rout, a decisive defeat, and I imagined that the Hangors would go on stealing Pangan herds indefinitely. We remained where we were until the victorious fleet started for Hangor with their prizes and their prisoners. Such disabled ships as they could move at all they towed behind undamaged Pangan battleships.

Now, assured that our flight had not been noticed, we came down into the canyon and made our way back to the 975, where we knew we could find food and water in her lockers.

Before it became too dark we examined the damage that had been done the little scouting ship, and discovered that a day's work might put it in running condition again; for there were tools and spare parts aboard.

We started to work immediately, but when darkness fell we had to abandon it.

After we had eaten we discussed our plans and decided to try to find Onar, the capital of Falsa, where we believed Duare

194

might be a prisoner. We thought that by hugging the foot of the northern mountain range we should be far enough away from any city, and off the beaten track so far that there would be no danger of our being discovered; and once in Onar I was sure that we would be well received, for we had fought with the Falsan fleet and no one there would know that we had also fought on the side of the Pangans. And so we laid our plans, and with such assurance of success that they seemed almost accomplished by the time we fell asleep.

The next morning we were up before dawn, had breakfast, and started working on the track the moment that it was light again.

We worked like a couple of galley slaves under the lash and by mid-afternoon the work was completed.

"There," I said, as we crawled out from under the 975, "in two shakes of a dead lamb's tail we'll be on our way;" and then I saw Ero Shan looking past me at something, and from the hopeless expression on his face, I guessed that what he saw was not pleasant.

I turned slowly around. Almost upon us were some fifty very savage-looking men mounted upon zorats, those weird-looking creatures which Amtorians use for saddle animals, but which I hate to dignify with the name of horse.

They are about the size of a small horse, with long slender legs suggesting great speed. Their feet are round and nail-less, and heavily calloused on the bottom. Their almost vertical pasterns suggest that they might be a hard-gaited beast, but this is not so, for their almost horizontal femurs and humeri absorb the jolts and render the zorat an easy-riding saddle animal. Above their withers and also just forward of their kidneys are soft pads or miniature humps, which form a perfect saddle with natural pummel and cantle. Their heads are short and broad with two large, saucer-like eyes and pendulous ears. Their teeth are those of a herbivore, but they can use them effectively as weapons when their short tempers are aroused, although their principal means of defense is their quickness.

The men who now surrounded us carried r-ray rifles and pistols as well as swords. They wore gaudy loincloths of many colors, and turbans of similar patterns, which were wound around their heads, leaving one end about a yard long, which hung down over their left shoulders. Their scowling faces were as hard as granite.

"What are you doing, Pangans?" demanded one of them.

"We are not Pangans," I said; "and we were trying to repair this ship so that we could go to Hangor and get directions for getting out of this country without being captured by the Pangans again."

"You were prisoners of the Pangans?" he asked.

"Yes," I said. "They brought us along with them when they came to attack Hangor yesterday."

"Will that ship run?" asked the man.

"No," I replied; "and it never will. It cannot be repaired."

"If you are not Pangans," the fellow continued, "you must be either Falsans or Maltors. Which are you?"

"Neither," I said.

"You must be lying," he said. "There are no other cities in Anlap."

"We are not from Anlap," I told him.

"Where are you from then?"

"From California," I replied. "It's a little country that's not at war with anybody, and certainly not with Hangor."

He had two of his men dismount and disarm us and then he ordered us up behind two others, and we set off in the direction of Hangor.

The zorats were very fleet and apparently tireless and we must have covered fifteen or twenty miles before we came to a camp just before dark. The camp was in a forest at the edge of a stream at the mouth of a canyon, in which I could see a large herd of Amtorian cattle.

In the camp of these herders, who were also warriors, there were a number of women, but no children; and when we arrived the women were cooking the evening meal. I say cooking the evening meal—they were cooking a part of it, boiling vegetables over many individual fires. The rest of the meal consisted of meat which they ate raw, the women passing it on huge platters and the men cutting strips from it as they went by.

They were certainly a rough lot, and during the meal and after it there were several bloody fights, mostly over women. I saw one man badly beaten up because he looked at a woman too long. Though they fought viciously upon the slightest provocation, or upon none at all, they did not use their weapons, relying entirely upon their hands, feet, and teeth to inflict damage upon their adversaries. It is a point of honor among them that they do not kill one another, and if one should transgress this unwritten law, the others would fall upon him and kill him.

There was quite a little discussion concerning Ero Shan and myself and the location of California.

"It is a little country that is not at war with us," explained one of the party which had captured us; "and they are going to Hangor to get someone to tell them how to get out of this country and get back to California."

At that everybody laughed.

"You just go right up to Jeft when you get to Hangor," said one of the men, "and tell him you want someone to show you the way back to California;" then everybody laughed again.

"What is so funny?" I asked one of them.

"You would think it funny, too, if you knew Jeft," he replied.

"Who is Jeft?"

"He is our jong; and he is a real jong, too. No slave has ever escaped from Hangor since Jeft became jong."

"You are going to take us back to Hangor to put us into slavery?" I asked.

"Of course," replied the man who had captured us.

"Have you ever been a slave?" asked one of them.

"Yes," I said.

"Well, don't think that you know what slavery is until after you have been one of Jeft's slaves. Then you can boast, if you live through it."

After a while they told us that we could go to sleep, and we curled up on the ground at one side of the camp. "Jeft must be a pleasant person," remarked Ero Shan.

"The Myposans were not pleasant people," I said; "neither were the Brokols, nor the Vooyorgans; but I lived through captivity with them, and I escaped."

"May your luck hold here," said Ero Shan drowsily, and fell asleep.

Early the next morning they mounted us on a couple of zorats and sent us with a guard of five men toward Hangor, which we reached late that afternoon.

Hangor is a mean little walled city, with narrow, crooked filthy streets, lined with hovels which one could not dignify with the name of houses. Slatternly women sat in the doorways and dirty children played in the filth of the streets.

The jong's house, to which we were immediately taken, was larger, but no less disreputable than the others.

Jeft was sitting in an open courtyard in the center of his house when we were taken before him. He was an extremely gross and brutal-looking man, wearing a filthy loincloth that had once had a pattern and a similarly disreputable turban. He was drinking something from an enormous tankard and spilling a great deal of it over his chin and down his front.

"What have we here?" he bellowed, as we were led before him.

"Two men from California who escaped from the Pangans during the battle day before yesterday," explained one of the men who had brought us.

"From California, hey?" demanded Jeft. "I've just been waiting to get my hands on one of you zorat thieves from California."

"Oh," I said, "so you are familiar with California, are you?"

"Of course I'm familiar with California," he fairly shouted. "Who says I ain't? You mean to call me a liar? What do you want in my country anyway, comin' in here and calling me a liar?"

"I didn't call you a liar," I said. "I was just pleased to know that you were familiar with California."

"There you go calling me a liar again. If I say you called me a liar, you did call me a liar."

"However, I am still pleased to know you are familiar with California," I said.

"You don't think I'm familiar with California; you don't think I've ever been to California. So! You don't think I've ever been to California, when I say I have. What do you mean, coming here and looking for trouble!"

I did not reply, and he immediately flew into another frenzy. "Why don't you answer me?" he demanded.

"What's the use of answering you when you know all the answers?" I said. "You even know about a country that you never heard of before, and it lies on another world 26,000,000 miles from Amtor. You are a big bag of wind, Jeft, and if I failed to call you a liar before, I do now."

I knew that we could expect no mercy from this man and that nothing I might say to him might make it any easier or any harder for us while we were here. He was an ignorant and a degraded bully and I had taken all from him that I intended to, let come what might. My words had an entirely different effect upon him that I had anticipated. Like the bag of wind that I had termed him, he deflated as though he had been punctured. He took a big swallow from the tankard, to hide what I imagine was his embarrassment, and then said to the men who had brought us, "Take them away and turn them over to Stalar; and tell him to see that they work."

FIFTY

We were taken through crooked streets, some of them ankle deep in filth, to what appeared to be the extreme limits of the city; and there in a filthy room beside the city walls we were turned over to Stalar. He was a tall man, with thin, cruel lips and close-set eyes. He wore two r-ray pistols and there was a heavy whip lying on the desk in front of him.

"Where are you from?" he asked.

"From California," I replied.

At that he leaped up and seized the whip. "Don't lie to me," he shouted; "you are Pangans."

I shrugged. "All right; have it your own way," I said. "What you or any of the rest of your filthy tribe think doesn't interest me."

At that he came around the desk, the whip in his hand.

"What you need is a lesson, slave," he growled.

I looked him straight in the eye. "If you strike me with that, I'll kill you," I said; "and if you don't think I can, just try it."

The yellow cur backed down. "Who said I was going to strike you?" he said. "I told you I was going to teach you a lesson, and I am—but I haven't got time to bother with you two now. Get on into the compound;" and he unlocked a gate in the outer wall, beyond which was a large enclosure crowded with men, nearly all of whom were prisoners taken from the Pangan fleet.

One of the first men I saw was Banat, the Pangan officer who had befriended us. He looked terribly dejected; but when he saw us, he came up and spoke to us.

"I thought you had escaped," he said.

"We thought so, too," I replied.

"My men on your ship told me that you had gotten away safely into the hills."

"We did, but we came down to the 975 again for food, and we were captured by a band of Hangorian herders. How are they treating you here?"

He turned his back toward me, revealing a dozen raw welts. "That is how they treat us," he said. "They are building an addition to the city, and trying to speed it up with whips."

"I don't think I can take it," I said.

"You had better take it," he replied. "I saw two men resist yesterday, and they were both shot dead on the spot."

"That might be the easiest way out," I said.

"I have thought of that," he said, "But one clings to life. There is always hope."

"Maybe Carson can get away with it," said Ero Shan; "he just got away with murder with the jong and with the fellow called Stalar; and they both backed down."

"Some of these slave-drivers they have over us won't back down," said Banat; "they haven't the mentality of a nobargan."

After a while some women entered the compound carrying food to us. It was a filthy mess, in filthy vessels; and not enough to give each man half a meal.

"Who are the women?" I asked Banat.

"They are slaves that have been captured in raids; their fate is even worse than ours."

"I can imagine so," I said, thinking of the bestial creatures who passed for men in Hangor.

The next morning we were given another similar meal, and taken out to work; and when I say work, I mean work. We were set to cutting and carrying the lava rock with which they were building the wall around the new part of the city. Twenty-five or thirty slave-drivers with r-ray pistols and whips stood over us; and if they saw a man stop even to wipe the sweat from his face, they struck him.

I was set to cutting rock at some little distance from the new wall, but I could see that there were women slaves working there, mixing and laying the mortar in which the rocks were set. After a while Stalar came out among us. He seemed to be looking for someone, and I had a rough idea that he was looking for me. At last he found me.

"How is this slave working?" he asked the slave-driver, who was standing over us.

"All right so far," said the man; "he is very strong. He can lift rocks easily that any two other slaves have to strain to lift."

"Watch him," said Stalar, "and beat him until he screams for mercy if he shirks his work or gives you any trouble; for I can tell you that he is a trouble-maker." Then he walked away.

"What has Stalar got against you?" asked the guard, after the chief slave-driver was out of hearing.

"I haven't the slightest idea," I said, "Unless it is that he thinks I am a Pangan."

"Aren't you?" asked the guard.

"No," I replied; but I was careful to keep on working diligently all the time, for fear the man was looking for an excuse for whipping me. I had decided that it was foolish to antagonize them up to a point where they would kill me; for there must always be the hope of escape and eventual reunion with Duare if she still lived.

"Stalar's a mean one," said the guard.

"Is he?" I asked. "He has never harmed me."

"Wait," said the man; "he'll get you. I can tell by the way he spoke that he has something against you."

"He wanted you to take it out on me," I said.

"I guess that's right," assented the guard; "but you go on doing your work and I won't bother you. I don't get pleasure out of beating the men the way some of the others do."

"I guess you're a pretty decent fellow," I said.

After I had cut a number of building blocks to the correct size, the guard told me to carry them over to the walls. The guard at the walls told me where to put them down, and I deposited them beside a woman slave who was laying mortar. As I did so, she turned and looked at me, and my heart leaped to my mouth—it was Duare.

I was about to speak, but she silenced me with a finger to her lips; and then she whispered out of the corner of her mouth, "They will beat us both if we speak."

I felt a stinging lash across my back, and turned to face the guard who was overseeing the work at this part of the wall. "What do you mean by loafing around here?" he demanded.

My first impulse was to kill him, and then I thought of Duare. I knew I must suffer anything, for now I must live. I turned and walked away to bring more rock. The fellow struck me again as I was going, the lash wrapping around my body and bringing blood.

When I got back to my rock pile the guard there saw the welts on my body. "Why did you get those?" he asked.

"The guard at the wall said that I was loafing," I replied.

"Were you?" he asked.

"You know that I do not loaf," I answered.

"That's right," he said; "I'll go with you the next load you carry."

I picked up two more of the building stones, which was one more than any of the other slaves could carry, and started back toward the wall, my guard accompanying me.

When I put the rocks down by Duare, I stooped close to her and brushed my arm against her body. "Courage," I whispered. "I will find a way."

As I stood up the wall guard came up, swinging his whip.

"Loafing around here again, hey?" he demanded, carrying his whip hand back.

"He was not loafing," said my guard. "Leave him alone; he belongs to me."

"I'll whip any lazy slave I want to," said the wall guard; "and you, too, as far as that's concerned;" and he started to lay the lash on my guard. I jumped him then and seized his whip. It was a foolish thing to do, but I was seeing red. I took the whip away from him as easily as though he had been a baby; and when he drew an r-ray pistol I took that from him, too.

Now Stalar came charging up. "What's going on here?" he demanded.

"This slave just tried to kill me," said the wall guard; "he should be beaten to death."

Duare was looking on, her eyes wide with terror—terror for what might be going to happen to me. I must say that I was considerable concerned myself, for my brief experience with these cruel, sadistic guards suggested that Stalar might order the wall guard's suggestion put into execution. Then my guard intervened.

"If I were you, Stalar," he said, "I'd do nothing of the sort. This guard was attacking me when the slave came to my rescue. He did nothing more than disarm the man. He offered him no harm."

I could see that Stalar was furious, but he only said, "Get back to your work, all of you; and see that there is no more of this." And then his eyes fell upon Duare. "Get to work, slave," he snapped, and raised his whip to strike her. I stepped between them. "Don't!" I said. Stalar hesitated. He will never know how near death he was then, but he was yellow all the way through, and he was afraid of me.

"Get to work," he repeated, and turned on his heel and walked away.

I went back to my rock pile then with my guard. "That was very decent of you," I said, "and I thank you, but won't it get you into trouble?"

"No," he said. "Jeft, the jong, is my uncle."

I looked at him in surprise. "I must say," I blurted carelessly, "you don't take after your uncle."

To my relief the guard grinned. "My mother was a Pangan slave woman," he said. "I think I must take after her. The Pangans are not a cruel people."

This guard, whose name was Omat, had revealed such a surprisingly sympathetic nature that I felt that I might with safety ask a favor of him, and I was about to broach the matter when he, himself, gave me an opening.

"Why did you risk your life to protect that slave girl from Stalar?" he asked. "It seems to me that you have already stirred up enough trouble for yourself without doing that."

"She is my mate," I said. "We were captured by the Falsans and separated. I had no idea what had become of her until I saw her laying mortar at that wall. I wish that I might talk with her."

He thought this over for a moment and then he said, "Perhaps I can arrange it for you. You are a good worker, and I don't think you would ever make any trouble if they left you alone. You have done twice the work for me of any other slave, and you have done it without grumbling."

FIFTY-ONE

That evening, when the female slaves brought our supper to us, I noticed that Omat was in charge of them. He called my name, and when I answered and walked over to him, I saw that Duare was with him. I had not noticed her at first because she had been hidden from me by some of the other slave women.

"Here is your mate," said Omat. "I shall let her remain here while you eat; and you needn't hurry," he added.

I took Duare's hand and pressed it, and we walked off to one side, a little way from the other slaves, and sat down on the ground together. At first neither of us could speak; we just sat there holding hands.

Presently Duare said, "I never expected to see you again. What strange fate brought us together again in Hangor?"

"Providence has been so unkind to us," I said, "that maybe it is trying to make it up to us a little now. But tell me what happened to you, and how it is that you are here."

"It is not a very pleasant story," she said.

"I know, dear," I said, "but tell me what you did after you killed Vantor—and of course it was you who killed him."

She nodded. "Yes. It was in the middle of the night. Everybody on the ship was asleep, including the sentry at the door, which had been left open. I simply walked out; it was that easy; but I didn't know which way to go. My only thought was to get away somewhere and hide, for I knew that if they caught me they would kill me because of what I had done. And in the morning I lay down in some tall grass and slept. When I awoke I saw the battle fleet of the Falsans moving toward the east. I knew you were with it, and though I never expected to see you again, I went along in the same direction, to be as near to you as possible.

"After a while I came to a little stream where I drank and bathed; and then, refreshed, I went on again; but by this time the fleet was out of sight. And then in the middle of the afternoon I saw one of those little scout ships coming toward me and I hid, but evidently they had seen me, for they came directly to my hiding place.

"Half a dozen of these terrible Hangors got out of the ship and seized me. It would have been as senseless as it would have been futile to try to escape them.

"I soon realized that I had fallen into the hands of some very terrible people, and that it was useless to expect either sympathy or kindness from them. Like the bandits they are, they were out looking for any sort of loot or prey they could find. They send these ships out constantly and sometimes in great numbers, especially after a battle between the Falsans and the Pangans, when they prey upon disabled ships, looting them and taking prisoners.

"The ship I was on was really scouting the battle that they knew was imminent, but in the meantime looking for anything else they could pick up. They continued on to the west and presently discovered our disabled anotar. They could not make out what it was, and when I told them they would not believe me, and one of them flew into a terrible rage because he thought that I was lying to them. I sometimes think that many of them are quite mad."

"I am sure of it," I said. "No normal mind could be as cruel and unreasoning as some of these Hangors. But go on with your story."

"There is not much more to it," she replied. "They stole everything that they could from the anotar, demolished the instruments and the engine, and then came back toward Hangor; and here I am and here are you."

"At least we are together again," I said, "and that is something; for now we can plan on escaping."

"You are always the optimist," said Duare.

"I have escaped before," I reminded her.

"I know," she said, "but somehow this seems so terribly hopeless. Even if we escape from Hangor, we have no way of escaping from the country. Our beloved anotar has been destroyed, and from what I have been told, the mountains to the south are absolutely impassable; and the land is full of enemies."

"I refuse to give up hope," I said.

"What became of poor Ero Shan?" she asked, after a moment's silence.

"He is here," I said; "and I have another friend here, a Pangan officer named Banat. Between the four of us we may be able to cook up some scheme for escape. By the way, where are you quartered?"

"It is just the other side of that wall," she said. "The men's and the women's compounds adjoin. They tell me that they used to herd them all in together, but there were so many fights, and so many men slaves were killed, that they had to segregate them."

The slaves had finished their meal by this time and the women had returned from their compound to take away the empty bowls. Omat came with them, and beckoned to Duare. We stood up, and I held her in my arms for just a moment; then she was gone. It was good to have had her to myself for even this short time and I felt far more hopeful than I had since she had been taken from the Falsan flagship, though I must admit that my hope lived on very meager fare.

After Duare left I went over and sat down with Ero Shan and Banat.

"Why didn't you come over and see Duare?" I asked Ero Shan.

"You could have so little time together," he said, "that I did not want to rob you of any of it."

"She inquired about you," I said, "and I told her that you were here and that we also had another friend in Banat; and that the four of us should be able to work out some plan whereby we might escape."

"Whatever it is," said Ero Shan, "you can count me in on it. I would rather be killed trying to escape than to remain here to be beaten to death."

The next day Stalar assigned me to another job. I was sent with a dozen other slaves, who, for one reason or another, he particularly disliked, to a large corral where a number of zorats were kept. It was so filled with accumulated filth that the animals were knee deep in it, and could move around only with the greatest effort.

While the work was offensive and nauseating in the extreme, it had one advantage in that the guards were not near enough to us to crack us with their whips; and as they wouldn't come down into the filth, they sat on the fence and swore at us.

This was all right while we were loading the carts, but we had to push them about a mile outside the city to dump them, where their contents could later be used for fertilizing the fields where they raised vegetables and grain for the zorats that are kept up. It was while we were pushing the carts that the guards could get at us, and then they made up for lost time. One of the guards soon discovered that I was much stronger and much faster than any of the other slaves, so he attached himself to me and made a game of it. He laid wagers with another guard that I could load faster, pull heavier loads, and get them out to the dumping ground sooner than any of the other slaves; and in order to encourage me, he laid on with his lash.

I took it because I had found Duare, and I didn't want anything to happen to me now.

The other guard had picked out a husky slave, on which he had placed his wager, and he stood over him, lashing him furiously to make him work faster. The wager was on the number of full loads we could take out to the dump during the remainder of the day and a certain amount of money was to be paid on each load which either slave took out more than the other.

It was soon obvious that I should win money for my guard, but the fellow was greedy to collect all that he could; so he lashed me out and lashed me back, until I was covered with raw welts and the blood was running down my back and sides.

Notwithstanding my anger and my suffering, I managed to control my temper until I felt that I could stand no more. On one trip I got out to the dump after the others had all unloaded and started the return trip to the corral. This left my guard and myself alone at the dump, a mile away from the city and with no one near us. I am a very powerful man, but I was about ready to drop from exhaustion. The afternoon was only about half over, and I knew that the fool would kill me if this went on until night; and as we reached the dump I turned and faced him, leaning on the forked tool which I had been using to load and unload the cart.

"If you were not a fool," I said, "you would not waste your energy and mine by beating me. Pretty soon I shall not have strength enough left to pull the cart after I have loaded it."

"Shut up, you lazy beast!" he cried, "and get to work;" and then he came for me with his whip again.

I jumped forward and seized the whip and jerked it from his hand; and when he started to draw his pistol, I raised the tool as though it had been a spear and drove it into his chest.

It must have pierced his heart, for he died almost instantly. I stooped over his body and took his r-ray pistol from him, concealing it beneath my loincloth; then I laid him near the cart and unloaded its contents upon him until he was completely hidden—a filthy thing buried beneath filth.

FIFTY-TWO

I had murdered a guard and I could imagine what the penalty would be, but I hoped that I had hidden the evidence of my crime sufficiently well to prevent detection. Unless the body were discovered, they couldn't very well establish the corpus delicti; in fact, they couldn't even know that a crime had been committed. However, I will admit that I was a little bit nervous as I returned to the corral alone, and I was still more nervous when the other guard, who had accepted the wager, accosted me.

"Where is your guard?" he demanded.

"He followed you back," I said. "He thought that you were having other guards' slaves help your slave load his cart, and he wanted to catch you at it."

"He's a liar," snapped the man, looking around. "Where is he?"

"He must be here," I said, "for he is not with me;" and then I started loading my cart again.

The disappearance of my guard might have constituted an absorbing mystery if the other guard had told anybody about it, but he didn't. He was too crooked and too greedy. Instead, he told me to slow down or he would beat the life out of me.

"If you will protect me from the other guards," I said, "I will work so slow that you will be sure to win."

"See that you do," he said; and so I took it easy all the rest of the afternoon.

At quitting time the guard whose slave had been pitted against me was really worried. He had won his wager, but there was no one from whom to collect his winnings.

"Are you sure your guard came back to the corral?" he asked me.

"That's where he said he was going when he left me," I replied. "Of course, I was working so hard that I didn't watch him."

"It is very strange," he said. "I can't understand it."

When the women slaves brought our food to us that evening Omat was not with them, but Duare was there and she brought my bowl to me. Ero Shan and Banat were with me. I had outlined a bold plan to them and they both had agreed to see it through or die in the attempt.

As Duare joined us we gathered around her, trying to hide her from the guards; and then we moved off into a far corner of the compound, in the shadow of one of the shelters beneath which the slaves slept.

Duare sat down on the ground and we crowded around her, effectually hiding her from view from any part of the compound. There were only two guards, and they were engrossed in conversation. One of them had come with the women, and when they left he would leave, returning only when they collected the empty bowls. The guards were always sleepy at night and they didn't bother us unless some slave raised a disturbance, and night offered the only rest that we had from their cruelty.

As I ate I explained my plan to Duare, and presently I saw that she was crying. "Why the tears?" I asked. "What is the matter?"

"Your poor body," she said; "it is covered with welts and blood. They must have beaten you horribly today."

"It was worth it," I said, "for the man who did it is dead, and I have his pistol hidden beneath my loincloth. Because of these welts, which will soon heal, we have a chance to escape."

"I am glad you killed him," she said. "I should have hated to live on, knowing that a man who had treated you so still lived."

After a while the women slaves came back and collected the empty bowls, and we were fearful that one of the slave women might discover Duare and expose her; but if any of them saw her, they said nothing; and they were soon gone, and their guard with them.

We waited until nearly midnight, long after the compound had quieted down and the slaves had fallen asleep. The single guard sat with his back against the gate that opened out toward the corral where I had worked that day. Another gate opened into the city and a third into the compound of the female slaves; but these it was not necessary to guard, as no slaves could escape in either of these directions. I stood up and walked over toward him, and as he was dozing he did not notice me until I was quite near him; then he leaped to his feet.

"What are you doing here, slave?" he demanded.

"Sh!" I said. "I have just heard something that you ought to know."

"What is it?" he asked.

"Not so loud," I said in a whisper; "if they know that I am telling you, they will kill me."

He came closer to me, all attention now. "Well, what is it?"

"Four slaves are planning on escaping tonight," I told him. "One of them is going to kill you first. Don't say anything now, but look over there to your left." And as he looked I drew the pistol from beneath my loincloth and placing it over his heart, pressed the button. Without a sound he died, falling forward upon his face.

I stooped and quickly lifted him into a sitting position, propped against the wall beside the gate; then I took his pistol from him, and looking back saw that Duare, Ero Shan, and Banat were tiptoeing toward me.

We spoke no word as I opened the gate and let them out. Following them, I closed it gently.

I handed the extra pistol to Ero Shan, and then led them down to the corral where the zorats were confined. Stealthily we stole among the brutes, speaking soothingly to them, for they are nervous and short-tempered. They milled a little and tried to move away from us, but finally we each captured one, seizing them by an ear, which is the way they are led and controlled.

We led them down to the gate, which I opened, and then we mounted. No saddles or bridles are used upon the creatures; one guides them and stops them by pulling on their long, pendulous ears. A pull on the right ear turns them to the right, a pull on the left ear to the left, and by pulling on both ears they may be stopped. They are urged forward by kicking them with the heels, while a gentle pull on both ears slows them down.

As the zorats' corral is outside the city wall, we were, for the time being at least, free; and as soon as we had left the city a short distance behind, we put heels to our weird mounts and sped up the broad valley at top speed. There was to be no rest for those zorats that night, nor for us either, for we must pass the camp of the herders before daylight, if we were to be reasonably safe from detection and pursuit.

It was a hard ride, but we felt that it would be a successful one. We had the hills on the left to guide us, and the big eyes of our mounts permitted them to see in the dim light of an Amtorian night.

Duare and I rode side by side, with Banat and Ero Shan directly behind us. The padded feet of the zorats gave forth no sound and we rode like ghosts through the darkness.

Presently Ero Shan moved up beside me. "We are being pursued," he said. "I just happened to look back and I saw a number of mounted men following us, and they are gaining on us rapidly."

"Give Banat your pistol," I said, "and then you go ahead with Duare. You will find plenty of arms and ammunition on board the 975."

"No," said Duare decisively, "I shall not leave you. We will stay together until the end."

I knew from her tone of voice that it was futile to argue, so I told them that we would have to ride faster; and I urged my zorat to even greater speed.

They may not be very beautiful, but they are really wonderful little saddle animals. They are almost as fast as a deer and have tremendous endurance, but they had come a long way and I didn't know whether they would hold out or not.

Looking back, I saw what appeared to be quite a number of mounted men bearing down on us rapidly. "I guess we are going to have to fight," I said to Ero Shan.

"We can get a few of them before they get us," he replied.

"I won't go back to Hangor," said Duare; "I won't! Kill me before they can get me, Carson; promise me that you will."

"If I fall," I replied, "you ride on to the 975;" and then I told her how to start the motor, which was quite similar to that of the anotar with which she was so familiar. The fuel used in the motor is the same as that which we used in the anotar. The element 93 (vik-ro) is released upon a substance called lor, which contains a considerable proportion of the element yor-san (105). The action of the vik-ro upon the yor-san results in absolute annihilation of the lor, releasing all its

211

energy. When you consider that there is 18,000,000,000 times as much energy liberated by the annihilation of a ton of coal as by its combustion, you will appreciate the inherent possibilities of this marvellous Amtorian scientific discovery. Fuel for the life of the 975 could be carried in a pint jar.

After a brief argument I persuaded Duare to promise me that if I fell she would try to reach the 975, and seek a passage through the southern mountains beyond which we were positive Korva lay. And then the pursuers were upon us.

FIFTY-THREE

As I turned on my mount, my r-ray pistol ready in my hand, prepared to sell my life dearly, I heard Ero Shan laugh and an instant later I had to laugh myself.

"What are you laughing at?" demanded Duare.

"Look," I said; "our pursuers are the zorats which escaped from the corral and followed after their companions."

We must have passed the herders' camp just before dawn, and later on in the morning we saw the 975, far ahead of us, where we had left it. I was greatly worried for fear the herders might have been there ahead of us and damaged it in some way, but when we reached it we found it in the same shape that we had left it; but we did not relinquish our zorats until I had started the engine and demonstrated to my own satisfaction that the 975 was in running order, then we turned them loose and they started grazing around us with their fellows.

I told Ero Shan and Banat to be prepared to fight either the port, starboard, or stern guns, if the necessity arose, and I kept Duare up forward with me, for she could fire the bow gun if we got into action, a thing none of us anticipated.

Banat wanted to return to Hor, where, he assured me, we would be well received, but I was fearful to risk Duare further, and Hor might again be in the hands of the Falsans. I told Banat, however, that I would approach Hor after dark, and that he could then make his way on foot to the city; and he agreed that that was fair enough.

"I should have liked, however, to have shown you some of the real hospitality of Hor."

"We were witnesses of the hospitality of Hor," I replied.

Banat laughed. "We are not such fools as the Falsans think us," he said.

"Look!" said Duare excitedly. "There is a ship approaching." We all looked then, and sure enough, off our starboard bow we could see a small scout ship racing toward us.

"The only way we can avoid a fight," I said, "is by turning back, and I certainly don't want to do that."

"Then let's fight," said Duare.

"What do you think she is, Banat?" I asked.

He took a long look and then he replied, "She is one of those fast Hangor faltars, as we call them." Faltar means pirate ship, and is a contraction of the combination of the two words fal, meaning kill, and anotar, ship. "And they are fast," he added. "I doubt if the 975 could run away from her."

I swung around and headed right toward her, and as soon as we were within range Duare commenced firing chemical shells. She made a clean hit on the bow, right in front of the pilot's seat; and then she sent a stream of t-rays for the mark. They were firing their bow gun, too, but they were not so fortunate as we, or else they didn't have as good a gunner, for they scored nothing but clean misses.

We had both slowed down to permit greater accuracy in our fire, and were approaching each other slowly now, when suddenly the faltar veered to the left and I could tell instantly from her erratic maneuvering that the pilot had been hit. Their starboard gun was bearing on us now, but Duare had the whole side of their ship as a target, and our starboard gun could now also be brought to bear. Several chemical shells hit us. I could hear the plop of their bursting, and both Duare and Ero Shan, who was manning our starboard gun, scored hits with chemical shells, which they followed immediately with their deadly t-rays.

In the meantime Banat had run a torpedo into the starboard tube and now he launched it. It went straight for its target, and the explosion which followed nearly capsized the faltar, and put her completely out of commission.

It was a short fight, but a sweet one while it lasted. However, I was glad to turn away and resume our journey toward Hor, leaving the disabled Hangor ship still firing at us futilely.

We drew off a few miles and then got out and examined the hull of the 975. There were several places where the t-ray insulation had been dissolved, and these we patched up with new insulation before we proceeded.

I asked Banat if it were true that no one had ever crossed the mountains to the south, or seen any indications of a pass through them.

"As far as I know," he said, "they have never been crossed, but on one or two occasions our herders have reported that when the clouds rose up, as you know they sometimes do, they have seen what appeared to be a low place in the range."

"Have you any idea where it is?" I asked.

"It is about due south of Hor," he replied. "That is where our best grazing land is."

"Well, we'll hope that the clouds rise up when we get there," I said; "but whether they do or not, we are going to cross the southern range."

"I wish you luck," said Banat; "and you'll need it, especially if you succeed in getting into the mountains at all."

"Why?" I asked.

"The Cloud People," he replied.

"Who are they?" I demanded. "I never heard of them."

"They live in the mountains, always among the clouds. They come down and steal our cattle occasionally and when they do, every portion of their bodies is covered with fur garments, with only holes for their eyes and a hole to breathe through. They cannot stand our dry atmosphere. In olden times people used to think that they were a hairy race of men until our herdsmen killed one of them, when we discovered that their skin was extremely thin and without pores. It is believed that they must perspire through their noses and mouths. When the body of the one who was killed by our herders was exposed to the air the skin shriveled up as though it had been burned."

"Why should we fear them?" I asked.

"There is a legend that they eat human flesh," replied Banat. "Of course, that may be only a legend in which there is no truth. I do not know."

"They wouldn't stand much chance against the 975," said Ero Shan.

"You may have to abandon the 975," suggested Banat; "a lantar, you know, is not exactly built for mountain climbing."

It was well after dark when we appraoached Hor. Banat

214

importuned us again to come into the city. He said that at the gate it would be revealed whether the Falsans were still occupying Hor.

"As much as I'd like to," I said, "I cannot take the chance. If the Falsans are guarding your gates, a single lucky shot might put us out of commission; and you well know that they would never let a strange lantar get away from them without some sort of a fight."

"I suppose you are right," he said; and then he thanked me again for aiding in his escape, and bidding us good-by, he started off on foot for the city and was soon lost in the darkness. That, perhaps, is the last time that I shall ever see the yorkokor Banat, the Pangan.

And now we moved slowly through the night toward the south, and our hearts were filled with thankfulness that we had come this far in safety, and our minds with conjecture as to what lay ahead of us in the fastnesses of the mountains which no man had ever crossed, the mountains in which dwelt the Cloud People who were supposed to eat human flesh.

FIFTY-FOUR

When morning came we saw the mountains far away to the south of us, their summits hidden in the eternal clouds. Only the lower slopes were visible up to an altitude of some five thousand feet. What lay above that was the mystery which we must solve. As we approached more closely we saw a herd of zaldars, the Amtorian beef cattle. Several herders, who had discovered us, were attempting to drive them toward the mountains, with the evident intention of hiding them in a canyon which opened in front of them and where they evidently believed a lantar could not follow.

A zaldar is a most amazing appearing animal. It has a large, foolish-looking head, with big, oval eyes, and two long, pointed ears that stand perpetually upright as though the creature were always listening. It has no neck and its body is all rounded curves. Its hind legs resemble in shape those of a bear; its front legs are similar to an elephant's, though, of course, on a much smaller scale. Along its spine rises a single row of bristles. It has no tail and no neck, and from its snout depends a long tassel of hair. Its upper jaw is equipped with broad, shovel-like teeth, which always protrude beyond its short, tiny lower jaw. Its skin is covered with short hair of a neutral mauve color, with large patches of violet, which, especially when it is lying down, make it almost invisible against the pastel shades of Amtorian scenery. When it feeds it drops down on its knees and scrapes up the turf with its shovel-like teeth, and then draws it into its mouth with a broad tongue. It also has to kneel down when it drinks, for, as I have said before, it has no neck. Notwithstanding its strange and clumsy appearance, it is very fast, and the herders, mounted on the zorats, soon disappeared with the entire herd into the mouth of the canyon, the herders evidently believing us to be raiders.

I should like to have had one of the zaldars for some fresh beef, but although the 975 could have overhauled the herd and I could have shot some of the beasts, I would not do so because I realized that they belonged to the Pangans.

As the canyon into which the herders had driven their charges seemed to be a large one, and as it lay directly south of Hor, I felt that we should explore it; and so I piloted the 975 into it.

We had advanced but a short distance into the canyon when we saw fully a hundred herders lined up across the mouth of a narrow side canyon, into which they had evidently driven their herd. The men were all armed with r-ray rifles, and as soon as we came within sight, they dropped down behind the stone wall which served both as a fence to pen their herd and as a breastworks behind which to defend it.

We had been running without colors, as we really didn't know what we were and couldn't have decided until we had been able to see the colors of any potential enemy, when we would immediately have run up his colors on the flagstaff that rises above the pilot's seat.

Positive that these were Pangan herders, and not wishing to get into a fight with them or anyone else, I now ran up the Pangan ensign.

A man stood up behind the breastwork then and shouted, "Who are you?"

"Friends," I replied. "Come over. I want to talk to you."

"Anyone can run up a Pangan ensign," he replied. "What are your names?"

"You don't know us," I replied, "but we are friends of the yorkokor Banat, whom we have just left at Hor."

"He was captured by the Hangors," replied the man.

"I know it," I said, "and so were we. We just escaped with Banat yesterday."

The herder walked toward us then, but he kept his rifle ready. He was a nice-looking young fellow, with a fine face and a splendid physique. As he approached I opened the door and dropped to the ground. He stopped when he saw me, immediately suspicious.

"You're no Pangan," he said.

"I didn't say that I was, but I fought with the Pangan fleet when it went to fight Hangor; and I was captured when the fleet was routed."

"Are you sure that the yorkokor Banat is safe in Hor?" he demanded.

"We let him out last night near the gates," I said; "and if Hor is not in the hands of the Falsans, he is safe. It was because of the fear that it might be that we did not go any closer to the city."

"Then he is safe," said the young fellow, "for the Falsans were defeated and sent home on foot."

"We knew that," I replied, "but things turn about so suddenly here in this country that we didn't know but what they had returned and conquered Hor. You knew Banat?" I asked.

"I am his son, and this is his herd. I am in charge of it."

Duare and Ero Shan had come out and joined us by this time and the young fellow looked them over curiously. "May I ask," he said, "what you are doing up in these mountains?"

"Our country lies beyond them," I explained, "and we are trying to find a pass to the other side."

He shook his head. "There is none, and if there were, the Cloud People would get you before you could get through."

"Your father told me that Pangan herders had sometimes seen a low place in the range when the clouds rose."

"Yes," he said. "That is about ten miles down the valley; but if I were you, I'd turn back, If you are friends of my father, you can go and live in Hor, but if you keep on you will surely die. No man has ever crossed this range."

"We are going to try it, nevertheless," I told him; "but if we find we can't make it, we'll come back to Hor."

"Then if you live I will see you there," he said, "for you will never get through this range. I have been in it a little way in several places, and I can tell you that the cliffs and gorges are simply terrific."

His men had followed him out and they were standing around listening to our conversation. Finally one of the older men spoke up. "I was up in that canyon ten miles from here about five years ago when the clouds rose higher than I have ever seen them. I could see sky beyond the low peaks. The canyon branches after you have gone into it about a mile and if there is any way to cross the range there, if would be up the righthand fork. That's the one I'd take if I were going to try it."

"Well, thanks for the information," I said; "and now we must be on our way. Tell your father that we got this far at least."

"How are you fixed for meat?"

"We haven't any," I replied.

He turned to one of his men. "Go and get a quarter of that zaldar we butchered yesterday," he said; "and you go with him," he said to another, "and help him with it, and bring along a bundle of smoked meat, too."

I was certainly grateful for these additional provisions. I had no Pangan money to pay for them with, but I offered him some of our ammunition. He refused, saying that we might need it; and after the meat was brought we bade them good-by and started in search of the canyon that might lead us to Korva, or to death.

FIFTY-FIVE

We found the mouth of a large canyon exactly where they had told us we would, and after going up it about a mile we came to the fork and took the one that led to the right. It was getting late and the clouds were pretty low above us now, so we decided to stop for the night. We were all armed now with rifles and pistols, but we were mighty careful to keep a sharp lookout as we descended from the 975 to gather wood for a fire to cook our zaldar steaks.

We finally had a good fire going and were broiling the steaks when we heard savage roars coming toward us from up the canyon. We were immediately on the alert, standing with our rifles ready, for I recognized the roars as those of the tharban, a lion-like Amtorian carnivore. But it wasn't any tharban that came in sight first, but the strangest looking figure that I have ever seen—a human being entirely encased in furs, with only holes for its eyes and for breathing purposes.

"One of the Cloud People," said Duare.

"And he is about to be not even that," said Ero Shan.

When the Cloud Man saw us he hesitated, but then a terrific roar of the tharban sent him on again.

"Get the tharban," I said, and raised my rifle. Ero Shan and I fired simultaneously and the great cat leaped high into the air with a piercing shriek and then Duare put another stream of r-rays into it as it hit the ground, but I think it was already dead. By that time the Cloud Man was right in front of us, and he stood looking at us, still hesitating.

"You had a close call," I said. "I am glad that we were here to kill the tharban."

He still stood looking at us in silence for a moment, and then he said, "Aren't you going to kill me?"

"Of course not," I said; "why should we?"

"All the plains people try to kill us," he replied.

"Well, we won't kill you," I assured him; "and you are free to go whenever you wish to."

"What are you doing up in these mountains?" he asked. "These belong to the Cloud People."

"Our country is on the other side of these mountains," I told him. "We were trying to find the way through."

Again he was silent; this time for a full minute. It is strange to stand looking at a man all muffled up like that and not to have any inkling of what is passing in his mind because his eyes and his face are hidden from you.

"My name is Mor," he said presently. "You have saved my life and for that I will guide you through the Mountains of the Clouds. You cannot go through by night, but in the morning I will come for you;" and without another word he turned and walked away.

"We must have left the jinx behind," said Duare.

"I think I buried him under the fertilizer back there in Hangor," I said. "This is certainly a lucky break if it is true, but it is almost too good to be true."

We ate our steaks and some dried fruit and vegetables which Duare had boiled in water for us, and then we went into the 975, locked the door, and threw ourselves down to sleep, utterly exhausted.

When morning came we were up early and while we were eating our breakfast we saw fully a hundred fur-clad Cloud Men coming down the canyon toward us. They stopped about a hundred yards from the 975 and one of them advanced.

"I am Mor," he said; "do not be afraid. We have come to take you through the Mountains of the Clouds."

"Those are about the pleasantest words I have heard for a long time," said Duare, in an aside to me.

"Can we get through in this lantar?" I asked Mor.

"There will be one or two bad places," he said, "but I think that you can get through with it. Can it climb?"

"It can climb," I said, "almost anything but a vertical cliff."

"Follow us," said Mor. "You will have to stay very close, for you plains people cannot see very far in the clouds. Some of my men will walk on either side to warn you of danger. Pay close attention to them, for after we have climbed a way the least mistake you make may send you into a gorge thousands of feet deep."

"I shall pay attention," I assured him.

Mor walked directly in front of us and I kept the nose of the 975 almost touching him. The canyon rose steeply, but it was broad and level at this point and we had no difficulty at all, and in about half an hour we entered the clouds. From then on it was one of the most nerve-racking experiences that I have ever endured.

We climbed continually and Mor turned and twisted up what must have been one of the most God-awful trails in existence. We made numerous hairpin turns, and on several occasions the side of the 975 scraped the rocky wall while on the opposite side there was nothing but billowing clouds, through which, at the level of the lantar, I could see the tops of trees waving, and I knew that we must be on a narrow ledge, little wider than the ship.

After we had entered the clouds Mor and the other Cloud Men whom I could see had divested themselves of their furs, which they rolled into neat bundles and strapped on their backs. Now they were entirely naked and as entirely hairless. Their thin skins were of the color of a corpse, and as they climbed they panted like dogs and their tongues hung out of the corners of their mouths. Their eyes were very large and round and they had tiny noses, the combination giving them a most owl-like expression. I think they were quite the most hideous creatures that I have ever seen.

When I thought that we must be at the top of the highest mountain that had ever existed on any planet, we rolled onto a level surface and after a few minutes Mor raised his hand for us to stop.

He came back then and said, "We will rest here. This is our village."

I looked about me, but saw nothing but clouds, or perhaps I should better say fog, through which the visibility was not over fifty feet, if that much. Presently women and children materialized out of it and came and talked with the men and looked at the lantar; but they seemed afraid of it and remained at a safe distance.

"How much farther," I asked Mor, "before we will be down out of the clouds on the other side?"

"If we are lucky, we will reach the summit tonight," he said; "and then late tomorrow you will be below the clouds on the other side."

My heart sank. The rest of this day and another day tomorrow was not very pleasant to look forward to. Our nerves were almost a wreck already, but we lived through it and late the next day we came down below the clouds into a beautiful canyon.

Mor and his companions had donned their fur suits and surrounded the lantar. I told Ero Shan to bring the quarter of beer, and I got out to thank Mor and say good-by; and I offered the beef to him when Ero Shan brought it.

"You have plenty?" he asked.

"We can get along," I replied, "with what food we have."

"You cannot tell," he said. "There are no herds on this side, only wild game, and sometimes rather difficult to get."

"But I want to repay you for what you have done for us," I said.

"No," he said. "You owe us nothing. You saved my life; for that I can never repay you. And know," he added, "that you are always welcome in the home of the Cloud People."

I thanked him, and we bade them good-by then, and started off down the canyon.

"And these were the impossible mountains," I said.

"And those were the man-eaters who would destroy and devour us," said Duare.

"Banat would be surprised if he knew how easily we had accomplished the impossible," remarked Ero Shan.

"And we have the tharban to thank," I said. "That was certainly a lucky break for us; for without Mor's gratitude we should never have come through. It would have been impossible to have found or negotiated that trail without his help and guidance."

We went on down the canyon to its mouth, where there opened before us a scene that was to us one of exquisite beauty, for I recognized distant landmarks of a terrain over which I had flown many times, and I knew that we had reached Korva; and in the distance I imagined that I could see the towers and spires of Sanara.

We had been gone a year or more. We had suffered appalling vicissitudes. We had survived unspeakable dangers. We had overcome seemingly insuperable obstacles, but at long last we were home.

NEL BESTSELLERS

T006 778	ASSIGNMENT IN ETERNITY	Robert Heinlein	25p
T007 294	HAVE SPACESUIT – WILL TRAVEL	Robert Heinlein	30p
T009 696	GLORY ROAD	Robert Heinlein	40p
T011 844	DUNE	Frank Herbert	75p
T012 298	DUNE MESSIAH	Frank Herbert	40p
W002 814	THE WORLDS OF FRANK HERBERT	Frank Herbert	30p
W002 911	SANTAROGA BARRIER	Frank Herbert	30p
W003 001	DRAGON IN THE SEA	Frank Herbert	30p

War

W002 921	WOLF PACK	William Hardy	30p
W002 484	THE FLEET THAT HAD TO DIE	Richard Hough	25p
W002 805	HUNTING OF FORCE Z	Richard Hough	30p
W002 632	THE BASTARD BRIGADE	Peter Leslie	25p
T006 999	KILLER CORPS	Peter Leslie	25p
T011 755	TRAWLERS GO TO WAR	Lund and Ludlam	40p
W005 051	GOERING	Manvell & Freankel	52½p
W005 065	HIMMLER	Manvell & Freankel	52½p
W002 423	STRIKE FROM THE SKY	Alexander McKee	30p
W002 831	NIGHT	Francis Pollini	40p
T010 074	THE GREEN BERET	Hilary St. George Saunders	40p
T010 066	THE RED BERET	Hilary St. George Saunders	40p

Western

T010 619	EDGE – THE LONER	George Gilman	25p
T010 600	EDGE – TEN THOUSAND DOLLARS AMERICAN	George Gilman	25p
T010 929	EDGE – APACHE DEATH	George Gilman	25p

General

T011 763	SEX MANNERS FOR MEN	Robert Chartham	30p
W002 531	SEX MANNERS FOR ADVANCED LOVERS	Robert Chartham	25p
W002 835	SEX AND THE OVER FORTIES	Robert Chartham	30p
T010 732	THE SENSUOUS COUPLE	Dr. C.	
P002 367	AN ABZ OF LOVE	Inge and Sten Hegeler	60p
P011 402	A HAPPIER SEX LIFE	Dr. Sha Kokken	70p
W002 584	SEX MANNERS FOR SINGLE GIRLS	Georges Valensin	25p
W002 592	THE FRENCH ART OF SEX MANNERS	Georges Valensin	25p
W002 726	THE POWER TO LOVE	E. W. Hirsch M. D.	47½p

Mad

S003 491	LIKE MAD	30p
S003 494	MAD IN ORBIT	30p
S003 520	THE BEDSIDE MAD	30p
S003 521	THE VOODOO MAD	30p
S003 657	MAD FOR BETTER OR VERSE	30p
S003 716	THE SELF MADE MAD	30p

— — — — — — — — — — — — — —

NEL P.O. BOX 11, FALMOUTH, CORNWALL

Please send cheque or postal order. Allow 6p per book to cover postage and packing.

Name...

Address ....

....

Title ....
(SEPTEMBER)